"What's Not to
the Novels of (

"Sizzling, irresistible, wonderful."
—*New York Times* bestselling author Lori Foster

"Each and every love scene explodes into fiery sensuality that will melt your heart. Tastefully written . . . blazing hot!"   —Joyfully Reviewed

"Scorchingly erotic, some of the hottest sex I've read. . . . The three heroes are mind-blowingly fabulous; the heroines are intelligent and likeable."   —*TwoLips Reviews

"Wonderfully written. . . . The sensuality level was off the charts!"
—The Romance Studio, 5 Heart Sweetheart Award

"Steamy stories sure to bring your blood to a boil on a cold winter's night . . . always satisfying."   —Romance Junkies

"Super-sexually charged erotic romance . . . hot-and-heavy tales. . . . Hearts will race and brows will rise."   —*Romantic Times*

"Humor, sex, science, relationships, and sex . . . a pleasing, prolonged pleasure read."   —*Midwest Book Review*

"Fun, sexy, and sassy—a Cathryn Fox book is a must-read great escape!"   —Sylvia Day, author of *Ask for It*

"[A] wonderful blend of passionate sex and witty intelligence."
—Fresh Fiction

"Hot, enthralling, and simply delicious . . . a must read!"
—Romance Reviews Today

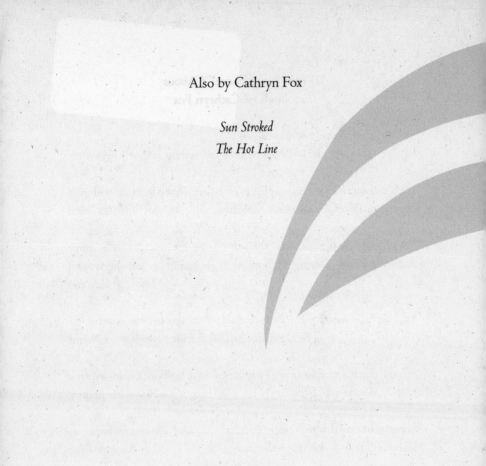

Also by Cathryn Fox

Sun Stroked
The Hot Line

Instinctive

An Eternal Pleasure Novel

CATHRYN FOX

HEAT

HEAT

Published by New American Library, a division of
Penguin Group (USA) Inc., 375 Hudson Street,
New York, New York 10014, USA
Penguin Group (Canada), 90 Eglinton Avenue East, Suite 700, Toronto,
Ontario M4P 2Y3, Canada (a division of Pearson Penguin Canada Inc.)
Penguin Books Ltd., 80 Strand, London WC2R 0RL, England
Penguin Ireland, 25 St. Stephen's Green, Dublin 2,
Ireland (a division of Penguin Books Ltd.)
Penguin Group (Australia), 250 Camberwell Road, Camberwell, Victoria 3124,
Australia (a division of Pearson Australia Group Pty. Ltd.)
Penguin Books India Pvt. Ltd., 11 Community Centre, Panchsheel Park,
New Delhi - 110 017, India
Penguin Group (NZ), 67 Apollo Drive, Rosedale, North Shore 0632,
New Zealand (a division of Pearson New Zealand Ltd.)
Penguin Books (South Africa) (Pty.) Ltd., 24 Sturdee Avenue,
Rosebank, Johannesburg 2196, South Africa

Penguin Books Ltd., Registered Offices:
80 Strand, London WC2R 0RL, England

Published by Heat, an imprint of New American Library,
a division of Penguin Group (USA) Inc.

First Printing, October 2009
10 9 8 7 6 5 4 3 2 1

HEAT is a trademark of Penguin Group (USA) Inc.

LIBRARY OF CONGRESS CATALOGING-IN-PUBLICATION DATA:

Fox, Cathryn.
Instinctive: an eternal pleasure novel/Cathryn Fox.
p. cm.
ISBN 978-0-451-22794-2
I. Title.
PR9199.4.F69I67 2009
813'.6—dc22   2009019824
Set in Centaur MT
Designed by Alissa Amell

Printed in the United States of America

To all the readers and writers who've purchased my books and supported me throughout the years. Your e-mails and kind words mean the world to me and have given me inspiration and encouragement during some trying times.

I'm excited about my new paranormal series and hope you enjoying reading it as much as I've enjoyed writing it. Keep those e-mails coming. I love hearing from each and every one of you.

Chapter One

In three days she'd be gone. Erased. Buried.

Dead . . .

Today, however, today was an entirely different story. Not only was Jaclyn Vasenty still alive and breathing—she was hell-bent on living the last few hours of her life to the fullest.

She glanced at the well-endowed man powering upward between her thighs, taking note of his smoldering blue eyes, dark, shoulder-length hair, the clench of his firm jaw, and the small beads of perspiration trickling down his bronzed skin. Every pleasure-seeking nerve in her body came alive as her gaze traveled downward to the tuft of curly black hair smashing against her naked, passion-drenched pubis as he drove his cock all the way up inside her.

Scrumptious . . .

Oh yeah, she was going to enjoy today, she mused.

She swung her long chestnut curls over her shoulders to expose her aching breasts. Brian's hungry eyes latched onto her pale pebbled nipples. When his tongue darted out to wet his sensuous mouth, a small moan slipped from the curve of her well-kissed lips and caught the attention of those around her. A few couples stepped closer, some eager to get a better look, while others coveted to get in on the salacious action. Jaclyn's libido fed off the sexual energy swirling around her, the intoxicating euphoria drawing her deeper and deeper into a cocoon of lust and desire.

Just knowing the voyeurs in the club were watching her fuck the dark-haired Adonis strapped to the plush sex chair, while she rode him like a feral animal in heat, brought on wild and wicked sensations.

She looked past Brian and glanced around Risqué, the erotic club where anything and everything goes. She took a moment to observe the explicit sex acts taking place on the nearby dance floor.

All in various stages of undress, hot naked bodies writhed in sync to the sensuous beat booming from the nearby speakers. Wet pussies and hard cocks were out in abundance tonight, all striving for one common goal—to get off using any means possible. In their single-minded pursuit of pleasure, some were fucking while others were licking, sucking, nibbling, or burying their faces in the juncture between their lovers' legs.

Her entire body vibrated in bliss.

As she took pleasure in the show, a rush of liquid heat rocketed through her and brought on one hell of a violent shudder. Jaclyn's pussy dripped in response to the stimuli, and her clit tightened with primal need, screaming for a little of that tongue action from Brian while she watched the hedonistic acts from afar.

God, she would miss this when she was dead.

With her pussy hot, wet, and ripe for the taking, she bent forward and loosened the silk rope from one of Brian's shackled hands. Settling for fingers over fellatio, she inched upward, her actions conveying without words exactly what she wanted from him. And she expected nothing less. Brian, the masterful lover that he was, shot her a grin and deftly parted her twin lips. With little finesse, he unceremoniously scraped the rough pad of his thumb over her inflamed clit, his perfect ministrations keeping her hovering on the precipice.

"Oh yes . . . ," she murmured, grinding her fleshy nub against him until pleasure bled into pain. "So good . . ."

"That's it, baby. Let me take you to heaven," he whispered and bucked against her, so his rock-hard erection toyed with her oversensitized G-spot.

Lust prowled through her and urged her on. Jaclyn cupped her engorged breasts, lifted herself clear off his cock and then swiftly impaled herself onto him. *Jesus . . .* As Brian's impressive length speared her, his girth stretched open the tight walls of her cunt until a creamy release was merely a stroke away.

She hungered to prolong the pleasure, to continue their fuck session clear on through to next week. But it couldn't continue and she damn well knew it. Because come Monday morning at eight a.m.—merely thirty-five hours and fifteen minutes away—she'd be dead.

Well, not *dead* in the biblical, or even the Wikipedia, sense of the word, but certainly in the spiritual sense. She knew her essence for life, the uninhibited sexual force deep inside that drove her pleasure-seeking hormones, would slowly be snuffed out until she became the proper girl her family demanded, and her upper-class, high-society community expected.

As a privileged socialite residing in Chicago's Gold Coast, she was supposed to play by her society's stringent rules, despite the fact that deep down she never felt she belonged. At times she attributed her loneliness to adoption; other times she was certain the hollow feeling stemmed from something else entirely—something she couldn't quite put her finger on, something that was just out of her grasp.

Nevertheless, in three days she'd have to bury her wicked ways and start playing the part of the good girl. Not an easy task considering she'd been sexually ravenous since hitting adolescence. Her stomach dipped in dismay at the thought, already mourning the death of her wild, sexual spirit.

It wasn't her fault she'd been born with a sex drive that would rival any man's, and she certainly hadn't meant for her enjoyment of kinky sex, ménages, voyeurism, exhibitionism, or BDSM to bring scandal to her family's name. Nor did she think her untamed, passionate nature would cause investors in her father's multimillion-dollar cosmetics business to turn skittish. And with the threat of a corporate takeover, any more rumblings about her after-hours activities would cause nothing but trouble for a company already treading on shaky ground.

But her daily desire for wild sex didn't mean she'd stand by while her father's empire collapsed around her. She was a high achiever, intelligent, resourceful, with a hard-earned marketing degree to back up her credentials—in addition to being her father's sole heir. It was a shame no one on the board could see past the paparazzi pictures. Sure she went to extreme measures to keep her private indiscretions, well . . . *private*, and she maintained a professional demeanor at the office, but as heir to a multimillion-dollar company, she continually found herself in the media spotlight—and not in a favorable way. Why couldn't anyone see that her sexual appetite would in no way hinder her ability to run her father's empire?

She pushed back a cold shiver and shelved those thoughts to the back recesses of her mind. It was not the time for thinking about such bleak matters. Right now was the time to focus on the orgasmic pleasure Brian was bestowing upon her. She was going to need these hot, erotic memories to draw on later when she found herself all alone in the quaint, isolated town of Serene, New Hampshire. A town where she suspected everyone lived behind white picket fences, resided in matching houses, and had two point four kids. The perfect location for her to mend her bad-girl ways and start over.

If the town was anything like Silver Springs, the neighboring community, where her grandmother used to reside—and Jaclyn suspected it was—she knew there wasn't a chance in hell she'd find herself another bad boy like the one between her legs. Which was exactly why Serene was the perfect spot to try on the good-girl persona and masquerade as something she wasn't. The less temptation she found in suburbia the better. Because when it came right down to it, where sex was concerned, she had little to no self-control.

If she was honest with herself, Jaclyn felt obligated to do

something to appease her parents. She owed them that much. Twenty-four years ago when her biological mother had ditched her in a Chicago subway station hours after giving birth to her, only to end up dead a few blocks away, Benjamin and Marie Vasenty rescued her from a life of foster care. They had also given her every luxury and privilege one could ask for.

She certainly hadn't wanted to disappoint them, or for them to abandon her because of her wicked ways. Sex had always felt right, never dirty or wrong. She had yet to find one man who could completely and thoroughly sate the incessant ache inside her. At least not for any length of time. When it came right down to it, she suspected no such man existed.

The door to the club opened and closed, and a pair of intense dark eyes swept through the room before settling on her. As she took in the man's watchful gaze, a wicked grin tweaked the corners of his mouth and seduced her already-heightened senses. Heart racing wildly, Jaclyn turned her attention back to Brian and redirected her thoughts.

She thrust her chest forward and placed one breast in front of his lips in offering. He flicked his wet tongue over her marbled nipple. The heat of his mouth felt like fire on her skin and escalated the tension between her legs. Brian continued to work his finger over her soaked clit. Small sinuous circles that drew out her pleasure as he feverishly pumped his thick cock in and out of her hot, tight pussy.

Pressure brewed inside her, demanding to be addressed before she went up in a burst of flames. In no time at all, every ounce of bottled lust rose to the surface, and a powerful orgasm ripped the air from her lungs. She gripped the chair and tossed her head from side to side. Her mind shut down and she gave a broken gasp, her muscles tightening and contracting as a violent shudder overtook her. Her hands went to Brian's hair. She grabbed a fistful, and she pressed against him harder, riding, rubbing and grinding out every delicious wave of ecstasy.

Goddamn, that felt good. . . .

Before she even had time to catch her breath, a warm hand curled around her waist, splayed out over her stomach, and began to ease her off Brian's lap. A hot, sexy voice loaded with promise whispered in her ear, sending a barrage of wicked sensations straight to her throbbing pussy.

She recognized the voice—lazy, laid-back, and a little rough around the edges, the callused hands, and the sinewy muscles leading up to broad shoulders. When Jaclyn inhaled, his rich, spicy scent singed her senses and slid over her bare skin like a powerful aphrodisiac.

Kane . . .

"Time to fuck, little lady."

Excited by the arousal in his dark, sexy tone, she sucked in a tight breath, the scent of her arousal and body language telling him just how needy she was, just how much she wanted to play it his way.

Before she could respond, Brian scowled, cupped her elbow and hauled her back against him. "Hey, back off. We're not done yet, Kane."

"Never said you were," Kane responded in that low, sensuous cadence that always got to her.

When she twisted her head to see him, those same gorgeous, intense eyes locked on hers again. His sheer strength and magnetism never failed to impress her. If they were pack animals, Kane would be their leader, their alpha—a trait that oddly excited the submissive part of her. When a guy like Kane said jump, the men in the crowd asked how high. He was a man who took what he wanted and never took no for an answer.

Since he wasn't much of a talker, Jaclyn had no idea what he did for a living. She guessed him to be some kind of hunter, but what he hunted was a question she thought best left unasked. All she knew was that he frequented the club once a week, and most times came looking for her. She suspected few women had the ability to keep up with his stamina, or the body to devour his thick, impressive cock. Even though Jaclyn was petite, merely five foot five, her body easily opened up and welcomed every fabulous inch of him, and dammit, he sure had a lot of fabulous inches.

"Then take a hike, so we can finish," Brian bit out.

Kane laughed and moved in beside them. The crowd surrounding the three quickly parted to clear a path. Even the loud music seemed to die down in his presence. Kane's head descended, his gaze settling on the greedy little spot between Jaclyn's legs. The slow sweep of his eyes over her clit was like an erotic caress, and she found herself getting a little hotter, and a whole lot wetter.

He flashed her a wolfish smile that was a dangerous combination of playful and naughty. "This little lady is far from finished." In a touch that was commanding yet soft, he eased her from the chair, turned her toward him, and enclosed her body in the circle of his arms. With promise in his eyes, he said, "And I know exactly how to take care of her." God, she loved a man with confidence, a man who was concerned with her needs.

A whimper escaped Jaclyn's lips as his jeans-clad knee slipped between her thighs, urging them apart. She gyrated against him, rubbing her pussy on his leg, fully aware of his mounting desire.

His eyes moved over her face before he shot Brian a quick glance. "Come with us, Brian, and we'll pleasure her together. The way she really likes it."

Brian tilted his head back, a challenging gleam in his eyes telling Kane he wanted her all to himself. When Kane leveled him with a glare, Brian grumbled in acquiescence and backed down. The two men exchanged a look of understanding before Kane bent to release the three remaining constraints holding Brian in place—a peace offering. His actions generated blatant appreciation in the depth of Brian's blue eyes. Even though Kane was a man who took what he wanted, he was still a stand-up guy, a man of character and integrity. Traits that he held in high regard, and everyone who had the pleasure of knowing him highly respected.

Jaclyn watched Brian's straps fall to the floor. Honestly, she loved when Brian played it her way, but she loved it more when they all played it Kane's way.

Jaclyn turned her attention to Kane, a dominant by nature, to consider his mood. Playful. Naughty. Commanding. Which room would he want her to join him in tonight? The dungeon? The schoolhouse? The lab?

The gentle placement of his hand on the small of her back made her shiver as he negotiated them through the crowd, up the stairs, and into the back bedroom. Brian followed close behind, the heat from his hard body reaching out to her, his stiff cock clamoring for attention.

Ah, so it appeared Kane was in the mood for romance. She supposed she should have guessed by the tame way he was handling her. Jaclyn quickly looked around, taking stock of the room and the large bed centered in the middle. Soft candlelight bathed the cranberry-colored walls in a romantic glow and created warmth, ambience . . . *seduction*. She turned to Kane and offered him a smile, her show of appreciation.

One large hand drifted downward to close over her bare sex. As the air around them charged with sexual energy, the smile fell from her face. Kane's nostrils flared; dark eyes burned and raced over her as his finger traced her plump lips.

"I've spent all week thinking about tasting your cunt, little lady."

His erotic words prompted her into action. Jaclyn inched back and dropped onto the quilted bedspread, her backside sinking into the plush mattress. When she widened her legs, her pink pussy glistened in the candlelight.

"Then by all means."

A low growl rumbled in Kane's throat as he sank to the carpeted floor, insinuated himself between her spread thighs, and made a slow pass with his hot, hungry tongue. A low, guttural, animalistic sound rose up from the depths of his throat. "Goddamn, girl, I swear you taste better and better every time."

After a small sampling, Kane inched back and ran his hands over her legs. He glanced at the café au lait birthmark that colored her inner thigh, and then traced the tip of his index finger over one of the three flamelike pigmentations. "I love the fire in you, baby. Let's see if I can help extinguish these flames tonight."

She nodded eagerly, even though no man had ever made her feel sated, complete. But by God, she was willing to let Kane try.

When Kane's tongue breached her opening, Brian slipped onto the cushiony mattress beside her. His hungry mouth crashed down on hers for a deep, thorough kiss. Their tongues lashed and dueled; the heat between them was wild and explosive. A moment later Brian's lips abandoned hers and trailed a path down her body until he reached her swollen nipples. Kane dipped a finger into her pussy at the same time Brian's mouth closed over one hard pebble, the dual assault severely impacting her ability to form a coherent sentence.

Jaclyn arched her back and bit down on her bottom lip. "Oh. God. Yes," she cried out as baser instincts took hold of her.

Kane pumped and withdrew repeatedly as Brian's hand slid lower to pair up with Kane's tongue. The two worked her inflamed clit until she nearly sobbed with pleasure. Minutes turned into seconds as they tended to her every primal desire in tandem, with each skilled lover ravishing her hot, needy body.

She moved restlessly against them, demanding more. Reading her body language, Brian applied more pressure to her clit, and Kane slipped another solid finger inside her and picked up the tempo.

Oh damn!

Kane's voice dropped an octave as he continued to finger-fuck her. "I want you to come for me now," he demanded, his voice dark and raspy and so damn arousing to Jaclyn. "Cream in my mouth."

He certainly didn't have to ask her twice. As if on cue, her body clenched, and she erupted, her hot flow of release pouring into Kane's eager mouth.

"Yesss . . . ," she cried out and raked her fingers through Kane's thick brown hair so she could hold his luscious mouth to her throbbing pussy.

The two men groaned in pleasure when they felt her first clench of fulfillment. Kane spent a long time on his knees, lapping up every last drop. Greedy boy that he was, he left nothing behind for Brian.

After her convulsions subsided, Kane climbed out from between her legs and shot a knowing glance Brian's way before turning to her. "Now I want you to get down on your knees and suck Brian's cock. He looks like he's in fucking agony. But don't make him come. Not yet. I have other plans for him."

Lust sang through her veins. God she loved his take-charge attitude. Obliging, she slipped to the floor as Brian eagerly shimmied to the edge of the bed. She nestled herself between his spread thighs and lapped at the precome pearling on the tip of his cock. His low growl filled the room.

"Mmmm," she moaned, then drew a substantial amount of his length into her mouth.

Brian jerked his hips forward as he fed her his cock. "Goddamn, that's good." He grabbed a fistful of her hair and followed the motion of her mouth, but it was damn hard to concentrate on sucking his cock with Kane parting her ass cheeks from behind.

A burst of cold liquid over her ringed opening caused her

puckered passage to clench. She gave a breathy moan, her thoughts in fragments.

"Relax, little lady." Kane burrowed a finger into her hole, stretching and widening her. "I know how to take care of you." Kane prepared her and her body shook in anticipation, since she had figured out Kane's plans for Brian's cock. "I know what you like," he added.

She turned her full attention on Brian and worked her tongue over his erection, until he fairly vibrated beneath her. His liquid heat lubricated her hand, and she used it to polish the length of his shaft.

"Fuck, baby, you're so good at that . . . ," he groaned and threw his head back.

Jaclyn cupped his balls, and gave a gentle squeeze while she circled her tongue over his bulbous head. His veins swelled with blood and she knew he was close. Too close. She eased back a bit, giving only light licks, not wanting to run the risk of ruining Kane's plans.

"Time to fuck," Kane announced again, his voice thick and gruff as he hauled her to her feet. He tore off his clothes, dropped to the bed, equipped himself with protection, and then pulled her on top of him. As she straddled his hips, he pulled open her pink lips and she moaned in bliss.

"Ride me, little lady," he said, and then exchanged a look with Brian. Brian nodded in understanding, sheathed himself with a new condom, and came around from behind.

Jaclyn positioned Kane's cock at her opening and slowly lowered herself, her cunt sucking him in, inch by glorious inch, taking ultimate pleasure in the depth of his penetration. Once their bodies fused, she bent forward and opened her back passage for Brian. Pleasure engulfed her as Brian gently worked his way into her tight backside.

She gave a soft whimper as her eyes met Kane's. He grinned, circled his thumbs over her areolas, and said, "That's it, darling. Be a good girl while we fill you."

A few moments later, once she had them both deep in her body, she began moving restlessly against them, the three finding an erotic rhythm that matched their rising passion. Long sensuous strides amplified the tension inside her. Kane ran his large hands over her body, his touch alternating between her nipples and clit.

Desire thrummed through her as their bodies moistened and scented the air. When Kane's simmering brown eyes moved over her face, it suddenly occurred to her that the two men were also fucking each other, rubbing their cocks together through the thin walls of her body. An erotic whimper bubbled from the depths of her throat. She began panting, gasping for air as pressure built up inside her. They began riding one another long and hard, her body tightening, shaking, her pussy muscles clamping hard around Kane's cock.

Her nails bit into Kane's skin as a powerful orgasm swept through her. Her body exploded and dripped hot cream over Kane's cock.

"That's my girl," Kane whispered, giving himself over to his own release. From behind, Brian joined in. He groaned out loud, plunged deeper, and came high up inside her.

"Oh, sweet Jesus . . . ," were the only words she could manage to say.

Temporarily sated, she collapsed on top of Kane's chest, and worked to recapture her breath. Goddamn, that felt good. These two men pleasured her so nicely, she was certain she'd died and gone to heaven. That last thought suddenly brought her passion-rattled brain back to the reason she'd needed a good hard fuck in the first place.

Because in three days, her true self would be dead.

Dead . . .

And it wasn't going to be from pleasure.

Chapter Two

Even though the summer sun had already given its final farewell, nightfall did little to ease the sweltering heat hovering over the small rural town of Serene. With his jeans and T-shirt clinging to his body, Slyck left his post at the nightclub and quickly made his way down Main Street. His heavy footsteps sawed through the moisture-laden air and echoed in the eerie silence.

Long, predatory, catlike strides carried him past the grocery store, the fire station, and the candy shop, before he reached the front door of the old town hall. The fluorescent light pouring from the window and lighting a long pale column on the dark sidewalk let him know the others were already inside, waiting.

As his hackles rose in foreboding, his skin instinctively grew tight and itchy—the lure of the shift pulling at him hard. Fighting down the animal springing to life inside him and working diligently to cling to his human form, Slyck felt perspiration gathering in the center of his palms, forcing him to draw deep breaths in a concentrated effort to shake off the alluring call of the wild.

Needing a distraction—something, anything, until the moment passed—he took a minute to examine the old wooden structure at the juncture of Main Street and Mulberry Lane. White chips of paint sailed to the ground and settled like dander on the overgrown mini rosebushes while ivy vines coiled around the two towering pillars flanking the solid front door. Even though the exterior of the nineteenth-century building needed a fresh coat of paint and a little tender loving care, the structure itself remained sound and would undoubtedly stand erect for years—Slyck should know, since he'd help raise it decades ago. He lightly tapped his knuckles on a cedar slat, reassuring himself that it'd be a long time coming before another reconstruction took place.

Outwardly, the aged landmark resembled an historical building that one would readily find in any small town. But Slyck knew firsthand that sometimes looks could be deceiving. Because Serene's town hall was far from typical, and the council members who were about to deliberate around a circular table were unlike any other council members in any other community.

With the clock ticking, Slyck collected himself, pulled the door open, and hastily made his way inside, his brisk movements stirring dust in the still night air. Silence fell like a death sentence as he perused the room and quickly took stock of those already seated around the oaken table at the other end of the long hall.

Satisfied that all members were present and accounted for, he secured the door behind him and proceeded toward his assigned chair to assume his familiar role of alpha leader. The old planked floorboards creaked and groaned like a wounded animal under his impressive size and alerted the others to his arrival. As he took his seat, his presence closed the powerful circle of five.

Even though the Overseers had been meeting here for centuries, it never failed to astound him to see such a diverse group of species—all of whom had once been mortal enemies—coming together for a greater good. A millennium ago it was unheard-of for any one of the five to be in the same territory, let alone the same room, but here they were: a panther guide, a demon guide, a vampire guide, a lycan guide, and a coven guide—five Overseers who were all working together to keep their brethren in line and maintain order amongst their kind, while keeping their existence a secret from the rest of the world.

Of course, to survive and walk undetected amongst humans, they'd had no choice but to join forces and form allegiances. Security and strength in numbers was a hell of a powerful thing.

After the Salem witch trials in 1692, humans had grown suspicious, even bloodthirsty, for anyone perceived as different. With their very existence at risk, each supernatural species had acknowledged the need to put aside their hatred and prejudice for one another and unite forces toward a common goal—survival. Shortly thereafter, secret communities were set up all over the world, with an even distribution of the five species in each district to prevent one brethren from growing too powerful and dominating the others. Natural-born leaders from the family bloodlines emerged, accords were made, and truces were forged, albeit uneasy truces at times. Especially between Slyck, the panther guide, and Vall, the lycan guide in the Eastern Chapter.

Cats and dogs just don't mix, but it went even deeper than that. Decades ago Vall had tried to sway Slyck's first-in-command—his enforcer of security—to overlook his pack's unscheduled night-time runs. In turn Slyck's security officer turned Vall in to the community leaders, only to end up dead a few months later. He'd left town to commute to the Western Chapter for a security meeting, and they'd later found his car wrapped around a guardrail, his head torn clear off his shoulders, ending any of the other nine lives he had left.

Although Slyck couldn't prove it, he had always felt Vall had had some sort of involvement in the gruesome incident, which left him with a deep-seated belief that Vall had ulterior motives and always acted with his own best interests at heart, not the community's.

Slyck had insisted Vall's position be challenged, but the ruling didn't go in his favor. The other Overseers sympathized with Vall and his pack, and their continual need to leash their wolf. In the end only a small reprimand had been handed down to the mongrel.

With that last thought in mind, Slyck avoided Vall's silvery glare, stretched his long legs out in front of himself, and turned his attention to Harmony, the coven guide, who was in charge of chairing this Sunday night's meeting, as per their assigned schedule.

Harmony was dressed in a floor-length black silk robe, with her long, thick, dark hair pulled back in a severe bun. Her violet eyes panned each council member for the briefest of seconds before she initiated the meeting. Then, for the next hour and a half, they discussed council policy, funding, agendas, policing, bylaws, and the threat of exposure from rogue members living outside their gates. Naturally, not every member of every species saw the beauty and benefits of their secret society, hence the need for the Western Chapter to set up a task force to track down and eliminate all rebels. Before the meeting came to a close, Harmony opened the floor to discuss any new business. With that opening, Slyck spoke up.

He hardened his expression and prepared for an impending confrontation with the canine. "It has been brought to my attention that a few of Vall's pack have been running in the woods, near the perimeter." He resisted the urge to add "again."

A moment of silence passed as Harmony absorbed that bit of information; then, "Vall, is this correct?" she asked in her usual, patient voice.

Vall smirked at Slyck, his ruthless pewter eyes narrowing to mere slits. His stony silence spoke volumes as he threaded his beefy hands—large paws that would look at home on a Kodiak—through his long golden mane. He groomed himself with a casual nonchalance that belied his primitive temperament.

In an attempt to lighten the situation, Vall rolled one broad shoulder, gave a humorless laugh, and said easily, "It was a little harmless run. A few of the teenagers enjoying the wind in their faces."

Slyck felt his temper flare from simmer to inferno. But since he was not a man who let emotions rule his actions, he worked to control his anger and fisted his hands beneath the table. His crescentlike claws bit into his flesh as his predatory instincts exploded like gunfire.

Slyck drilled his gaze into Vall and held his ground as he leaned forward—a battle of wills. Since Slyck wouldn't tolerate stupidity or insubordination, he continued with his litany. "As you know, a rule is a rule, Vall. No matter how big or how small. And these rules are in place for the *community's* best interest." He shot Vall a distrustful look, the underlying message clear in his tone. It didn't take a genius to translate the meaning of his words, only a lycan. "We all have responsibilities that we must uphold. If we don't, our community will collapse around us," he added. "You know it, and I know it."

"No harm was done, Slyck," he barked out, undaunted. "If your little kitties hadn't—"

Slyck unfurled his fingers and cut him off, refusing to tolerate his juvenile conduct. "Since I'm chief of security, it's their job to report to me." Slyck turned the conversation back onto Vall and his irreverent behavior, refusing to let him sidetrack the council, a technique the mongrel had skillfully mastered over the years. "The full moon was three days ago. They should have gotten their run out of their system then. We all know shifting at any other time during the month is purely for pleasure, an aphrodisiac, or to procreate, and such behavior is not tolerated, never has been, especially during our temporary halt in population." Even though he had no solid proof, deep down Slyck believed Vall was trying to grow his pack, to build his army and shift the town's power to his advantage. "If you don't discipline them, then this matter will have to be handed over to Devon—"

At the sound of his name, Devon, the demon guide, who had seemed rather quiet during tonight's meeting, perked up. Christ knows, if there was one thing the town needed to worry about, it was a quiet demon.

When Vall lifted his brow in a challenge, Harmony broke in. Her ancient, knowledgeable eyes silenced Slyck with a glance. She angled her chin and spoke in a placating manner. "Vall, please see to it that it doesn't happen again."

Slyck bit back a response and pinched the bridge of his nose in disbelief. Was it his imagination, or lately was Harmony always siding with Vall? Everyone knew there were no second chances in this town, except, it seemed, where Vall was concerned. Devon was chief of discipline, and the matter should now be in his hands, his to deal with. Slyck shook his head, unable to believe that Harmony was letting Vall off the hook so easily. Yet despite his incredulity with the coven guide's ruling, since she was chairing tonight's meeting, council directive stated the others must abide by her dictum. And since he *always* abided by the rules, he swallowed a protest and sat back in his chair, suddenly feeling much older than his nine hundred years. And maybe even a little burned out.

Slyck panned the table, and then focused on Quinn, the vampire guide, who seemed rather peaceful tonight. His eyes flashed a contented black as he sipped on a fresh bag of blood to sate his hunger upon his recent awakening.

Vall let off a little of his puppy charm and smiled at Harmony. "Of course, Harmony," he said, his voice as smooth as aged scotch—and just as intoxicating. "I'll see to it that it doesn't happen again," he amended, then brandished his familiar, insidious smirk when he glanced Slyck's way.

"Thank you, Vall." Her tone softened, and dark lashes blinked over violet eyes. "Of course we all understand the desire to be in primal form, but you know it's forbidden for a lycan or even a panther to change at will outside the privacy of your home. With the exception of your full-moon runs, we must always hide our identities. Exposure to the real world is a never-ending threat, especially now with an outsider about to set up residence. That"— she paused to tap her finger in the air—"and you can't always be accountable for your actions in your natural state."

Devon's raspy voice sounded from across the table, and his gaze flashed gold. Effortlessly redirecting the conversation, he asked, "Speaking of the newcomer, what do we know of her? Will she be making her stay permanent? Or, rather, will *we* be making her stay permanent?"

Ah, so at least Slyck now knew what was wrong with Devon. Boredom. Demons were only happy when they were wreaking havoc on others and it had been a hell of a long time since he'd slain anyone, taken them "home," and returned to Serene with a new plaything.

"As far as I can tell, her stay is temporary." Harmony pulled a file from her briefcase and placed it on the table. "Meet Jaclyn Vasenty, heir to Vasenty Cosmetics, her daddy's multimillion-dollar company."

All sets of eyes were trained on the striking young woman in the photo. Slyck spent an extra-long minute taking in her expensive business suit, and the sexy way it clung to her curves like a second skin. So prim. So proper. So human.

So not his type.

His gaze lingered on her pretty face, and he noted the way long lashes shadowed dark, tortured eyes, and he wondered what had made her so sad. Chestnut hair tumbled in waves over her slender shoulders, and her full pouty mouth was slightly turned down at the corners.

His focus shifted and fixed on her luscious, kissable lips. He aimed a longing glance and afforded himself a moment to devour the plush smoothness. He moved restlessly in his old wooden seat, suddenly uncomfortable. *Goddamn.* Lips like those belonged to a wild, uninhibited woman, a woman far different from the one portrayed in the picture. Full, sensuous, erotic—everything a young panther's wet dreams were made of. He wondered if that sweet, lush mouth of hers ever got her into trouble.

He felt a curious clench in his gut as lust jumped up to kick him in the groin. Okay, so if she wasn't his type, then why the fuck was he wondering how that pretty pink mouth of hers would feel wrapped around his ever-expanding cock?

Jesus . . .

Berating himself, he resisted the urge to take his dick into his palms and stroke it as it hungered for sexual attention.

Her sexual attention.

He quickly marshaled his wayward thoughts and considered the matter at hand. What would bring a cultured, well-to-do city girl like her to Serene? He turned his attention back to the group and worked to play catch-up on the conversation.

"A princess, then," Devon murmured. Slyck could feel the pleasure resonate through the demon's body as he thumbed through the pictures, his amber eyes thoroughly devouring every delicious detail. "It's been a long time since I've sampled a princess," he mumbled under his breath, a reminder that even though they'd all come together for a common cause, at the root of their existences, they were all still primal beings ruled by lust, hunger, and primitive urges.

Vall arched a brow. "I give her a month before the town eats her alive."

"Mmm." Quinn flashed his white teeth, then brushed his tongue over his protruding incisors. "Can I go first?"

Harmony leveled Quinn with a glare. "Down, boy. You won't be eating anyone alive."

"Killjoy," Quinn shot back, an edge of humor in his voice as he turned his attention to his near-empty sack of blood. It was just like Quinn to find amusement in the situation, absurd master vamp that he was.

Slyck remained quiet during the whole exchange. Oddly fascinated, he found himself drawn to the pictures, despite a hard-fought battle to look the other way. There was something about the young woman in the photo that caused his blood to rush a little faster and his heart to beat a little stronger, which went completely against his feline nature. His skin prickled, and suddenly it took effort to breathe and organize his thoughts.

"Children, please." Harmony gave a light laugh and toyed with the charm dangling around her neck. "Sometimes it's like being in a room full of fledglings," she teased, then tapped her fingertip on the picture. "From what I understand she comes from Chicago's Gold Coast and is here to turn around cosmetics sales at the department store. I put her in the rental property on Mulberry

Lane. The house across the street from you, Slyck, so you and your team can keep a close eye on her actions in the interim."

An eye on her.

A hand on her.

A tongue on her.

Oh boy . . .

Warmth spread out over Slyck's skin as an odd tingling caused the hairs on his nape to rise. What the fuck was the matter with him? No woman had ever elicited such a bizarre response from him—especially of the nonpanther variety. He bit back a raspy moan of pleasure before it rumbled to the surface, and tried to make sense of his reactions to her.

"So if we buy her product and help her turn around cosmetics sales, won't that get her out of Serene quicker?" Quinn asked.

"It's only a temporary solution," Harmony assured him. "If sales decline after she leaves, who's to say the company won't send more employees in the future? And if we're forced to continually make their stay permanent, it would raise too much suspicion."

Slyck remained quiet through the exchange, his mind racing, his cock thickening.

"What's the matter, Slyck? Cat got your tongue?" Vall questioned, ever determined to get under Slyck's skin.

"Fuck off, Vall," Slyck returned, no longer in the mood to humor him. With passion segueing to anger, Slyck quickly pulled himself together and splayed his hands on the table, needing the meeting to end immediately. "You all know the routine. If she's still here after one month, we reconvene and decide her future. Until then tell your brethren to keep their distance, and make her stay as unwelcome as possible." His eyes met and locked with Vall's. "And remember, no council member is to 'play' with her, or 'mark' her before judgment, should it come to that."

Jaclyn had but one month to get out of Dodge. Otherwise she ran the risk of making her stay . . . *permanent.*

With Slyck's nonnegotiable parting advice, Harmony tapped the table with the tip of her finger, a habitual gesture, and called the meeting to a close. Desperately needing air, Slyck hastily made his exit. He stepped out into the warm night and drew a sharp breath, his mind racing, trying to figure out what it was about Jaclyn Vasenty that held his attention and aroused the hell out of him—because never in his nine hundred years had a *human* female enticed him.

Physical discomfort apparent, he adjusted his jeans and berated his traitorous cock as he made his way back to the bar, but there was nothing he could do to bank his desires. What he needed was a cool drink, and a hot woman to help take the edge off. That would help numb the familiar, incessant ache for a while, but the only one who could help sate the bone-deep loneliness that stirred his insides was his true mate—a mate he'd yet to find.

Obviously such things weren't meant to be.

In search of his partner, he'd visited the other secret communities over the years but had no real answer as to why he'd yet to find the one woman meant for him. Other panthers were able to unite with their true mates by the time they reached maturity, around their third lifetime, but for some unfathomable reason his soul mate continued to elude him. Slyck worked to fight down the pang of envy that ate at him.

As he walked past the candy store, he looked through the plate-glass window to see a few of Vall's pack inside devouring a bounty of sugary treats. Christ, that sweet confectionary was like catnip to dogs. The townsfolk tolerated it in moderation, but what they wouldn't tolerate was demons and alcohol. Talk about hell on Earth.

Retracing his earlier steps, Slyck sauntered past the fire station and then the grocery store. He glanced at the men washing their already-spotless trucks outside the station, then turned his attention to the women milling about inside the store. To an outsider, the town of Serene looked like any other rural community. In order to keep up the appearance, they offered all the amenities of small-town living and even kept a few rental properties.

In a town that didn't welcome outsiders—for fear that they'd reveal their secret community—one rarely stayed long. And those who insisted on making their stay permanent quickly understood the repercussions behind that rash decision, because eventually straws were drawn, and species were made.

Since the folks in Serene couldn't risk exposure, the unsuspecting humans would soon find themselves going head-to-head with one of the five species. With primal instincts governing the actions of the chosen breed, the human would inevitably be turned into an immortal being in one of five ways: through a lycan's bite, a vampire's blood transfer, a witch's spell, a demon's slaying, or a panther's mating.

When a panther mates with a human, and fluids are exchanged, it alters human DNA, and eventually that human would be gifted with the ability to shift, and brought into the brethren.

Sometimes it took but one mating; sometimes it took more. If a male panther filled his "true mate" with his seed, however, the mating was for life, and without her true alpha at her side, the panther inside her would grow weak and die.

Tension eased from his body as he entered the bar, his sanctuary. The only place where music, as opposed to loneliness, stirred his soul and made him temporarily forget that he'd spent far too many lifetimes searching for the one woman meant for him and him alone.

Sure he'd had sex, plenty of bang-me-up-against-the-wall sex, with a myriad of different partners. After all, he was a panther, the most libidinous cat by nature. But those encounters merely sated his physical needs, not his emotional ones.

Slyck moved farther into the club and nodded to Drake, his first-in-command, who was serving up drinks and covering for Slyck in his absence. After an exchange of pleasantries, Slyck scanned the dance floor. Heat fired his blood when he spotted Brandy and Gina dancing under the flashing lights. Together they moved sensuously to the fast-paced music, mewling and brushing up against each other like they were two animals in heat. The entire scene was most erotic, stimulating, and just what he needed at the moment.

He inhaled. The scent of their arousal reached him clear across the room and brought out the carnal beast in him. He needed to fuck. Hard and fast. With his mind racing, and his cock throbbing for attention, he negotiated his way through the crowd and closed the distance between himself and the two sex kittens.

Brandy turned and grabbed a fistful of his T-shirt, her heat scorching him as she pulled him from the dance floor, away from the lights. Her eyes widened in pleasure when they met his.

"Slyck," she purred, and rubbed her face up against his, trailing small kisses over his jaw. "We were wondering where you've been."

He fingered her long dark locks. Soft. Silky. Suddenly his mind wandered to Jaclyn. Would her hair feel so luscious? Would it feel smooth against his naked flesh? *Damn.* He quickly shook his head to clear it. "Out on the prowl tonight, are you, kitten?"

In the darkened corner, Slyck could barely make out Brandy's pretty features as he traced the pattern of her long, sleek body. He toyed with the light, barely there material of her blouse before his fingers stole underneath her satin miniskirt. He brushed her smooth thighs with the pad of his thumb and climbed higher and higher until he found her sweet pussy dripping with desire. He arched an inquisitive brow, and growled low in his throat.

He gave her a knowing smile, and even though he already knew the answer, he questioned in a low, aroused voice, "Are you wet like this for me?"

When his fingers connected with her moist cunt, raw desire seared his insides. Lust bombarded his body and a tremor raced through him. Oh yeah, this was exactly what he needed to get his mind off Jaclyn Vasenty, because nothing good could come from his strange fascination with her.

In answer to his question, Brandy's fingers spiraled through his hair, pulling greedily as she pounced. Making no qualms about how hot she was for him, she wrapped her long, lithe legs around his back. With blatant sexual need ruling her actions, she mewled and shifted, positioning his hard cock on her soft mound.

Slyck's hands began shaking with desire, and his mouth watered for a taste of her skin. Ever determined to take the edge off, he took charge of their pleasures, gave a lusty groan, and backed her up against the wall. His large body hovered over hers, camouflaging them in the dimly lit corner. When his mouth found hers, a violent shudder ripped through his body.

The talented flick of her tongue over his lips aroused him to the point of no return. Fire pitched through his body; his heart pounded against his rib cage.

Although fucking Brandy in the dimly lit club was completely uncharacteristic for him, he couldn't seem to help himself. Normally he'd have taken her home and pleasured her thoroughly before he got off himself, but this fierce hunger and this foreign need burning through his veins had him acting completely out of character.

Gina pressed her full breasts into his back. As her hard nipples indented his flesh, he shuddered in heated bliss. Going up on her tiptoes, she positioned her mouth close to his ear and whispered, "What's the matter with you tonight, Slyck? You're acting so . . . *feral.*"

Without answering, he pinned Brandy against the wall and, wasting no time, slid into her, burying himself in her hot, tight pussy. He moved urgently against her, driving into her moist heat hard and fast, each velvet stroke bringing them both closer and closer to the edge.

"Yesss . . . ," she cried out and clawed at his skin.

Blood pulsed so hot and hard through his body, it was all he could do to keep himself upright. He plunged harder, deeper, ramming her with everything inside him as he strived to assuage the strange need he couldn't seem to identify.

Suddenly, his mind drifted, and as his orgasm mounted, a burst of bright light danced before his eyes and brought illumination to his darkest corners. The image of a beautiful feline muzzle flashed before his eyes. And he knew instinctively it wasn't Brandy's face that had just manifested itself in his mind.

It was Jaclyn's.

Chapter Three

So this was it.

Home, sweet home for the next few months, or more, depending on how quickly she could turn a profit and whip Vasenty Cosmetics sales into shape. Uncertainty wormed its way through Jaclyn's veins as she thought about the daunting task ahead of her. Huge corporate accounts she could handle. But coming in from the head office to restructure, reorganize, and improve marketing strategies in a small town where research had proven that folks preferred to age naturally just might pose more of a challenge. Then again, research had also proven that the elderly bought the greatest amount of skin-care products, and if Serene was anything like its neighboring community, she certainly expected to see her fair share of elderly people.

She briefly glanced at her sleek black cat, Ruby, and gave a heavy sigh. Although the town of Serene was Jaclyn's destination choice, and her father had readily agreed that it was the perfect location to prove her loyalties to the company, she was beginning to have second thoughts.

"What have we gotten ourselves into, Ruby?" Ignoring Jaclyn, Ruby pawed at the passenger-side window in search of an escape. Jaclyn chuckled. "Forget it, girlfriend. We're in this together."

When Jaclyn's tire hit a pothole, she turned her attention to the road ahead. Peering through her windshield, she slowed her sporty BMW down to a near stop and absently tapped her fingers on the leather steering wheel. She surveyed the unfamiliar surroundings analytically as she crept forward with caution. She took in the uninviting, cracked, and pitted road and the main gate that seemed to have materialized before her eyes. Her gaze panned the wide expanse of quaint little houses that slumbered in the picturesque village just beyond the entrance.

She'd picked Serene of all places because she thought there'd be little to no sexual temptation in the Podunk town, but it was more than that. She couldn't deny, nor could she explain why, that there was something about the town that called out to her. That she was drawn to it in some inexplicable way.

On many occasions while out driving on the highway with her granny during one of her childhood visits, she'd glimpsed the long, winding road leading into the secluded community. Her grandma had always refused to stop, insisting the inhabitants of Serene gave her heebie-jeebies. Which made it all that much more fascinating to Jaclyn, she supposed.

The static on her radio began to grate on Jaclyn's last nerve, and she went to work on finding another station. Was it too much to hope for a decent station? Or even a damn road sign, for that matter? She had no idea that that long, winding road went off in so many different directions, and if she hadn't been equipped with BMW Assist, she never would have found her way.

Unlike Silver Springs, with its branching communities, Serene was smack-dab in the middle of nowhere. She glanced to her left, then to her right, only to be greeted by miles of wilderness and mountains off in the distance—as if she needed another reminder that she was a far cry from her beloved clubs in Chicago.

Her stomach churned as her eyes followed the path of the fence until it disappeared into a dense cluster of spruce trees. It occurred to her that the entire town was imprisoned behind that sturdy security fence. No wonder the place gave her grandmother the creeps. Jaclyn too was beginning to feel a bit distressed, almost a little claustrophobic. As shivers of unease slithered down her spine, she diligently tried to shake off the unsettling feeling.

She shifted in her seat and took a moment to consider the quirks of small-town living. Was the barrier to keep outsiders away? To keep the inhabitants in? Or both?

She fiddled with her radio for a moment longer, then gave up, flicked it off, and cast her eyes heavenward. She might have chosen to spend an indeterminate amount of time in Serene, but that didn't mean she wanted to live here any longer than she needed to accomplish her goals, especially since setting sights on that impenetrable gate. She prayed that she could improve marketing strategies fairly quickly and turn around lagging cosmetics sales in the town's only department store—yes, she'd done her research—and could then get back to the real world. Otherwise she feared she'd shrivel up and die in the isolated village. Even though she was director of marketing at the head office, her father had assured her that moving product and increasing sales in a town where sales were practically nonexistent would be a strategic move on her part. Time and energy spent at the retail level would ultimately prove to investors and the board of directors that she had a vested interest in running the empire from the ground floor up upon Benjamin's retirement. Then again, maybe her parents just wanted to get her out of the city before she brought any more scandal to her family's name—now that she was out of town, the *Chicago Social* had turned its attention to the next misbehaving debutante. Or a way for her to find a nice respectable God-fearing guy she could bring home to Daddy. But in all seriousness, if restructuring to improve sales of skin-care products, antiaging creams, and makeup to the folks in Serene was the only way to appease her family and the board, then she'd happily do it. Okay, maybe "happily" was an overstatement.

When a car pulled up behind her, and she caught the driver's scowl in her rearview mirror, it set her into motion. She drew a fueling breath and hit the accelerator with much more force than necessary. A second later she pulled up to the security booth before passing through the armored gate.

She lowered her window down and stuck her head out to greet the guard. The warm summer sun beat down on her chilled, air-conditioned flesh and helped melt the tension inside her.

"The purpose of your visit, ma'am?"

She gave the guy a quizzical look. *Purpose of her visit?* Was he serious? Lord, she was entering the town limits, not crossing the border to Canada. Still, she decided to soften the path and use charm to lighten his mood.

She flashed him a genuine smile. "Jaclyn Vasenty," she said. "From Vasenty Cosmetics."

His eyes narrowed in displeasure. He gave her a hard look before turning his snarl on her cat. His dark glare let her know that her attempt at altering his hard-ass disposition had failed. That, and he wasn't a cat lover, apparently.

"How long will you be staying?" he asked.

Damn . . .

Within two minutes, she'd come across two men who'd both given her nasty scowls. And here she thought everyone who lived in small towns was friendly and accepting. So much for that theory. She hoped the women were friendlier and more open to purchasing the product once she educated the sales staff how to promote it, since going to backyard barbecues to gain trust with chatty, altruistic PTA members wasn't really her thing.

For some reason she didn't always play well with other females. Sure it was strange, but as far back as she could remember, she had preferred the company of men—or her cat—because most women seemed threatened by her. From kindergarten on through high school she'd always been a loner—aloof some had called her. And because she refused to bend to the will of those "mean girls," the ones who ruled school hallways and wielded their lipsticks like weapons, she'd found herself in a catfight a time or two.

Speaking of cats. Ruby jumped onto her lap and hissed at the guard, obviously not a fan, either. Offering her kitty an apologetic look, Jaclyn gently stroked her fur to calm her down and answered the guard, "As long as it takes."

"Excuse me?"

The guard's abrupt tone sent her eyes flashing back to his, and it was the first time she noticed the color. Such an odd shade of silver. As he continued to glare at her with those artic eyes, frustration caused her to throw her arms up and blurt out, "I don't know. A month. A year. Forever."

He turned to write in his little notepad, and she could have sworn he whispered something under his breath that sounded like, "We'll see about that."

Once he gave her the go-ahead, she stepped on the gas pedal and glanced at the open notepad on the seat beside her. Twenty-five Mulberry Lane. Since the town seemed to have only one main street, she was pretty certain that finding her house wouldn't prove too much of a task. She was right. Less than two minutes down the main drag, past the post office, the bank, and the schoolhouse, she spotted Mulberry Lane. She negotiated the turn, pulled into the stone driveway, and killed the ignition. With her window still down, she took a moment to drag the fresh, aromatic country air into her lungs. Suddenly, the floral scent roused happy memories from the recesses of her mind. Was that lilac?

The scent immediately took her back to her grandmother's old house. God, she had loved those overnight trips, and how she and her granny would get up extra early to feed all the robins and blue jays littering her vast backyard. Honestly, Jaclyn had forgotten how much she enjoyed those mini vacations—she smiled at the memory of how much she loved nature in all its splendor. Maybe she'd pick up her own bird feeder and see what kind of birds she'd find in Serene.

"How would you like that, Ruby?" She gathered her mewling

cat into her arms. "You can bird-watch, but you can't bird-feed," she added. Ruby purred her consent and rubbed against Jaclyn's arm. Then another thought struck her. Mosquitoes. Her skin itched as she recalled the way the flies had peppered her childhood clothes.

Cringing and fully expecting to be bombarded with insects, she climbed from the car and began waving her hand in front of her face like an escaped mental patient. The scarcity of divebombers stilled her movements. Okay, that was odd. Not an insect to be found. In fact, she couldn't even hear one single cricket chirping.

Bugs forgotten, Jaclyn grabbed the luggage from her trunk and glanced up at the house. She shaded her eyes and panned the quiet neighborhood. Apparently it seemed her arrival had garnered quite a bit of attention. Women and small children all stopped to stare, watching her over the rims of their lemonade tumblers.

She plastered on a smile and waved. Time to make nice. A few of the children waved back. The women, on the other hand, not so friendly. She drew a deep breath and let it out slowly as visions of backyard barbecues and neighborhood clambakes danced in her head.

Damn.

When she realized Ruby had yet to exit the cool car, she scooped her up. "What's the matter, girl? You couldn't wait to escape earlier." Ruby hissed, bolted from Jaclyn's arms, and took off to find shelter under the front steps of her rental bungalow.

"Ruby," she called and crouched down on all fours to peer

under the two stone steps. She really didn't have time for this. "Come here, girl." Unfortunately, she only succeeded in staining the knees on her new white capris. For some reason, her cat seemed to have taken up permanent residence under the dark stairs, and despite her efforts, there wasn't a damn thing Jaclyn could do to lure her out. After a few minutes she decided to deal with her cat's bizarre behavior later. She climbed to her feet and fished her keys from her purse. Now it was time for a quick exploration of the town she'd forever wanted to visit before she headed over to the department store and set things into motion. The quicker she became productive, the quicker she could accomplish her mission and head home.

Jaclyn slipped her key into the dead bolt, but noticed that the door was unlocked. Another quirk of small-town living, no doubt. She dropped her luggage inside and took a quick tour to familiarize herself with the furnishings and layout. A pretty blue vase on the coffee table caught her eye. She walked over to it, picked it up, and carried it to the windowsill, which she decided was a much better spot for it. Satisfied with her new rental property, she stepped back outside, and then automatically locked the door behind her, a habitual response compliments of big-city living.

She walked the footpath to the backyard and cringed when she spotted the huge swimming pool. She was not a lover of water, even preferring quick showers over long, luxurious bubble baths. Still, it'd be a great spot for a barbecue should she need to host one.

Leaving her car in the driveway, Jaclyn hitched her handbag high on her shoulder and glanced behind the houses across the street from hers. She spotted a beautiful, albeit deserted, tree-fringed jogging park. Oddly enough, there wasn't one dog walker to be found—not that she was a dog person. She shivered at the thought, really. But still, since it was such a familiar sight in Chicago, she expected to see a few people in the small town playing catch, or at least running the track with their pets.

Taking in her surroundings and looking for the department store, she made her way down Main Street and walked past the candy store. The enticing smell of ice cream and chocolate called out to her and slowed her down. Mmm. Chocolate.

The next best thing to sex, she decided. And since she was off sex . . .

A bell above the door jingled as she dashed inside the air-conditioned building. After purchasing a bag of dark chocolate mints, she popped one into her mouth, dropped the rest into her handbag, and made her way out into the early-afternoon sunshine, to take another look around at the small town.

Back out on the sidewalk, a woman and her child sidestepped her, barely sparing her a glance as they made their way inside for some candy. A few other people milled about, no more friendly than the mother and child. Jaclyn gave a heavy sigh and leaned against the hot brick building for a second, fearing this stint was going to be a hell of a lot harder than she had expected.

The warm sun beat down on her as she glanced up and down the streets in search of the department store. Her gaze settled on Vibes, the nightclub adjacent to the firehouse, one that brought back rich, decadent memories of Risqué. Not to mention Brian.

Or Kane.

Her salacious mind conjured up heated memories of her night with the two men, the provocative slide show sending shivers of warm need all the way to the tips of her toes.

Okay, speaking of alphas . . .

She spotted a man with more testosterone than both Brian and Kane combined stepping from the club. Heck, he had more than all the muscle-bound men who frequented Risqué, actually. Her blood began pulsing in hot waves, and her nipples tightened almost painfully beneath her crisp white blouse. Tiny beads of perspiration broke out on her upper lip as she studied him from afar.

Oh yeah, now there was a man who could corrupt her virtues with a blink of an eye. Looking sexy, completely groomed, and not at all uncomfortable in the blazing heat, he turned toward her. The mere sight of him from some twenty feet away had managed to reduce her to a wanton hussy. She could only imagine how she'd react if he was up close and personal. Her entire body shivered with longing, and deep between her thighs, her flamelike birthmark began to warm, tingle even. How odd.

The guy was temptation. Pure and utter temptation.

And *so* not what she needed right now.

As heat flared on her cheeks, she pressed her thighs together in an attempt to rein in her lust. The last thing she expected to find was a badass like him in Serene. A badass who was tall, with broad shoulders, sun-kissed skin, and a delectable body designed to satisfy.

A badass who was coming her way.

He moved like an alley cat with slow, easy, confident strides.

Something about him told her he was a man who knew what he wanted and took what he needed.

Damn, that excited her.

He turned those gorgeous green eyes of his on her, and she considered what he saw. Stepping into her role of the good girl, she'd forgone makeup that morning, and had pinned her long hair up in an artful coiffure. Thanks to her assistant's help, and her weekend shopping spree, she'd given up her professional yet still sexy work wear and now wore a pair of casual cotton capris that reached midcalf, and a starched blouse that was buttoned up to her neck and practically suffocating her. Damn, she must look like the headmistress from her all-girl prep school, and felt as comfortable as a cat caught in a summer downpour. As though moving of their own accord, her fingers found the top button, where she began to fiddle restlessly. Her tongue flicked out to lick the moisture from her upper lip.

As she shifted from one foot to another in her sensible flats, it occurred to her that this man was Dangerous with a capital D, and she needed to keep her distance, especially if she wanted to modify her wicked ways.

That realization soured her smile. She shot him a wary glance and, needing to escape, took a measured step backward. When her leg connected with something solid she spun around.

Oh shit.

"I'm sorry," she said quickly as she watched the little girl's big scoop of strawberry ice cream splatter to the sun-scorched sidewalk. "Let me get you another," Jaclyn hurriedly offered.

Watery eyes took in the big, gooey blob and then stared up

at Jaclyn in quiet distress. A second later, the child made a move to retrieve the liquefying ball, but Jaclyn bent down on one knee and stopped her. Unfortunately, the five-second rule didn't apply to ice cream.

"It's dirty, sweetie." Fearing the child was about to burst into tears, Jaclyn grabbed a handful of chocolate mints from her handbag and placed them in the girl's palm—a temporary peace offering. "Have these and I'll be back in two seconds, okay?" Jaclyn climbed to her feet just as the mother came through the door.

Jaclyn caught the disappointed look on the mother's face as her glance went from her child to the puddle of melting pink cream.

Hands out, palms up, Jaclyn said, "It was my fault."

Ignoring Jaclyn, the mother grabbed her child by the arm. "Candace, look what you've done. How many times do I have to tell you to be careful? You should have listened to me when I told you to choose a cup over a cone." She pulled the child away from the spreading mess and whispered, "So clumsy," under her breath.

Jaclyn's heart skipped a beat as she looked down at the whimpering little girl. Having been the recipient of many disappointed parental glares over the years, Jaclyn felt sorry for the child. Little Candace couldn't help her clumsy nature any more than Jaclyn could help her sexual one.

Jaclyn intervened. "Uh, it was my fault."

The woman spun around and Jaclyn felt herself wilt under her pewter glare. If looks could have killed, Jaclyn's family would have been picking out their funeral attire.

Seconds before the child put a chocolate in her mouth, her mother's eyes widened and she grabbed all the mints from her hands. "Where did you get these?" she shrieked.

The child pointed to Jaclyn.

Oh shit, Jaclyn thought again, realizing her day had just gone from bad to worse.

The mother waved the candy in Jaclyn's face. "What do you think you're doing? You can't just give candy to children."

Jaclyn shrugged. "I never thought—"

Enraged, the mother cut her off. "That's right. You never thought. This stuff will kill her. She's allergic."

Jaclyn frowned. Sure chocolate made babies sick—heck, it could even kill dogs—but she'd never heard of anyone being allergic before. "I'm sorry. I didn't know."

"Is there a problem here?"

Jaclyn spun around and came face-to-face with Mr. Testosterone in a T-shirt. Well, actually it was more like face to chest. Her face. His chest. And oh what a magnificent chest it was. She quickly tipped her chin to meet his eyes. When their gazes connected and locked, she felt like she'd just received a blow to the midsection.

His commanding manner drew the attention of all those surrounding them. A hush fell over the sidewalk. The mother physically retreated, even the child stopped whimpering in his presence.

Jaclyn strived for normalcy. "We had an accident."

He stepped toward her to peer over her shoulder, and she was certain she heard him inhale. She took a quick moment to wonder if he liked her new jasmine-vanilla perfume.

He inched closer. His nearness made her breathless, and the earthy scent beneath the clean smell of soap made her feel a little wild and wicked. When bewitching green cat eyes turned back to hers, Jaclyn faltered, her legs turning to overcooked noodles beneath her. Warmth flooded her system as one large hand circled her waist to support her, preventing her from escaping, which, ultimately, would have been the smart thing to do. Too bad common sense wasn't ruling her actions at this particular moment.

At first contact, sexual energy swirled throughout her body and exploded her senses. As life surged in her veins, she became hyperaware of the way her flesh began to itch and burn. She clawed discreetly at herself, scratching her arms as though she were trying to shed a layer, to crawl out of her skin.

His brow furrowed in concern, and a lock of dark hair fell over one eye. She fought the sudden urge to flick it back.

"Are you okay?" he asked, meshing her body to his.

She nodded and tried not to think about the powerful tingling sensation rushing its way through her bloodstream as her flesh connected with his in such a personal way.

As though he could read her every thought, feel her every desire, the corner of his mouth twitched. His smile was slow, inviting. "Then why are you turning red?"

Jesus, she hadn't even realized she'd stopped breathing. She inhaled and filled her oxygen-deprived lungs with the aromatic country air. She waved one hand in front of her face, fanning herself.

"Heat," she managed to get out, and tucked a wayward strand of hair behind her ear as she righted herself and escaped the enticing circle of his arms. She watched the way Mr. Testosterone carefully tracked her every movement, studying her intimately as she took a tiny step back. The hungry look he sent her way had her body quivering almost uncontrollably. As her body shifted into overdrive, foreign emotions and sensations ripped through her and practically rendered her speechless.

With remarkable success she managed to form a coherent sentence and answer the unasked question still lingering on his lips. "I spend most of my days in an air-conditioned building. I'm not used to prolonged exposure to sunshine. I think I'm prone to sunstroke," she rambled on. God, was that her voice? She hardly recognized that deep, desirous tone.

A flurry of emotions passed over his face. "I see," he said slowly, deliberately, as though tasting the electrically charged air around them.

She perused his sensuous mouth while lust sizzled between them. As his primal essence overwhelmed her, she spent one agonizing minute considering how that sexy mouth would feel on her skin, between her legs. Oh hell.

"Then we should get you inside before you pass out." A bad-boy grin curled his mouth as his warm breath brushed over her skin, eliciting a shiver from deep within her core. Jesus, he had to be the sexiest man she'd ever encountered. "I'm not quite up on my CPR," he confessed.

Desire slammed into her as she visualized herself lying horizontal while he pressed his mouth to hers. She placed her hand over her stomach, where need gathered in a ball. It was a need unlike anything she'd ever felt before.

Oh God, she really needed to pull herself together before she dragged him into the nearest alleyway and had her wicked way with him. Lord knows she was trying to be a good girl, but his body called out to her in ways that even she couldn't understand.

He turned his attention to the child and spoke in a calming voice, reassuring her that she'd have a brand-new ice cream in just a few moments. With his back to her, Jaclyn took that opportunity to pull herself together.

When Mr. Testosterone turned her way, Jaclyn physically pulled back, arched her spine, and put on her best professional face, cloaking her true sexual nature. Her sudden change in demeanor seemed to perplex him.

He held his hand out, eyeing her cautiously. "I'm Slyck."

Oh he was Slyck, all right. So was she. Slick between her thighs.

She accepted the offered hand and worked to summon a defense against his charm. "Jaclyn."

He gestured to the candy shop. "Shall we?" There was a rich cadence to his voice that heated her from the inside out and did the most amazing things to the moist little spot between her legs.

Okay, so maybe her trip to the department store could wait a minute or two. When she nodded, he pressed his hand to the small of her back and guided her into the store. The intimacy of his gesture caught her off guard and had her pussy clamoring for his attention. Not to mention his tongue.

"You can cool off while I grab the child another cone."

And here she'd rather *get off*.

Mercy!

Chapter Four

After Slyck had bought Candace another ice-cream cone, he'd escorted Jaclyn to the department store and then briskly walked away, spending the next two days trying to figure out what it was about her that called out to him like a beacon in the night. Christ, just knowing she was in town, living across the street from him no less, had his mind in an uproar, and his cock rising at will, like he was nothing more than an untrained kitten. But there was something special about Jaclyn—something that brought out the animal in him, and had his panther itching in a way it had never itched before.

Night had fallen as Slyck left Vibes and made his way home. He shook his head in bewilderment, trying to make sense of it all, yet still unable to figure out who Jaclyn was, and what it was about her that intrigued him to the point of distraction.

In a town that never slept, streetlamps lit his path along the sidewalk and fanned out into the streets, illuminating a handful of vamps who'd just recently awakened and were now making their way to the blood bank for replenishment before they hit the nightclub.

With an abundance of deer in the outskirts—deer that continually jumped the fence—keeping the vamps well fed never posed a problem. The deer, as well as the coyotes that managed to dig their way under the gate, also served to keep the lycans satisfied when they went for their compulsory monthly run. Since they'd rather avoid a bloodbath, the townsfolk remained inside on lockdown during that particular night.

Restless and edgy, Slyck walked down Mulberry Lane, slowing his pace as he passed Jaclyn's house. His gaze strayed to her backyard, to the milk carton hanging from a tree. Was that some kind of homemade bird feeder? He shook his head. Honestly, the woman kept surprising him.

He turned his attention to her big bay window and hunger consumed him when he spotted her inside, dancing sensuously as she prepared dinner in her small kitchenette. Music blared from her stereo and cut through the still air. His muscles bunched, and his cock thickened as he took in the erotic sway of her body. Jesus, his attraction to her just wasn't normal.

Slyck inhaled the enticing scent of warm barbecued chicken that seeped from her open window, making his stomach growl. Unfortunately, despite his own hunger, the delicious aroma did nothing to override the pressure brewing deep in his groin.

He took a long moment to gaze at her, then turned his attention to her fluttering curtain. Slyck spotted two glowing eyes cautiously watching him from behind the sheer lace.

"Hello, kitty," he murmured. "You'd better stay inside where it's safe."

Sidestepping a blue vase, her kitty studied him carefully and swiped its paw at the window. He suspected the poor kitten had to be shaken by its new home and all the creatures roaming the streets. Especially the lycans. That thought even made Slyck shiver.

Slyck crossed the road and slipped through his back door. His house was cool, a welcome contrast to the hot outdoors. Without bothering to turn his lights on, he made his way to his upstairs bedroom. The perfect spot to keep his new neighbor under surveillance. He tried diligently to focus on the job, and keep his mind off his raging libido—he really did. But he had to admit that watching her had more to do with wanting her in his bed with his tongue tasting her skin, and less to do with keeping tabs on her actions for the town's safety.

His exceptional night vision allowed him to easily see Jaclyn inside her kitchen. He scrubbed his hand over his jaw and inhaled. Her heavenly scent, a sexy combination of jasmine and vanilla, still lingered on his skin. He'd bet she'd taste just as exquisite between the legs.

As he watched her, he loved everything from the way she moved to the delicate way she ate her dinner and licked her fingers clean. She was mind-blowingly sexy, and it was all he could do not to cross the lane, grab her, bend that sweet little ass of hers over the sofa, and fuck her until sunrise. Christ, what was it about her that spawned such peculiar reactions in him?

Rattled by the lust rushing through his veins, he ripped open the front of his jeans to release the pressure on his cock, and let his lust-drunk mind wander. He ached to unleash himself on her, to greedily pull her marbled nipples into his mouth, to part her nether lips with the tip of his tongue and taste her sweet cream.

God, he'd never felt so aroused by a human female before. As a were-cat he was only attracted to his own kind. He stroked his engorged cock as he mulled that thought over for a moment. Was it possible that underneath that prim exterior she was panther? Surely that wasn't possible. Because if it was, she'd never be able to suppress her wild, sexual nature or keep her body buttoned up beneath that starched white blouse. She'd also have a distinct feline scent. A rich, earthy aroma that would be recognizable to him, as well as every other lycan in town.

Then again, there had been moments when he caught a glimpse of something primal beneath her staid clothing, and when he'd anchored her body to his outside the candy store two days previous, he felt desire stirring inside her before she quickly banked it. But how could she suppress it? It was impossible for a "she panther" to keep her femininity hidden. It went completely against their natures.

An uneasy feeling closed in on him. It couldn't be possible.

It just couldn't be.

Of course, there was one surefire way to find out.

After Jaclyn finished her meal, she deposited her dishes in the sink, switched all her lights off except the dim bulb above her range, and made her way into the front room. She moved in front of her bay window. Her position afforded him with an unobstructed view of her gorgeous body.

Slyck's ears perked up as she punched up the volume on her stereo. With her hands on her hips, Jaclyn bit down on her bottom lip, and then, with a look on her face that Slyck didn't understand, she scanned her living room. Seemingly unsettled she paraded across the carpeted floor. After a quick glance out her sheer curtains, she picked up a blue vase. With tension visible in her stance, she crinkled her nose in thought. Turning, she positioned the vase on an end table, then paced back to her stereo, where she fidgeted uneasily with her blouse.

Then suddenly, in a move that took Slyck by surprise, she let out what appeared to be a long, resigned breath, sensuously widened her legs, and leaned against the wall. Her hands left her waist, slid over her stomach, and then climbed higher, until she reached her breasts.

His brain stalled and liquid fire pitched through him as he perused her, immediately understanding her strange look, as well as what her agitated state was all about.

Arousal.

With her body shrouded in darkness, her hands spent a moment teasing her nipples before continuing to explore her flesh. She caressed her flat stomach and then dipped her fingers into the waistband of her pants.

Slyck's entire body moistened. He moaned, a heady mixture of agony and pleasure rushing through his blood. He shook his head to clear it, not wanting to focus on his own lust and miss a thing as Jaclyn licked her lips and threw her head back.

His cock grew another inch and he ached to sink into her warm, wet mouth as she pulled her pants wide-open and shimmied out of them. Her panties quickly followed. When she turned toward the window, he got a gorgeous glimpse of her naked pubis. He stroked his cock. Hard.

His mouth watered, thirsting to taste her pretty pink clit, to watch it swell before his eyes as he laved it with his tongue. He was dying to taste her entire body, and his mind conjured up the path his tongue would take, and the ways he'd make her quiver beneath his erotic assault.

She stroked the nub between her soft feminine folds and his thoughts went haywire. White-hot desire claimed him as lust hit him like a high-voltage jolt.

"Come on, sweetheart. Spread your legs for me, just a little bit," he whispered in a quiet plea as basic, elemental need took hold.

What she did next blew his mind and fueled his hunger in ways he never knew possible.

Jaclyn disappeared into the bedroom for a moment and came back with a pink rabbit vibrator. She stripped off the rest of her clothes, dropped down on the sofa, and widened her legs to give him a beautiful view of her sweet pussy.

Little white beads moved in a circular motion when she turned her vibrator on, and the clitoral stimulator lit up and buzzed to life.

She spanned her legs even more and brushed the tip of the fake cock over her clit before pushing it all the way up inside her.

Holy fuck.

His eyes widened in surprise. His body began shaking; air rushed from his lungs. Feeling crazed and frantic, he began morphing, his flesh stretching, his bones elongating. His skin itched and burned with his panther clawing to get out. Everything inside him urged him to run naked in the wild with Jaclyn, to fuck her hot body beneath the star-studded night.

Summoning all his strength, he quickly focused on something else. Now was so not the time to shift to his primal form, where his senses were enhanced, his strength was doubled, and his sexual appetite was most powerful and would be clamoring for attention. Jaclyn's attention.

Good goddamn thing he had control over the animal inside him; otherwise, like any one of his undisciplined teenagers, he'd have already been on all fours. With the inexplicable pull he felt for her, and the raw need ruling his baser instincts, he feared he'd turn into a mere kitten himself, unable to harness his animal urges for any length of time. Once in animal form, panthers, like other shifters, couldn't always be held accountable for their primitive actions—hence shifting outside the home was prohibited.

Slyck shook his head to clear it, and once he had himself under control he turned all his attention back to Jaclyn.

With a heated expression on her face, Jaclyn slipped her hand between her legs, parted her twin lips and worked the stimulator over her clit. He was sure he could hear her moans of pleasure clear across the street as she ravaged her sweet fissure.

Her eyes glazed with heat and hunger, and with slow controlled movements, she began to rotate her hips. He studied her carnal expression as the erotic show mesmerized him. Oh Jesus, he wanted her. Needed her. But he couldn't go over there and fuck her like she needed to be fucked, and he damn well knew it.

As his body thrummed with need, she shifted her position

and started to pump the cock in and out of her pussy. Raw lust flashed inside him and he almost came.

Okay, so maybe he couldn't physically be with her while she masturbated, but that didn't mean he couldn't talk to her, to hear her aroused voice while she pleasured herself with that sexy toy.

Even though he knew he should just walk away, as every instinct he possessed told him to, and even though it went against his better judgment, he picked up the phone and dialed her number anyway. It was a mistake. He knew it. But he couldn't help himself. That little vixen had him acting out of character and breaking policy—responding with his own best interests in mind, not the town's.

Wasn't that the very thing he always accused Vall of doing?

He pushed that thought to the back of his mind because he *needed* to talk to her, more than he needed to release the panther inside of him as it strived to claw its way out and ravish the hell out of her. He also needed to find out why she hid her sexy vivaciousness—a quality that she'd tried valiantly to hide, but he'd caught fleeting glimpses of over the last couple of days when she thought no one was looking.

The sexy vivaciousness of a female panther.

A surprised expression crossed her face at the sound of her ringing phone and he hoped—no, prayed—that the distraction wouldn't deter her from her solo act. Although he had to admit, the carnal look on her face told him it wouldn't slow her down one little bit.

Jaclyn leaned over, turned the music down until it was barely audible, hooked on a handless earpiece, and said, "Hello."

Her soft cadence quickly pulled him under and every nerve in his body immediately came alive. He tried to keep his voice light but failed. Need thickened his tone when he said, "Hello, Jaclyn."

She drew a shuddery breath. "Slyck?"

It pleased the hell out of him that she recognized his voice. Then another thought struck. Was it possible that she'd been thinking of him while she masturbated?

He pitched his voice low. "Yeah, it's me."

Without slowing down her sexy pumping action she asked, "What's up?"

My cock. You?

Before he could formulate an intelligent response, she furrowed her brow and went on to question in a low tone, "How did you get my number?"

"I, uh, small town, and the number on that rental property has been the same for years."

Lust danced in her simmering blue eyes as her gaze passed over her lace curtains cautiously. "Oh. What can I do for you, Slyck?"

Fuck me instead of that vibrator.

But he couldn't fuck her. Hadn't he said it himself earlier—no council member was to "play" with her or "mark" her before judgment, if a judgment call was made.

He took a quick moment to compose himself and for a lack of anything better said, "I was just wondering how you're making out at the department store. Cosmetics sales still down?"

"My, news sure travels fast around here, doesn't it?" She

drove the base of the shaft between the cushions. With the toy supported upward, she lifted her hips and slowly sank down onto the cock. An erotic whimper bubbled in the depths of her throat.

Sweat broke out on his forehead and he struggled to keep the lust from his voice. "Yeah," he managed as all his blood rushed south. "Real fast. So how are things going?"

He heard her sigh. "Not so great. The cosmetics clerks, Brandy and Gina, are more interested in gabbing and painting their nails than they are in listening to my strategies. And have you seen the women around here?" She laughed and said, "Of course you have. Silly question."

"What about them?" As chaos erupted inside him, Slyck rubbed his palm up and down his cock, moving his hand to the rhythm of her body. He pinched his eyes shut for a brief second as he stroked himself, imagining he was the one sitting on that sofa beneath her while she rode him hard.

"The women are gorgeous," she said, her voice pulling him back. "Flawless, really. No wonder the cosmetics don't move. These women don't need them. Everyone looks . . . *ethereal*. Must have something to do with clean country living."

Slyck's body tightened. Shit. Jaclyn was too observant for her own good. For the town's good.

"So tell me, Slyck. You're a local. What do you think is the key to selling cosmetics to these women? And please don't tell me I have to throw a backyard barbecue." Her soft chuckle curled around him and nearly drove him to his knees.

"What do you have against barbecues?"

"Uh, let's just say I never really learned how to play well with others."

"Well, since the women don't seem to need the product for wrinkles, why don't you market it as a product that can make them look and feel sexy. All women want that, don't they?" He couldn't believe he was actually giving her advice. Then again, maybe that was the key to getting her out of town. Which was exactly what he wanted, and the town needed. Right?

Her voice came out low, sexy. "You're a marketing genius, Slyck," she whispered, not bothering to mask her surprise.

After nine hundred years on earth, he'd learned a thing or two.

Her mouth curved enticingly when she went on to ask, "What exactly is it you do around this town, anyway?"

"I own Vibes."

She rocked her hips and he could hear the light buzz of the beads working her G-spot. "Oh. Nice. What kind of music do you play there?"

"The kind you're listening to," he said automatically, and then winced, realizing he'd given himself away. Before she'd answered the phone, she'd turned her music down so low; there was no way a mere human could hear it on the other end.

Her body stiffened. "How do you know what kind of music I'm listening to?"

His pulse leapt and his mind raced. "I heard it earlier when I was walking home from Vibes."

"You live near me?" Her voice sounded husky, sensual.

"Yeah. Listen," he said, redirecting the conversation. "I'm

heading back to Vibes shortly. Maybe you'd like to come and listen to some music."

Okay, that was a mistake. A big, fucking mistake. Talking to her on the phone from the privacy of his house was one thing, but meeting her in public was something else entirely. Something that Vall could grab on to and use against him. And if there was one thing Slyck was certain about, it was that Vall would love to see him taken down a notch, and for Drake, Slyck's first-in-command, to move into alpha position. After his last first had been decapitated, he'd chosen Drake to replace him. Slyck recognized that Drake possessed all the qualities of a good leader—intelligence, power, speed, and authority—thereby making him the next logical choice. Unfortunately he'd yet to develop the ability to fight with intellect instead of emotion—such things took time and had to evolve naturally—and therefore he wasn't quite ready for the role. Both Slyck and Vall knew it, which led Slyck to believe that Vall wanted to overpower Drake, manipulate him, and use the shift in balance amongst the community for his own gain.

After a long moment of hesitation, she said, "I, uh, no. I have an early morning tomorrow."

He blew out a breath, not sure whether it was disappointment or relief that stirred his soul. Since he knew better than to voice an argument, knowing her decline was for the best, he continued to rub his cock, and when she began to pump harder, faster, there wasn't a damn thing he could do to stifle the groan in the back of his throat.

Jaclyn undulated her hips. "You okay, Slyck?" she asked, her voice breathless. "You sound funny."

He could feel his composure vanish. Urgent need colored his voice. "Yeah, I'm doing just fine," he lied and rubbed his precome over the tip of his cock. Any second now he was about to lose it.

Squeezing her legs together she rocked harder, her voice coming out a little deeper as her pussy muscles gripped the cock. The sight of the sweet torture made him throb.

"What exactly are you doing?" she baited.

"You wouldn't believe me if I told you."

"Try me."

He drew a fueling breath. How would she react if she knew? Would she be angry? Excited? Damned if he didn't want to find out. Figuring nothing ventured was nothing gained, he took the bait and said, "I'm watching you."

Her body froze and her glance darted to her window. After a moment she squared her shoulders and asked in a suspicious voice, "Where are you?"

"I'm across the street."

Her glance swept over his windows in search of him. He took in her watchful eyes. "How can you see me?" she asked. "It's dark in here."

Fuck.

How was he supposed to answer that? Oh, I'm a were-cat with exceptional night vision. Jesus, if he kept this up by the end of the night he could write the manual *101 Ways to Give Away That You're a Shape-Shifting Panther Living in a Town Full of Deadly Secrets.*

"The kitchen. The light above your stove is on. It's casting shadows."

"Oh," she said, sounding a bit skeptical. She made a move to get up.

"Don't," he said firmly, stilling her.

He was almost certain he saw her whole body quiver at his commanding tone. "Why?"

He sucked in another tight breath and went for broke. "I want to watch. It's hot. You're hot, Jaclyn."

One perfect eyebrow arched. "Yeah?" Her tone deepened and she shivered with something that looked like a mixture of excitement and nervousness. Turbulence danced in her eyes as though she was struggling, trying to decide her next move, and then by small degrees, something in her expression changed, darkened when she said, "You're a very bad boy, Slyck."

Fuck, she didn't know the half of it. "Yeah, I know," he murmured.

"So all this time we've been talking, you've been watching me."

It was a statement, not a question, but he answered, anyway. "Yeah. I'm a regular voyeur."

"Tell me, does watching me masturbate excite you?"

"Uh-huh."

Her edgy laugh morphed into a heated moan, and Slyck got the sense that she wasn't at all stepping outside her comfort zone. That she was really adventurous, daring, and perhaps even an exhibitionist.

Her pretty pink tongue darted out to moisten her plump lips. "So your cock is hard then?"

He heard the longing in her voice and wondered where she

was going with this. "Real hard," he said, deciding to play along to see where this led them.

She whimpered with pleasure, obviously pleased with his admission. "And you thought you could just spy on me, without consequences?"

"Yeah, I kinda did."

"Spying is very naughty, Slyck."

"Mmmm. And masturbating in front of your window isn't?"

One hand went to her chest. She feigned offense, but the gleam in her eye turned wicked. "But my lights were out and I didn't think anyone could see me."

"I can see you."

With that, the little vixen cupped her breasts, held them high, and flicked her tongue across her nipples. "I think naughty boys need to be punished."

"Me, too."

Her soft chuckle bombarded him with need and a wave of possessiveness swamped him.

She shot him a smoldering look. "So here's what you're going to do. You get to watch, but you don't get to touch. Take your hand from your cock, Slyck."

He grinned. "Intuitive, aren't you?"

Amusement laced her voice when she said, "Well, you *are* a man."

Okay, he'd give her that. "So if I stick to your rules, you'll continue?"

"Yes."

"And if I don't?"

"Then I just might have to punish you."

Her words told him she liked the control, the power. "Okay," he agreed, shivering in anticipation. "I'll just watch then," he added, urging her on.

With that, Jaclyn threw her head back and began to ride the come-soaked vibrator. His mouth went dry as he ached to touch her all over, to taste the cream dripping from her cunt.

The soft, sexy bedroom noises she was making had him trembling uncontrollably. Her skin glistened with moisture and he licked his parched lips in response.

Savoring the moment, he whispered softly, "Come for me, baby. Let me watch you drip."

Her body began shaking and he suspected an orgasm was pulling at her. Her eyes strayed toward his window and swept over his silhouette as he briskly worked his hand over his cock, desperately needing to release the tension inside him.

Okay, so he was still whacking off. So what? And, yeah, once again she had him breaking all the rules, even self-imposed ones.

When her face flushed hotly, Slyck ground his teeth together and braced himself. His skin grew tight, and his balls constricted as pressure brewed.

"Yessss . . ." Her soft cries of ecstasy pushed him over the precipice, and he came. Hard. His muscles contracted, his liquid heat filling his hand. With her breathing labored, she continued to feed the rubber cock in her hot pussy as she too tumbled into orgasm.

As she worked the cock in and out of her, her head fell forward, spilling her hair over her breasts while her body clenched.

She exhaled a whimper of relief. "So good," she mumbled and blew a wispy bang from her forehead before sinking back and resting her head against the sofa's cushiony headrest. After a long, quiet moment, she glanced his way, lightly brushed her finger over her clit in a soothing motion, and cut the easy silence encompassing them. "Slyck, did you come?" she asked. There was something deeply intimate in the way she was talking to him. It caught him off guard and filled his darkest corners with warmth. He felt his whole world shift.

His heart began to slowly return to a steady rhythm. "Yeah," he admitted, noting the easy intimacy between them after what they'd just done.

She *tsk*ed. "Now you're really looking for trouble," she teased.

"I think I already found it," he responded, suspecting this woman was panther, and she was his mate. He didn't know how and he didn't know why, but everything inside him told him she was the one woman meant for him, even though she didn't seem to know it herself or know *what* she was. There was only one way for him to confirm that she was indeed a panther, and that was to get between her legs and breathe in her feminine scent.

Another thought struck him and his stomach clenched. If she truly was panther, that meant her life was in danger. After all, council rules were in place for a reason. He drew a deep breath and worked to center himself. Oh shit, this wasn't good. Not good at all.

Grinning seductively, she said, "Well, I think you need to be properly punished for not adhering to my rules, Slyck." Jaclyn climbed from the sofa, walked to her window and stared into his bedroom window. When intense blue eyes met his he could barely form a coherent thought. "But right now it's time for me to go to bed."

"Jaclyn."

"Hmmm." Her voice sounded sleepy, and not quite satisfied.

"You're not really that prim and proper girl you're pretending to be, are you?"

A pause, and then: "Good night, Slyck."

Chapter Five

No, it wasn't a good night. Hell, it wasn't even a great night. It was a fabulous night. An absolutely, unequivocally, blissfully, fabulous night.

And it never should have happened, dammit.

What in the hell had she been thinking?

So much for masquerading as a prim and proper city girl. Her act was as flimsy as rice paper, and it only took a bad boy like Slyck one meeting to rip through that thin veil.

With the intention of calling it a night, and cooling her heated body down, Jaclyn made her way to the bathroom, and took an icy-cold shower. Unfortunately the cool spray against her heated nipples only managed to arouse her more. She spent the next few hours tossing on her bed, with sleep continuing to elude her. Frustrated, and deciding she needed air, to clear her head, and her libido, she climbed from the mattress and reached into her closet for something to wear.

After pulling on a knee-length floral sundress—a dress that would make any debutante in her high-class society proud—and a pair of flat sandals, Jaclyn dabbed her neck with perfume and stepped from her house. Of course, no debutante she knew would be caught leaving her house without panties, she mused. It was naughty, for sure, but her pussy was just too damn hot to keep covered up.

It was nearing midnight as she made her way to town, convincing herself that her trip down Main Street had nothing at all to do with the hopes of seeing Slyck at his club, and everything to do with cooling off her heated flesh.

She took note of the people milling about, and watched them wander in and out of Vibes, as the lure of the music called out to her like an aphrodisiac.

She walked the streets, noting how there seemed to be an abundance of partygoers out on a weeknight. She found it odd that all the stores were lit up. Didn't anyone in this small rural town sleep? Back in her grandmother's quaint village, the majority of shops all closed up after dinner.

Treating her the same way they treated her at the department store—as though she was invisible—townsfolk passed her by, barely sparing her a glance. Waves of energy came off them, charging the warm air around her and creating static in the night sky. It made her feel antsy, like she wanted to run away, yet familiar enough that she wanted to stay.

Jaclyn pressed her back to the wall of the candy shop and hugged herself, suddenly feeling very alone and agitated. As the bar crowd sailed past her, she knew what they saw: a buttoned-up prude not worth talking to. But not Slyck. No, Slyck saw the real her. And she wasn't certain that was a good thing.

As her mind raced to Slyck, and their erotic phone call, her entire body quivered in yearning. She'd only gone along with the sexy game to get him out of her system, but the truth was, masturbating on the phone with him had left her needing the real thing.

Once again Jaclyn's skin grew itchy without warning, and she wondered if there was something in the town that she was allergic to.

"Hey."

Her breath stalled, and she didn't need to turn toward the voice to know who it was. His rich tone bombarded her with need, and her skin grew more irritated, inflamed. Jeez, maybe it was Slyck she was allergic to.

She turned to face him. Unlike the well-groomed guy she'd first met a couple of days ago, he now looked rumpled, dark, and somewhat dangerous. As she wondered what got him in such a disheveled state, she fought the urge to squirm. Right into his powerful yet scrumptious arms.

"Hey," she finally managed to respond.

He pitched his voice low and dipped his head. "What are you doing, Jaclyn?"

"I needed air," she rushed out quickly.

She noticed the way Slyck glanced over her shoulder, his expression guarded, and how he pressed himself deeper into the shadows.

She gestured with a nod toward Vibes. "So I thought I'd check out the music."

In a move that took her off guard, he caught hold of her hand and hauled her into the dark alleyway between buildings. Breath ragged and body tense, he put his arms on either side of her head, caging her between him and the wall. The clean scent of his freshly showered skin reached her nostrils, and she pulled it into her lungs. His seductive aroma curled through her blood, reminding her she was a libidinous woman—a libidinous woman with so very many unsated needs. Slyck touched a damp lock of her hair and searched her face.

His gaze was so dark and intense it took two locked knees to keep herself upright. The air grew ripe with the scent of her arousal. She watched Slyck's nostrils flare when he caught her excited tang as it saturated the narrow alleyway. His eyes closed for the briefest of seconds.

She touched his face. "What—"

He cut her off and brought his mouth closer and she could have sworn she heard him purring. "You need to get out of here."

"Why?"

He pulled her against him. Turmoil flashed in his green eyes. "Because if you don't, I'm going to ravish you. And I don't think it's in your best interests," he said with quiet certainty.

She gulped air. "What is in my best interest?"

His lips hovered over hers, and she got a heady whiff of aged scotch. "Leave town."

That took her by surprise, especially after the sexy voyeur game he'd played with her. She crinkled her nose, wondering what was going on. Why was he suddenly pushing her away? "You want me to leave?"

"Yes. It's for your own good." He pulled her in tighter, his actions seeming to contradict his words.

"It doesn't seem like it's for *your* good," she said, stating the obvious as his hard cock pressed into her stomach.

His nostrils flared again, and he growled into her mouth. "Tonight, Jaclyn. Leave tonight."

God, the steady way he held and touched her made her feel so edgy, so out of control. She wanted him more than she had ever wanted any other man, which gave credence to her logic to stay away, because sleeping with him wasn't conducive to her new image. Then again, the phone sex hadn't helped either. But the fire that brewed between her legs and the way her birthmark began to burn and sizzle urged her to answer the demands of her body.

Just once.

Just for tonight.

Then tomorrow she'd get back on track.

She had no idea what possessed her to say it, but without censoring her thoughts she said, "But you haven't been properly punished yet."

His hands fisted. His jaw clenched. She could feel his heart pounding so hard against his rib cage, she was sure it was going to burst wide-open.

"And I'm just the girl to do it," she added.

"Oh, fuck, Jaclyn. You have no idea what you're getting yourself into."

She thrust her pelvis forward. "Maybe we should be thinking about what you could be getting yourself into."

The invitation in her voice seemed to unleash something wild

inside him. His hardened expression changed and took on a resigned look. Gone was his will to push her away.

"Come with me." He roughly shackled her arms and pulled
her deeper into the alleyway. A moment later she found herself
cutting through the deserted park with him, taking a shortcut
back to his place.

Silence hovered in the air as he guided her through his back
door. They entered the kitchen, where he reached into his cupboard and poured them both a stiff drink of scotch. Jaclyn definitely wanted something stiff. But scotch wasn't what she had in
mind.

A sliver of moonlight outside the window provided sufficient
light for her to see him in the dimly lit room. She shook almost
uncontrollably as she watched him recap the bottle and put it
away. There was something very sensual in the way he moved, she
decided. He turned back to face her and pushed the glass into her
hand.

"Drink," he said.

"Thanks." She took a small sip. As the liquid burned a path
down her throat, she watched him, noting how he never once took
his dark, seductive gaze from hers as he downed his glass in one
gulp.

"Thirsty?" she questioned, barely able to keep her voice from
shaking and her body from quaking as she hungered for him with
an intensity that both scared the hell out of her and excited her
just the same.

"Yup." He put his glass down and stalked closer. He took her
glass from her and put it aside; then he grabbed her firmly by the

hips and backed her up against the wall. Slyck breathed a kiss over her mouth and surfed his lips over her cheek. "But the only thing that is going to quench my thirst is your sweet cream, Jaclyn."

She gave a broken gasp. Overwhelmed by need, she opened her mouth in invitation. He pressed his lips to hers and kissed her deeply. Her nails bit into his shoulders as their tongues tangled and thrashed. His mouth went to her neck and he breathed in her perfume.

"You smell so fucking good."

A moment later he inched back. His lips, warm and silky, hovered over hers as he whispered into her mouth, "I need to fuck you, baby. I need to fuck you real bad."

She gyrated against him, desperately needing him to assuage the ache inside her. Barely able to reply she managed to get out, "Yes. Please . . ."

A growl ripped from his throat and his cock pressed against her so hard, her entire body shuddered in response. His knuckles brushed her heated cheek. Ripples of sensual pleasure danced over her skin, urging her to give herself over to him completely.

His eyes locked with hers. He thumbed her lips. "But first I need to kiss you. Every square inch of your body. I want to taste your mouth, and your nipples, but mostly I want to taste right here." He slipped his hand between their bodies and cupped her moist pussy through her thin dress.

"Please . . . ," she murmured. "Now." She widened her legs so he could feel her heat.

His eyes smoldered. "Oh fuck, baby, you're not wearing any panties." Raw excitement laced his voice. In one swift movement, he gathered her into his arms and carried her up the stairs to his bedroom. He deposited her onto his mattress and stood back to look at her.

She whimpered, unable to vocalize what she needed, or just how crazed this man, this stranger, made her feel.

Slyck quickly removed his clothes and stood before her, looking completely comfortable in his own skin. After she took in the sexy artistic ink on his upper arm, her glance traveled to the plethora of deep clawlike scars marring his flesh and everything inside her softened.

"Slyck?" she questioned.

"It's okay. They're from a long time ago."

She understood that he didn't want to talk about it now, so she nodded her head and continued with her slow perusal. Even with the scars, he had the most beautiful body she'd ever set eyes on. Athletic, with broad shoulders, striated muscles, a magnificent chest, rock-hard abs, and an even harder cock.

She bit down on her bottom lip with longing when she saw the impressive size of his erection. Impatience thrummed through her, and she flushed hotly. "Come here." She reached for him, needing intimate contact.

When he didn't make a move, her glance traveled to his face, questioning him.

"Open your legs." His voice was a low, velvet seduction. "Show me your pussy."

Muscles tightening with arousal, Jaclyn eased her legs open, offering her naked sex up to him. "Like this?" she asked.

A muscle in his jaw twitched. "Exactly like that."

He stood there for a long time, just looking. Desire coiled deep in her belly. Oh God, was he ever going to fuck her?

"Slyck, please," she begged shamelessly. "I need you inside me."

Then he did the strangest thing. He climbed between her thighs, buried his nose into her pussy, and inhaled. Taking long, deep breaths as he filled his lungs with her scent.

Warmth streaked through her when a low growl rumbled in the depths of his throat. Then he flicked his tongue out and swiped it across her sensitized clit—a furtive brush that reminded her of a kitty lapping at its cream. A purr resonated through her body and brought on a shudder.

"So delicious," he whispered against her trembling sex.

She quivered beneath his invading tongue and gripped the bedsheets, hanging on for what she suspected was going to be the best ride of her life. As though sensing her mounting desire, he took full possession of her pussy. His light, delicate laves turned into long, luxurious strokes, and just like that, he made her come.

Her entire body clenched as an intense orgasm took her by surprise. "Oh God, Slyck," she cried out, racing her fingers through his thick hair as his mouth devoured every drop of her release. Good Lord, nobody had ever made her come so quickly before.

When her tremors subsided, he pushed on her legs, spreading them even more. His gaze raced over her skin, as though searching for something. His eyes widened when he caught a glimpse of her birthmark. "Jaclyn," he whispered, his voice edgy, raspy, and very, very shaky.

"What?" she asked.

She hadn't expected to see such tenderness in his gaze when he looked up at her. "You have the mark of fire."

Jaclyn glanced between her legs. Her pale café au lait birthmark now flamed red. She touched it. "I think I might be allergic to something," she said breathlessly. "It's been inflamed ever since I arrived in town."

His fingers dug into her thighs. With a tone that was both rough and emotional, he murmured, "Jesus, Jaclyn, you really don't know, do you?"

With no idea what he meant, and not wanting her allergic reactions to spoil her night, she gripped his head and guided it back to her sex. "I know that I want you to make me come again."

And make her come again he would.

Fiery birthmark temporarily forgotten, he turned his attention to fucking her. Which he planned on doing today, tomorrow, forever. Because everything from the way she aroused and stimulated his panther, to the taste and scent between her legs, and the mark of fire on her thigh confirmed that she was indeed his mate.

With a flash of possessiveness, he climbed up her body and pressed his mouth to hers, seeking more than just a physical connection. After a deep, heated kiss, he worked a path down her body. His hands tugged on her dress, ripping it from her skin like he was a wild animal in heat. He kissed her breasts, sucked on her pert pink nipples, and then positioned himself between her legs.

He wanted to slow down, but he couldn't think; he could only feel. And this was the most important moment of his life.

His eyes met hers as his cock probed her slick opening, his actions completely consumed by lust. As he pushed his thickness into her, she easily opened up for him, welcoming every inch of him into her body. Her warmth and heat closed around him, completing his soul in ways that he never thought possible, and empowering every inch of his body, the way only a true mate could.

After he fully entered her, a burst of energy swirled around them, explosive, powerful, all consuming. The look in her eyes told him she felt the powerful pull between them every bit as much as he did.

She gripped his shoulders and held him to her as he pumped into her with fevered passion. Moisture sealed their bodies as they rocked together. Blood pounded through his veins so hard, he thought he'd black out, and when her liquid heat singed his cock, he knew he wouldn't be able to last long.

As though sensing his urgency, she whispered in an unsteady voice, "Come for me, Slyck."

Something about the way she said his name, so softly, so gently, immediately pulled him into a cocoon of need and desire and propelled them to a deeper level of intimacy. Tenderness stole over him when he sought out her mouth again. His hands crushed through her long silky hair as he pushed deeper and harder. In no time at all, he felt her muscles tighten again, and at that point he let his own orgasm take hold.

He filled her with his seed, splashing every drop high up inside her as he surrendered to the pleasure. Her hands raked through his hair, and she pulled his mouth to hers as she too rode out her climax.

"Oh wow," she whispered as he rolled beside her and pulled her in close.

"Wow?" he teased.

"Yeah, that was totally wow worthy," she replied, her breath still ragged.

When she rested her head on his chest, Slyck gathered the blankets and pulled them over her. He ran his fingers through her hair, thinking about how perfect sex was with her, about how perfect she was.

Slivers of light seeped through the opening in his curtain and cast warm shadows across the bed as they lay there and basked in the afterglow of great sex—the greatest sex of his life, as a matter of fact.

A long while later, in search of answers, he broke the comfortable silence. "Jaclyn?"

"Yeah?" she murmured sleepily.

"What really brought you to Serene?" He wondered if she was here to turn around company sales, or if she had been drawn to the place, drawn to him.

She got quiet for a moment and then said, "It's a long story."

He brushed her bangs back, and when he caught her glance, he nearly sobbed with joy. *We-Sa.* His kitten. His mate. "I'm not going anywhere, sweetheart. Talk to me."

She blew out a breath, and then began to open up to him. "I did it to appease my parents."

"Your parents." He touched her cheek, coaxing her to continue.

Jaclyn then went on to explain everything, from always wanting to visit Serene, and not wanting to disappoint her adoptive parents after they had rescued her from a life of foster care, to the board of directors looking down on her wild behavior.

As he listened, he took it all in, understanding so much more about her and her actions. "So that's what the conservative clothes are all about?"

"Yeah, I'm changing my image, so you can't tell anyone about what we did," she whispered, her lids slipping shut as sleep pulled at her.

"I have no intentions of telling anyone," he said adamantly, because if he did, there'd be hell to pay.

"Tomorrow we'll go our separate ways and pretend nothing ever happened," she added.

Like hell they would.

As she drifted off to sleep in his arms his mind raced, trying to make sense of it all. Once her breathing deepened, he climbed from his bed, flicked on his computer, and went through years of files.

How was it possible that she was panther?

Something in his gut told him this wasn't the work of a rogue living outside the protective walls. Panthers weren't attracted to humans, and it wasn't in their animal nature to change them at will.

After a bit of research, Slyck began to piece together the time frame, recalling the shifter who'd escaped from the walls some twenty-four years ago. Back then, acting with the community's best interest at heart, Slyck was personally forced to hunt him down and dole out suitable punishment to the shifter. It was the only way to keep peace amongst all the species and keep the rogue panther's escape a secret. Slyck glanced at Jaclyn and then back at the computer screen. What he didn't know at the time, and could only conclude now, was that *his* rogue had impregnated a female during the ordeal—a female panther.

And Jaclyn was the offspring.

Slyck had handled the incident secretly—something he wouldn't normally do—because if the lycan guide had found out that one of Slyck's species had turned mutinous, he'd have demanded Slyck's authority and leadership position be challenged by his first-in-command. And Slyck couldn't let that happen. Drake might be more prepared now than he had been back then, but he still wasn't quite up for the tremendous task. And now, as the offspring of the rogue shifter, Jaclyn would automatically be terminated, as per their governing rules, for fear that such offspring would retain rebellious traits of the mutinous parent and uncover their secret community. After all, despite their civilization, they were all still primal beings ruled by instincts, and survival of the fittest.

Which meant that Jaclyn's life was in danger.

Torn between protecting Jaclyn and following council's rules, he looked down at the woman in his bed. *We-Sa.* His heart pounded harder in his chest as deep-rooted need unfurled inside him.

Even though it went against everything his community demanded of him, he knew he'd protect her with his life. He also knew he couldn't let anyone know what she was.

Christ, he was barely keeping peace with the lycan as it was.

The cat-dog relationship was already far too strained, not to mention that Vall was furious with Sunray, one of his strong females. Sunray was an alpha wolf who had a strange fetish for all things kitty, and who just happened to be growing more powerful and restless, challenging Vall's wolf far too often.

Slyck could no longer force Jaclyn out of town, not now, not after they had mated. It was far too late for that. There was a bond between them that would only grow stronger with time, and without her true mate by her side, she'd eventually die. There was no turning back for him now.

His mind raced, sorting through matters, searching for an option and finding none. His gut rolled.

Oh God, what had he done?

Chapter Six

Off in the distance, just past the edge of the town, fingers of warm golden light crept toward the towering mountains while Jaclyn lay beside Slyck in bed. As she took in his warm, rumpled look and listened to his soft breathing sounds, her entire body trembled with longing. Even though she was covered in blankets, she'd never felt so exposed, bare, or vulnerable. This man did something to her. Something that made her feel things she'd never felt before. Truthfully, she'd never responded to anyone the way she responded to him. What was it that made it feel so good, so right with him? She shook her head, unable to put her finger on it.

Even though she wanted him inside her again—she craved the feel of his warm lips on her body and his gentle hands stroking her flesh in the way that only he knew how—she had to admit that for the first time in her life, she actually felt sated. Like the incessant need inside her had finally been assuaged—the hollow filled.

But despite that newfound satisfaction, Jaclyn was here to

change her wild ways, and Slyck certainly wasn't the kind of guy she could bring home to Daddy. That last thought made her stomach plummet and prompted her into action.

Quietly slipping from his king-sized bed, she gathered her dress off his carpeted floor. She stepped around his computer desk and dresser—the only two pieces of furniture in the sparse room—and not wanting to wake Slyck, she tiptoed toward the window to glance out. The small community remained shrouded in darkness as off in the distance the brand-new day fought its way out of the black. She glanced at her bungalow across the street, noting how she could see straight into her living room and clear on into her kitchen. As she thought about the sexy performance she'd given Slyck, her entire body shivered.

"Good morning, sunshine."

Jaclyn's breath caught at the sound of his warm, sexy tone. God, he moved so quietly and so stealthily, she hadn't even heard him approach. His delicious earthy scent closed around her and did the most amazing things to her insides. Moisture broke out on her skin just from his close proximity. Before she turned to face him, she had to work hard to gather herself, because the sound of his voice alone had her wanting him between the sheets again. It suddenly occurred to her that one could take the naughty girl out of the city, but definitely not the naughty out of the girl. No matter how hard she might try.

She began to turn. "Slyck . . ."

"*Shhh.*" Big warms hands touched her body, pinning her against the window frame. "You look so fucking beautiful standing here, Jaclyn."

He buried his face in the side of her neck, and when his mouth pressed hungrily against her flesh, her dress fell to the floor, completely forgotten. Her resolve to flee melted faster than the strawberry ice cream on the hot pavement had a few days earlier.

"I don't want you to move." His warm lips feathered over her skin. As he reacquainted his mouth with her body, her entire flesh broke out in goose bumps. "Because I haven't been inside you yet."

She gulped. "You've been inside me."

His fingers slid over her ass, and he gently parted her cheeks. "Not everywhere," he murmured. "And you see, Jaclyn, that just won't do." His voice was so calm, collected, and confident it made her shake.

"So I'm going to fuck your ass while you stand here."

With that, moisture gathered between her legs, and there wasn't a damn thing she could do to summon a defense against his slow seduction.

"Then, and only then, will I have been inside you— everywhere—like I need to be."

God, the way he was acting—like a wild animal ready to claim its mate—had her wanting to submit to all his demands. Because deep down, she wanted him inside her everywhere too.

Marking her.

Before she could consider the intelligence of that decision, or where that primitive thought had even come from, he slipped his hand between her legs and all thoughts were forgotten.

"I can't get enough of you," he murmured, then added in a soft voice, "You need this too, don't you?"

Obviously the moisture between her legs had given her away. "Yes," she whispered.

That seemed to please him. "Mmmm. So nice and wet for me," he murmured as he pushed a finger into her pussy. He spent a long time stroking her, brushing the rough pad of his finger over her sensitive G-spot. Jaclyn gripped the window frame for support.

Using her cream, he lubricated her back opening, and worked his finger inside. Once he had her widened and stretched, he breached her ass with his cock, slowly pushing past her tight ringed passage, ever so gently, letting her get used to his thickness. Jaclyn moaned in pleasure. Her head fell forward to press against the cool glass, ribbons of hair spilling over her bare breasts.

After he worked his way inside, he began rocking his hips, slow at first as he raised her passion to new, never-before-known heights. Jaclyn met and welcomed every delicious thrust, her responses conveying her needs. Her body opened for him so easily, because they were made for each other. He bent forward and cupped her pussy, his thumb toying with her engorged clit.

"Oh Jesus," she bit out. Jaclyn closed her eyes and concentrated on the delicious points of pleasure.

The growl in his throat told her he was close. "You're so tight, baby." But it was the need and passion in his voice that pushed her over the edge.

"Oh yes . . . ," she cried out and erupted all over his hand, amazed that he knew just how to touch her.

He pushed deeper inside as her warm cream pooled in his palm. His cock throbbed twice as hard in response. "I love how responsive you are to my touch. You have no idea what that does to me."

The intimacy in his words filled her with warmth. "I have a pretty good idea," she whispered, as she rode out the waves of ecstasy.

With that, he stilled his movements. She could feel his cock pulsate as he let go, splashing his seed high up inside her. She clenched her ass muscles, milking him dry, not wanting to lose a single drop of his liquid desire. As his hot come filled her body, it seemed to bring on yet another orgasm, and she began to shake uncontrollably.

Not really understanding what was happening to her, she glanced at Slyck over her shoulders; their eyes met and locked. "Slyck . . ."

"It's okay, babe. I've got you." His tender tone caused her heart to skip a beat. Slyck tightened his arms around her waist as she rode out the tremors. Oh God, her body had never reacted in such a bizarre way before, climaxing simply from a man releasing inside her, as though his hot seed had the ability to bring on another orgasm. What the hell was that all about? When the wave finally passed, he spun her around and pulled her to him.

Seconds turned into minutes as they stood there holding on to each other, each seeking solace in the other person's arms. She wasn't sure what the strange tremors were all about; all she knew was that they'd yet to use a condom, which was so unlike her. But they'd been so caught up in the frenzy, desperate to fuck, she'd never given protection another thought. Her body tightened with unease. Yes, she was on the pill, but she always took safety precautions.

Slyck brushed her hair over her shoulders and put his mouth close to her ear. "Are you okay?" he whispered. From the protective way he held her to the intimate way he talked to her, she instinctively felt this man would never do anything to harm her.

She talked into his chest. "We didn't use a condom. I always use a condom."

He blew a slow breath. "I'm clean, babe, if that's what you're worried about."

"Me too," she whispered, suddenly feeling unusual and strange.

He licked her earlobe and she shivered. "Come back to bed."

She touched his face and summoned all her control. "I have to go," she murmured, even though she liked his idea much better.

A teasing grin curled his lips, and he slipped a hand between her legs to stroke her swollen clit. "No, you don't. You have to come," he teased.

She moaned and pushed against him. "Oh, I have, many times. Thank you very much," she said, chuckling. He pinched her clit. Good Lord, if he kept that up, she'd never get out of there. "But I want to get home before sunrise, before the neighbors find out that I'm a wanton hussy, sleeping with the first man I met after only a few days in Serene." She frowned. "They're already unfriendly as it is."

He stepped back, his hand falling from her pussy, his face taking on a serious look, like he'd just remembered something. Something important. "I'll walk you."

"It's just across the street."

"And I'll walk you." Slyck bent down and gathered her dress.

Jaclyn watched a flurry of emotions pass over his eyes. "It's okay. I'll be fine. It's almost dawn," she assured him.

"All the more reason."

"What is that supposed to mean?"

"I'll explain it when we get you safely inside."

"Jeez, you're acting like the bogeyman is out there."

"He is."

She waited for an explanation, but when none came, she quickly got dressed.

The morning sun began its ascent as they cut across the lane and slipped through the back door of her bungalow. Jaclyn stopped to check her bird feeder and frowned when she found it empty.

When she got inside, Slyck got right to the point. "Jaclyn, you can't go out alone at night."

"Why?" She made a face, but it didn't seem to amuse him. "Because the bogeyman is out there?"

"Yes."

She tossed him a skeptical look, dropped her purse onto her kitchen table, stretched out her fatigued body, and stepped into her living room. Slyck followed close behind. "And here I thought your need to see me home was just a quirk of small-town living."

He watched her move the vase from the side table back to the window. He arched a brow. "I guess we all have our quirks."

"Touché," she said, grinning.

His voice took on a hard edge as though to prove his seriousness. "Jaclyn, I need you to listen to me, to understand what I am about to tell you."

His brisk tone stilled her. She turned to face him and took in his watchful, protective stance. Her stomach clenched, her pulse leapt. "What?"

He captured her hand and led her to the sofa. When he had her nestled in beside him, he said, "Your whole life you had this emptiness inside you, right? This hollow feeling?"

She narrowed her eyes and nodded at him. "How did you know that?"

He brushed his thumb over her bottom lip, and it was all she could do not to lean into his touch. "I also know that you have an insatiable appetite for sex."

"Yes, but I told you that."

He angled his head and studied her carefully. "But what you don't know is why you have it, and I do."

Okay, he was starting to freak her out. She began to inch away. "Listen, Slyck—"

He cupped her elbow to stop her from escaping. "It's because you're a shifter, Jaclyn," he announced.

She blinked several times as her sleep-deprived brain took a minute to digest and assimilate what he was telling her.

"Shifter?"

He looked at her carefully, gauging her reactions. "Yes, a shape-shifting panther. A were-cat."

All righty, then.

Breaking his tenacious hold, she jumped to her feet and stepped behind the coffee table, putting some much-needed distance between them. So she'd slept with a weirdo, an escaped mental patient perhaps. And here she'd always prided herself on her exceptional intuition, and her ability to judge character. Her sixth sense had never let her down before. Why had it suddenly failed her now?

She lowered her voice and spoke in a calming manner. "It's been a long night, Slyck. And we're both in need of sleep." She blinked at him and smiled. "I'll see you later, then," she added for good measure, with every intention of avoiding him for the rest of her stint in Crazyville.

He shook his head slowly and studied her eyes. "You really had no idea, had you?"

"No, but thank you for enlightening me. Maybe we can discuss this later after I've had some rest."

Or not.

His voice softened. "Jaclyn, I know it sounds bizarre, and that it's hard for you to take in and assimilate, but trust me when I say I'm not insane." He angled his head and took in her stance. "So you can stop looking at me like I am."

She planted her hands on her hips and questioned, "Well, how am I supposed to look at you after listening to you spout something so crazy? Shifters are folklore, Slyck. So are vampires, demons, and monsters under the bed."

"You forgot witches and werewolves. They're real too."

Oh boy! He was crazier than she thought.

She pointed to the door and demanded, "I think it's time for you to go."

"Were-cats are very sexual beings, Jaclyn." Undeterred by her rising hysteria, he stood and began to walk toward her. The closer he came, the weaker her knees felt. "They're unable to sate the incessant ache inside them unless they mate with the one and only panther meant for them. It's the way of our pride, Jaclyn. The way of our bloodline."

As he inched closer, her thoughts raced, and she recalled how for the first time in her life she had actually felt satiated, the hole inside her closing, the ache abating after mating—err—having sex with Slyck.

"Your parents were shifters."

"Slyck, you're crazy. I grew up in Chicago, with two very normal parents."

"And your biological mother?"

"I never knew her. She abandoned me."

"No, she didn't."

"She didn't?" After harboring fears of abandonment her entire life, she brushed her tongue over her bottom lip and entertained the idea for a brief moment. She truly wanted to believe her mother had never ditched her in a Chicago subway on purpose.

"No. She was panther too. Which was why my rogue shifter broke through the town's barriers and went in search of her. The panther in her called out to him. Just like your panther calls out to me, and the reason you were drawn to Serene."

Okay, so she couldn't deny that she felt a very strange pull toward this town, toward him. But still, she was hardly a panther.

What a weirdo.

"Then after I hunted down my rogue shifter, he was forced to accept his just punishment for putting the colony at risk."

Her eyes widened with a mixture of disbelief and fear. "You killed him?"

He lowered his head, as though taking a moment to remember and respect a lost loved one. "Mandate rules, Jaclyn."

Oh God, she couldn't believe he was telling her that he had killed her biological father, that he'd stolen her opportunity to know and love him. Her legs weakened as her emotions went on a roller-coaster ride. Tears threatened and she choked them back, reminding herself that none of this could be true, that Slyck was a wacko.

He looked sad. "I'm sorry, Jaclyn. I never knew it would come to this, but we have strict rules."

"And you never break the rules," she challenged, overwhelmed by everything he was telling her.

His eyes clouded for a quick moment; then he said in a low voice, "Never."

Frightened, Jaclyn took a quick glance around her living room, searching for something big and hard to hit him with, although judging by his size, it would take more than her glass vase. She remembered the mace in her purse, but before she could get to her kitchen, her head began spinning, and she felt dizzy. Slyck wrapped his arms around her waist as her rubbery legs began to give out on her.

He continued with his explanation, and she struggled to make sense of his words. "The female's panther stays dormant until she's introduced to male seed. And after finding a true mate and joining as one, an impenetrable bond is formed. And because of that bond, without your mother's true mate at her side, the panther inside her died, killing the human part of her as well." He put his palm on her cheek and looked deep into her eyes. "So you see, Jaclyn, your mother never abandoned you. Never would have. You would have been her pride, and she would have loved you and protected you with everything inside her. It is our way, the way of the panther."

Her mother had never abandoned her?

She touched her stomach, comforted by that. Then she shook her head, forcing reason back to her brain. "This is crazy. Wouldn't I have exhibited some panther traits?" she said, humoring him.

"You're very libidinous, aren't you? Unable to play well with other females, aloof at times. Not a fan of the canine. Never felt sated before until you slept with me . . ."

"Yeah, but—"

"You're my mate, Jaclyn. I'm your alpha and you belong to me."

"So what does that mean, I'm your subordinate?" she challenged.

"It means I'll always protect you and take care of you." He softened his voice. "It also means I belong to you."

She swallowed as something inside her gave. She'd never really belonged to anyone before or had anyone belong to her. It gave her a weird sense of comfort.

"You have the mark of fire, Jaclyn."

"You mean my birthmark?"

"It's more than just a birthmark. It's the mark of the panther. We're all descendants of the courageous Indian maiden Tallie."

"Tallie?"

"Native American legend says the Indian maiden had a vision of an injured panther. As if drawn by the animal, she traveled great lengths, putting herself in danger in an effort to rescue the wounded animal. When she found the panther, she wasn't strong enough to carry it back to her grounds to care for it, so she stayed with it to provide warmth and give it food. That night she dreamed the panther had turned into a man and made love to her. Come morning she had gained the strength of the alpha and was able to bring it to safety and nurture it to good health. Tallie was then able to summon other panthers and, soon after, had taken on the animal characteristics herself." His hand trailed down to the juncture between Jaclyn's legs, to where her birthmark was hidden. "Tallie wore the mark of fire because she was as bright and beautiful as the blazing sun. The sun that gave us crops, sustenance, and life."

Jaclyn became acutely aware of her birthmark, and the way it burned and itched whenever Slyck was near.

"I have the mark too." He lifted his shirt and then his arm, showing her the same mark etched on his side. The only difference was that his had bright yellow flames, where hers had gone from pale to red-hot. As if he read her thoughts, he said, "It's not a coincidence."

Jaclyn got quiet, trying to sort through everything he'd just told her.

"You can't mention this to anyone," he said, his voice taking on a hard edge.

"I would think not," she said. A trip to the hospital that Slyck had obviously escaped from was not on her list of things to do today.

"Because as the offspring of the rogue shifter, you'd be terminated."

Okay, that totally got her attention. She gulped air. "Terminated?"

"Our town isn't what you think it is. You see, you would automatically be killed, as per our rules, for fear that the offspring—you—would retain rebellious traits of the rogue parent and reveal our secret community."

Her stomach knotted. What the hell had she gotten herself into? None of this could be true. She needed to go to the police to report this lunatic. But what if they were just as crazy as he was? She had to leave. To get the hell out of Dodge.

"You can't leave, Jaclyn. Because we've mated, bonded in a way that you don't yet understand. And like your mother, the panther in you will die without me, your true mate, at your side."

She decided to humor him for another moment. "You mean mates die when they're not together?"

"It's complicated."

"Then uncomplicate it for me."

"Like Tallie, females can gain strength from their alpha. The longer mates are together, the stronger the female becomes, and upon prolonged separation, such as death, she can absorb his strength through their life bond and live on, should she so choose. But if the male dies, most females choose death, not wanting to live on without their partner."

Jaclyn shook her head. "That's one hell of a bond."

"Yes, it is. And that bond empowers each mate. Someday you'll understand."

"Like my mother understood?"

Slyck pitched his voice low. "Jaclyn, your mother probably didn't understand any of this. And she wouldn't have chosen death over her daughter. She just hadn't been together with your father long enough to have gained his strength to live on without him."

Jaclyn gave a heavy sigh. "Why are you telling me this, Slyck?"

"To protect you."

"So you're telling me I'm a shape-shifting panther, and you're my mate, and if anyone in the town finds out *what* I am, they will kill me, and I can't leave because my panther will die?"

"Yes."

Her entire body stiffened. "That's some pretty fucked-up shit, Slyck."

His green eyes darkened. "I know you can feel it."

"I don't feel anything," she said, angling her chin in defiance.

The air around them charged as his head descended and his sensuous lips came down on hers. Her entire body melted against him. No longer able to ignore the sensations, everything inside her screamed for more. For him to ravish her, for her to give herself over to him.

That he was her mate.

Oh hell!

"Tell me you feel it, Jaclyn," he whispered into her mouth.

Breathless, she said, "I feel nothing."

Their tongues played and tangled. Fire licked over her thighs. Pulled by a strange commanding force, she pressed harder against him, unable to help herself because what he did to her was both frightening and exhilarating.

Slyck inched back and caught her glance. If she wasn't so god-damn hot for him, she would have smacked that "told you so" look off his face.

"Your words say one thing, Jaclyn, but your body says another."

Chapter Seven

Five days had passed since Slyck had last set eyes—or hands—on Jaclyn, and the separation was damn near killing him. But he knew he had to back off, to give her the time and space she needed to sort matters through. After all, it wasn't every day one was told she was a were-cat. And truthfully, he couldn't blame her for thinking he was a psychopath. Hell, he'd have reacted the same way.

Sure she was dubious, fearful even of what he'd told her. And, sure he could have presented her with his panther as proof. But he suspected it would have been far too much for her to handle, especially seeing the way she'd stood there staring up at him with those big disbelieving eyes of hers. Not only would it have frightened her, but showing one's true self to an outsider before a council ruling was strictly forbidden as it risked exposing their colony. He scoffed at that last thought. Not that he'd been abiding by any rules lately anyway. Even though he'd always been levelheaded and analytical, in a matter of a few short days, Jaclyn had drawn him into a place where emotions ruled his actions, and because he was an alpha leader who needed to govern with logic and patience, that really wasn't a good place for him to be.

But Jaclyn was smart, observant, and curious, and it would have only been a matter of time before she discovered the truth behind the town, and the people in it.

Especially when her panther tried to get out.

They'd mated only twice, but she had enough of his seed running through her system to bring on her change. He was positive she'd come to him when she was ready, or when she needed answers, which he suspected would be very soon. Until then he would spend his time watching over Jaclyn to make sure she didn't try to escape, as well as training his first-in-command. Slyck had no idea what Jaclyn's future held—or his own, for that matter. Now that he'd found his mate he just didn't want any part of a future without her, and he needed to prepare Drake for Vall, should he suddenly need to assume the alpha position.

In the basement of the old town hall, Drake kept a tight berth, walking small circles around Slyck as they practiced their martial arts. Having only lived two lives, Drake was still a kitten in Slyck's eyes, and he still had so very many skills to learn.

With lightning speed, and practiced agility, Slyck did a round-house kick, easily knocking his opponent off balance. He wanted to anger Drake, to bring out his panther, knowing anger was one of the many things that roused the animal in them. Other things that stirred the kitty were fear, passion, lust. . . .

It took Slyck many lifetimes and a great amount of self-discipline and patience to gain control over the shift, and he was hoping to speed up the process for Drake, because one needed to work with intellect, not passion, when going head-to-head with a lycan.

"Stand up," Slyck demanded when Drake began to morph, his bones elongating and crackling, his jaw shifting, extending. "Fight it," he boomed out.

Too late. Drake ripped off his jeans and T-shirt, letting the call of the wild rule his actions. A moment later, standing before Slyck was a sleek black panther, eyes enraged, razorlike claws prolonged, ready for battle.

Cutting through the air, Drake lunged, hurtling toward him. Slyck immediately assumed a combative stance and easily side-stepped him, angling his large body and widening his legs in defense. Drake flew past him and landed with a thud against the wall.

A moment later, Drake climbed to his feet, bared his teeth and prowled closer, his long, sharp nails clinking and clattering on the old wood floor. Slyck took that opportunity to shed his own jeans and T-shirt. Once he was completely naked, he drew a breath and welcomed the change, mentally and emotionally distancing himself from the all-too-familiar pain associated with the transformation as he prepared for the inevitable catfight.

The two panthers faced each other, circling slowly, sizing each other up. A low, savage growl rumbled up from Slyck's throat. With years of battle experience, and the scars to prove it, Slyck made the first move. Both cats went up on their hind legs, but within seconds Slyck had the weaker cat pinned to the ground.

Drake struggled beneath him, swatting at Slyck's face as he

strived to right himself. Using his beefy paws to hold him down, Slyck put his mouth on the other man's neck, showing his dominance as he held him firm. When he felt Drake's body loosen, he said, "Let it go, Drake."

As though knowing he couldn't win in a power struggle against the pack's alpha, Drake began to purr, his show of submission. With that, Slyck slowly backed away and returned to his human form. Drake shook away his panther, his thick black coat receding as he too morphed from cat to man.

Slyck paced the floor, calming the animal in him. A moment later Drake sat on his heels, cautiously staring up at him with a confused look on his face. Intense green eyes full of questions locked gazes with Slyck. Slyck held his hand out and pulled him to his feet.

"What's going on, Slyck?" Arms folded across his chest, Drake tipped his head to meet Slyck's glance. Even when Drake was at his full height, Slyck still towered over his first-in-command.

Slyck shrugged. "Nothing," he hedged. "Just thought we should add more intensity to your training sessions."

Drake rubbed his neck. "I'd say."

"And we need to go from once a week to daily."

"Daily?"

Slyck reached for his clothes and handed Drake his. "You need to learn to control your panther, Drake, and fight with intellect. There is no place for emotions in the battle of wit and skill."

Slyck felt Drake's eyes on him, gauging him carefully. A suspicious look crossed his first's face as he began pulling his clothes back on. Even though they were as close as any friends, Slyck was still Drake's leader, and Drake knew better than to question him or challenge him about his current actions or his decision to up the intensity of their training.

"You sure you don't want to talk about it?" Drake asked.

"Nothing to talk about," Slyck assured him, and pushed his hair from his face. "You're my right-hand man, and it's time for us to get serious about your training."

Drake scoffed. "I don't think we need to worry about that too much. You do have nine lives, you know."

"Yeah, and I've already used up seven of them." That thought suddenly made him tired. He'd dedicated the better part of his life to maintaining order amongst the community, keeping his brethren under control, and holding the balance in place. Unfortunately, the fact that Jaclyn's mother had panther in her meant that in the past, well before her mother's generation, others had escaped the gates and impregnated women without his knowledge. Had the years and strain from fighting and trying to maintain balance taken their toll on him? Maybe it really was time for someone younger to take over. Maybe he'd lost his edge.

After they dressed they made their way to the café on Main Street for refreshments. Since a shift always took a great amount of strength and energy, nourishment afterward was necessary.

They grabbed a booth by the window, and Slyck looked out at the sky. "Another scorcher," he murmured, thinking about how the heat drove the lycans to stupidity. No doubt he'd find a handful down at the pond, swimming and playing when they should be working. They all had their daily duties to fulfill, and everyone

needed to pull together if they wanted to keep the town running smoothly. Slyck's pack was in charge of security. The demons
were in charge of discipline. The vamps, having been on the earth
the longest, and having seen just about everything, were in charge
of education. The coven took care of medicine, healing, and all
things pertaining to nature. The lycans oversaw training of all species, keeping the town prepared should an attack from a government agency take place. After all, the Western Chapter wasn't the
only one with a task force in place to hunt rogues. The government had long ago set up a secret branch to rid the streets of
all supernatural beings. Other responsibilities—from managing
the stores and manning the front gate, to keeping a fresh supply
of food and blood and taking away the garbage—were delegated
amongst the species on a rotating basis.

Besides being a council member, Slyck also ran Vibes. Other
council members had their own "hobbies" as well. Slyck dubbed it
a hobby because inside the town of Serene, they exchanged money
for show only. Thanks to smart investments, the vamps alone were
worth billions.

Slyck turned his thoughts back to the present when Lily came
with their menus and coffee.

"Mmm, thanks, Lily," Slyck said and took a much-needed
sip of caffeine. Lily's warm yet guarded violet eyes glistened as
she listed the daily specials. She then left to give the two men a
minute to decide.

As Slyck's glance strayed to the street, he spotted Jaclyn turning
the corner and coming his way. Just the sight of her took his breath
away. Slyck sucked in air and fought to retain his composure.

Dressed in a prim, knee-length skirt and a neutral blouse that matched her skin tone buttoned to her neck, she hustled across the street in a pair of low heels, and made her way to the café. Slyck glanced at his watch and guessed she was on her lunch break.

Despite her staid attire, everything in him perked up and he felt his cock tighten in his jeans. Aware of the way he began to tremble with want, he slipped his hands under the table and in desperate need of a distraction gripped his thighs, hard. He bit back a curse and shifted uncomfortably in his seat as his mind recalled the feel of her skin, the delicious taste of her sweet cream, and the way her body had opened for him, the way only a true mate's would. His nostrils flared, his body urging him to chase across the street and pounce, to leave his final mark on his mate. Of course, he couldn't leave his final mark and fully claim her as his until they completed the mating ritual in panther form.

Drake's glance went from Slyck to Jaclyn, and back to Slyck again. He cleared his throat. "You okay, Slyck?"

Slyck tore his gaze from Jaclyn and glared at Drake. "Fine. Why?" he bit out with much more force than necessary.

"Your hackles are up."

He nodded toward Jaclyn. "My hackles are always up when we have a newcomer in town."

"Not like this they're not."

Drake was the closest friend Slyck had, and for a quick moment, he thought about confiding in him, but then shook it off. Even though they were friends, family actually, and he trusted Drake, he suspected that in a battle Vall still had the means to

force Drake's submission, should he want to. Best not to put anyone else in danger.

"Yeah, well, seems a few townsfolk are already complaining
about her," Slyck went on to explain. "She accidentally tried to
feed chocolate to a lycan."

Drake cringed. "Shit. That couldn't have gone over well."

"It's not like she knew," he said in her defense, and then realized what he was doing. Hoping that slip had gone unnoticed, he
went back to studying his menu and added, "If she causes any
more trouble, folks are going to demand we do something about
her, and do it fast."

"Maybe that's what the barbecue tonight is all about."

Slyck's head snapped up with a start. "What barbecue?"

"She's having a barbecue tonight." He paused to reach for his
coffee. "A meet-and-greet-the-neighbors sort of thing."

That caught Slyck's attention. "You've got to be kidding
me?"

"No, she passed out flyers. Didn't you get one?"

"Haven't checked my box." Not that he expected one.

Drake took a sip of his coffee and studied Jaclyn as she came
rushing through the door. "You think she's going to be trouble,
Slyck?"

Oh yeah, she was all kinds of trouble.

Slyck thought more about this barbecue. "It's not like anyone
is going to show up. Everyone is under strict orders."

"Yes, well, we're not dealing with the most authoritative people here, now, are we? Especially with the promise of food, alcohol, and . . . *fresh meat.*"

"Dammit . . . ," he murmured. "We could demand they don't go."

"Why? Truthfully, this is the perfect opportunity for her to see that she's not a good fit to the community. Folks will go, eat, drink, and have a good time without bothering to give her the time of day."

So Drake did have a point. But Slyck didn't want her social-izing. What if the lycans got a whiff of the panther between her legs? And if she started asking questions, raising suspicions, the shit would hit the fan and the townsfolk would demand straws be drawn. Her panther had yet to show, which meant that if she hadn't fully transformed yet, it was possible a "marking" could change her into another species. If she was full panther, however, already having completed her first shift, and one of the others tried to claim her, it would temporarily weaken her or, worst-case scenario, kill her. Yet if they knew what she was, they'd also kill her. Fuck. It was a lose-lose situation.

Slyck planted his elbows on the table and rested his forehead in his palms. Jesus, he had to figure out what the hell he was going to do about this mess. Restlessness and anxiety urging him on, Slyck climbed to his feet, cut across the café, and came up behind Jaclyn.

Jaclyn spun around, her hand on her chest. "Oh, I didn't see you there." Her blue eyes flared hot when they met his, and he could see from the welt marks that she'd been scratching her skin. It was happening. Quickly.

He pitched his voice low. "This barbecue. It's not a good idea."

She leveled him with a stare and lowered her voice to match his. "I can't think of a better way to get to know the neighbors."

"These aren't neighbors you want to get to know, Jaclyn."

Just then the door opened up, and Vall walked in. His suspicious pewter eyes met Slyck's before he sidled up to the counter. As he moved in beside them, Slyck noticed the way Jaclyn's body tightened, her panther's instinctive reaction to the wolf in Vall. Under the guise of needing a straw, Slyck leaned over Jaclyn and grabbed one from the dispenser. "Cancel the party, Jaclyn, or I'll crash it."

"Over my dead body."

"That's what I'm afraid of."

Jaclyn paid for her egg salad sandwich and soda, and decided to eat back at the store. She told herself it was because she didn't like the company at the café, but the reality was that Slyck's close proximity was playing havoc with her senses. Her skin had begun to itch, her birthmark to burn.

She glanced at Slyck as he slid back into his booth. Her gaze shot to the man he was with. Lord, she never expected to find so many hotties in Serene. Not that she wanted to sample any of them, not now, not after Slyck.

Oh boy.

Needing escape, she darted outside and hustled back to the shop. Even though the rest of the townsfolk ignored her, she had made one friend at the department store. A female friend at that.

As Jaclyn entered through the front doors, and welcomed the rush of cool air on her heated flesh, she replayed Slyck's parting words. She wasn't so sure she had to worry about him crashing her party, since she was pretty certain no one would show up anyway. She was hoping to soften the women up and gain their confidence with fine wine and good food. Then maybe they'd trust her enough to purchase her company's cosmetics.

Jaclyn made her way back to the empty cosmetics counter—she had no idea where Brandy and Gina were off to—and Sunray—her one and only friend, who worked in lingerie and who didn't at all seem threatened by her—sauntered over.

"That was fast," Sunray said.

Jaclyn felt so frumpy next to the vivacious Sunray. She took a moment to peruse her friend. Although they were the same height and build, Jaclyn had chestnut hair and blue eyes whereas Sunray had thick golden hair the color of a wheat field and big, beautiful silvery eyes. Jaclyn had never seen such an interesting color outside Serene before. Sunray dressed in sexy clothes, with her hot lingerie peaking out underneath. She wore her pants low on her hips, and when she bent over, Jaclyn always got a glimpse of her lacy thongs and her tattoo. Jaclyn took a moment to wonder if the kitty paw print represented something, but didn't really know the other woman well enough yet to ask. Her gaze traveled to Sunray's mouth. Good Lord, no one could pull off red lipstick the way Sunray could. The woman looked good enough to eat. Heck, not that Jaclyn swung that way, but after five days without a man, she was about ready to take a nibble.

"The café was busy, so I decided to bring lunch back." She held out half her sandwich. "Bite?"

Sunray's graphite eyes glistened as she licked her painted lips, except it wasn't Jaclyn's sandwich she was looking at when she nodded her head eagerly.

Jaclyn would have taken her for a lesbian, except she'd seen her leaving Vibes the other night with a couple of guys, and the way they were all fawning over one another told Jaclyn they weren't going for coffee. Heck, maybe her thong swung both ways. Not that it mattered one iota to Jaclyn. She liked Sunray and didn't judge or label people. Okay, so maybe she had labeled Slyck as crazy, but who could blame her? The way Jaclyn saw it, if anyone showed up at her barbecue, and she had a chance to talk to them, she'd prove to herself that the town wasn't full of make-believe fairy-tale creatures; it was just a town where the people were suspicious of outsiders.

She put her mind on the matters at hand, chewed her sandwich, and said, "So, Sunray, tell me: What marketing strategies would you put in place to sell cosmetics to all these beautiful, flawless women?"

Sunray gave her a quizzical look, gauging her for a moment.

Jaclyn recognized that look, had seen it on Slyck's face a time or two. Slyck. Why the hell was she going there again?

"Any ideas?" Jaclyn pressed.

"Maybe if you wore it yourself, you know, showed the women how sexy they can be."

Okay, so she'd just recounted Slyck's advice. Although it made sense, she didn't want to give off the wrong image. If she did, she'd never attract a nice churchgoing boy—someone who was the opposite of Slyck, someone she could bring home to Daddy. She blew out a long sigh. Not that any of the men she'd come across in Serene fit that description, however. Who would have thought that the small town would be filled with so many hunky alphas?

"Not to offend you or anything, Jaclyn," Sunray went on to say, "but maybe I could lend you some clothes. You have a great body underneath all that starch."

"Thanks. I'll think about it," she murmured around a mouthful of sandwich.

The rest of Jaclyn's workday crawled by. She found Brandy and Gina lounging in the staff room and summoned them to the counter so she could introduce and explain the benefits of each and every product. Then she went over sales and marketing reports, phoned a few contacts, and reorganized the shelves. At the end of her shift, she left the building and took note of the threatening clouds moving in from the west. Praying the rain would hold off, she hurried home to prepare for the night's barbecue and tried to keep her mind off Slyck, and keep her gaze from straying to his bedroom window.

Was he up there watching?

She strung lights over the pool, not that she planned on getting in, whipped up a few salads and desserts, avoiding anything and everything chocolate just in case, and tossed the steaks on the grill. Once the preparations were complete she changed into a pretty floral dress that would be right at home on any one of the Stepford wives. Now all that was left to do was wait.

As she walked the perimeter of the pool, enjoying the cool breeze that had just blown in, a strange energy brewed in the air. Yes, the storm was coming. But it was more than that. As the sun began its nightly descent, there was an eeriness, a stillness over the town that caused the hair on the back of her neck to tingle. She hugged herself to stave off a shiver.

A noise behind her gained her attention. She brushed off her uneasy feeling, and spun around to find Sunray and the same golden-haired man she'd spotted at the café coming up her walkway. Jaclyn's eyes widened when she saw the pack of people in the driveway behind them.

"Sunray," she cried out, rushing forward to give her a big hug.

The man at her side cupped Sunray's elbow and eased her back to him, seemingly displeased to see the two of them embrace. His nostrils flared, anger flashed in his eyes.

Wearing a sassy smirk that matched her hot little outfit, Sunray ignored him and smoothed a hand over her short, flirty skirt. "Jaclyn, this is Vall. My . . . *date.*"

Jaclyn turned to Vall and fabricated a smile, even though it felt like her skin had suddenly been bitten by a million insects. With every instinct in her body urging her to flee, she gave him a quick glance that took in his worn jeans, navy blue T-shirt, and combative military-issue boots. Who the hell wore heavy boots in the middle of summer?

"Nice to meet you. I remember you from the café earlier today."

His charcoal eyes slithered over her body, a cold, calculating perusal that turned her blood to ice. But underneath that scrutinizing gaze, she spotted something else, something that looked like carnal desire. Vall inched closer and then drew a deep breath, like he was pulling her scent into his lungs.

She grew extremely uncomfortable under his inspection and fought off a shiver before saying, "Feel free to have a swim." The delicious aroma of her barbecue reached her nostrils, and it suddenly occurred to her that over the last few days, everything had started smelling better, tasting better. It must have something to do with good, clean country living, she decided. "The steaks will be done shortly," she added, waving for them to enter her backyard.

With Sunray anchored to his side, Vall shot Jaclyn one last longing look and walked around her, eyeing her pool as his heavy boots pounded against the cement and serrated the moisture-laden air. When he brushed up against her, Jaclyn wasn't able to suppress a shiver. There was something about that man that she just didn't like.

A few more folks had found their way over, and before Jaclyn knew it, darkness had fallen and her backyard was full of people. Some were swimming, some were lounging, and others were moaning in bliss as they dug into her food with fevered passion. That made Jaclyn smile. All those years spent under her mother's thumb learning how to be a proper hostess hadn't gone to waste, after all. Another group, acting like they had a touch of the devil in them, were causing havoc as they tried to swing from the lanterns that she'd strung earlier. Perhaps they'd all had one too many shots of tequila.

After spending most of her evening talking with Sunray, Jaclyn now walked amongst the crowd, working hard to make small talk with the women, who seemed no friendlier toward her now than they had been upon her arrival Monday morning.

When she spotted a group of three women huddled together in conversation, she decided it was time to make her move. As she walked toward them, Ruby ran from the house and jumped into her arms, hissing at the guests in the pool.

"Ruby," she admonished and ducked under her bird feeder as she moved in beside the women. "Hi, ladies," she said. "Did you all get enough to eat and drink?"

They nodded, and after a round of introductions were made, Harmony's violet eyes turned to Ruby. "This is Ruby," Jaclyn offered. When Harmony looked at her cat longingly, Jaclyn asked, "Do you have any pets?"

"No," Harmony said, a sadness in her eyes. Her bangles jangled when she reached out and petted Ruby's fur.

"I haven't really seen anyone around town with pets," Jaclyn said, trying to lighten the mood. "Nor have I seen one dog in the park since I've been here."

"Too many coyotes," Alexis piped in.

"Coyotes eat the pets?"

"Yes," all three ladies said in unison.

Jaclyn gestured toward her bird feeder. "I guess they must also be eating all the birds too, then. I haven't seen one little robin."

"Yes, they do," Harmony added, in a very patient yet firm voice, reminding Jaclyn of her stern but fair headmaster back in prep school.

She shot the lady a dubious glance. Okay, even that seemed a little far-fetched to her. It was starting to look like everyone was as crazy as Slyck. "Is that what the gate is for? To keep the wild animals out?"

Harmony angled her head, her long black curls tumbling in waves over her shoulders. She really was a beautiful woman, Jaclyn mused. The look in her warm violet eyes, as well as the humorless smile on her face, told Jaclyn this was a conversation she had no interest in pursuing. "Sometimes they crawl under."

Despite the admonishing regard in Harmony's gaze, Jaclyn decided to push—partly because she wanted answers, and partly because she wanted to prove to herself that the strange goings-on were just the quirks of small-town living. Things like the cluster of people who came out only at night. Heck, if she didn't know better, she'd think they were vampires.

Damn Slyck for putting such crazy notions into her head.

Unnerved with the direction her mind had gone, she shook her head and marshaled her thoughts. Her cat swatted at the bird feeder behind her, and it brought back memories of her grandmother, which raised another question.

She shifted Ruby in her arms. "Tell me, where are all the elderly?"

"Excuse me?" Harmony asked.

"The elderly. Where are they?"

"Why do you ask?"

"Well, the elderly purchase the highest percentage of skin-care products, and since I'm here to sell cosmetics, I was wondering why Serene has no elderly residents. Do you ship them all off to a retirement home or something?" she asked, only half teasing, because she certainly expected to see a high number of geriatrics in such a quaint town.

"Yes, that's exactly what we do," Harmony said, and then

excused herself, taking her friends with her, and leaving Jaclyn standing there all alone, a little pissed off and a whole lot more concerned.

Where were the elderly? The birds? The animals?

Suddenly her flesh began to burn and she sensed Slyck's presence. She felt him long before she saw him. She could even feel his hot gaze caressing her body. God, she was so aware of him. It was all she could do not to come unhinged.

Jaclyn spun around. Her gaze surfed through the crowd, and despite the darkness at the back of her yard, she spotted him in the shadows.

Her body came alive just knowing he was watching her. Moisture grew between her thighs, and her nipples turned sensitive beneath her sundress, every little movement of the fabric causing them to tighten, swell. Ignoring Slyck, Jaclyn shook off her arousal and moved through her backyard, where she tried to mingle with her guests, albeit unsuccessfully.

Less than an hour later—no further ahead with the townsfolk than she had been when they'd arrived—Jaclyn stifled a yawn and began to pick up the discarded dishes as the crowd slowly began to disperse. Soon the backyard fell quiet, and she strived to hear one cricket chirp, one bat squeak. Nothing.

She gave a heavy sigh, planted her hands on her hips, and glanced around.

"Well, that didn't go as well as expected," she mumbled under her breath.

"It shouldn't have gone at all."

Slyck pressed his chest to her back, and it was all she could do to remain standing. Awareness hit like a wrecking ball. God, her body called out to him in ways that confused her and left her breathless.

She turned around and worked to sound casual. "I don't remember giving you an invitation." She tried to keep her eyes on his face and off his rippling muscles as he shifted his stance and deliberately leaned over her.

Smoldering green eyes met hers, and it took every ounce of control she could muster not to rip her clothes off and offer herself up to him. She linked her hands together and fought the natural inclination to touch him.

He wet his lips, and before she realized what she was doing, she moistened her own. When his head dipped, her breathing grew shallow. In a voice that was deep and sensual, he said, "The look in your eyes and the way your body reacts to me is all the invitation I need, Jaclyn."

Before she could come back with some smart-assed response, a noise in her driveway pulled her focus. She caught a glimpse of Sunray exchanging words with Vall, and by the intent look on his face, she would have hazarded a guess that they weren't tossing around friendly words. When Vall forcefully grabbed Sunray's arm, she quickly jerked it away. There seemed to be some sort of power struggle between the two.

Jaclyn made a move to go to her friend's aid, but Slyck stepped in front of her, his huge body blocking her path. "Stay out of it."

"I don't like that man, Slyck." It didn't appear that Sunray did either. So why would she date him? A strong, outgoing woman like Sunray didn't seem the type to be pushed around or dominated by any man. Did he have something over her?

"That's because he's a werewolf and you're a were-cat. The two don't always mix."

"Slyck—"

"Look at their eyes, Jaclyn. Their behavior. I know you've noticed."

She took a moment to entertain the idea. Okay, so she couldn't deny that their eyes were a strange color. That seemed to be a definable characteristic amongst everyone who'd come tonight—a definable characteristic that clumped them into a group of five. From the silver eyes of the group that loved the water, to the gorgeous green eyes of the group that didn't. From the black eyes of the group that only surfaced at night, to the amber-yellow glow of the rowdy group that liked to create chaos. And of course she couldn't forget the quiet group with the violet eyes and dark black hair.

She transferred her thoughts back to her friend when the sound of Vall's rising voice echoed in the air.

"Why are they fighting?" she asked quietly.

"Because Sunray has a fetish for all things kitty."

"Meaning?"

"Meaning she's not like the other wolves and she likes you. A lot. Even though I suspect she doesn't quite know why yet."

"I like her too." She turned to see Vall grip Sunray's upper arm tighter, forcing her compliance as they moved into the shadows.

"Even though she's a lycan?" Slyck questioned.

Jaclyn gave Slyck a deadly glare. "She's my friend, and she's the only one in town who's been nice to me."

Slyck brought his lips close to hers, and despite a hard-fought battle, she could feel the heat rising in her. Her lips automatically parted.

"I'm nice to you," he whispered into her mouth.

Her eyes slipped shut, and she waited for his kiss. What she got instead infuriated her.

With a light shove, Slyck threw her into the pool.

A moment later she surfaced, sputtering and cursing and wanting to kill the man. She finally found her footing and stood. "What the hell do you think you're doing?" she asked, pushing her wet hair off her forehead and madly blinking droplets from her eyes.

Instead of answering he let his eyes race over her wet dress, and the way it clung to her body. When his green eyes darkened with desire, her nipples hardened in response, alerting him to her arousal. Damn him.

"Are you insane?" she bit out.

"I thought you already established that I was."

"What are you trying to do? Drown me?"

"Nope, trying to anger you."

"Well, congratulations. Mission accomplished." She shot him an indignant glare before making her way to the ladder. "Why the hell did you want to anger me?"

"So your panther will show."

"Okay, Slyck, I've heard enough of this." She climbed from the pool, but there was no ignoring the niggling in her stomach—a familiar intuitive reaction. She didn't want to believe Slyck—she really didn't—but she couldn't ignore her gut feeling any more than she could ignore his blatant sexuality. As she ran over the events of the night, she couldn't deny that there was something very unnatural about this town and the people in it, making it hard for her to cling to the belief they were merely fearful of outsiders. There was something more unnatural than just their eye color. Everything from the aloof way they treated outsiders to having no pets, no birds, insects, or elderly. And their skin, it was flawless. Eternal-looking, really.

Oh Jesus.

Her stomach knotted. She worried her bottom lip. Surely to God she was caught up in some bad nightmare. Maybe if she pinched herself . . .

With two easy steps Slyck closed the distance between them. "Still angry?"

"Yes," she bit out, then challenged, "If anger causes one to shift, why haven't I shifted before? Trust me, I've felt anger many times over."

"I told you, you need male seed."

"So you really expect me to believe your seed brings out the panther? Sounds like some kind of trick to get into a woman's pants if you ask me. God, leave it to a man to come up with something so ludicrous."

He ignored her comment and continued. "It also changes DNA in humans."

She planted her hands on her hips. "I thought you said I wasn't human."

"You're panther. And a female's panther lies dormant until the male seed is introduced," he reiterated.

Jaclyn's head began swimming, and she tried to hold on to her anger. She nibbled her bottom lip as her body tightened. Christ, this was becoming all too much for her to comprehend. "Slyck—"

He brushed the backs of his fingers over her cheek. His familiar caress combined with his close proximity caused all her anger to evaporate, her resolve to crumble.

The heat from his body reached out to her and she grew moist, but that moisture had absolutely nothing to do with her unexpected dip in the pool. Oh God, she needed him again. There were no two ways about it. There was something so right, so comforting about his touch, and it almost hurt when she wasn't in his arms.

So maybe he was crazy, an escaped mental patient even. Or maybe he was as sane as she was and this town really was full of fairy-tale creatures. To her lust-drunk brain, what had seemed so important earlier now suddenly seemed insignificant. Especially when she had other things to think about. Things like slipping between the sheets with Slyck again. Things like spending the rest of the night making wild passionate love with him. Things like riding his mouth, his fingers, and his beautiful cock. God, she wanted to give herself to him in a way she'd never given herself to a man.

She couldn't deny the way her body craved him, *needed him*, in a way that she'd never needed another, and she swore if she didn't feel him inside her again within the hour, she'd die of want.

He lowered his head, and she caught a whiff of his earthy scent as it assailed her senses.

"Jaclyn . . ." The soft way he said her name instantly brought them to a deeper level of intimacy.

The air around them suddenly felt heavy, suffocating, and it was all she could do to inflate her lungs.

"Yeah," she managed.

Slyck's eyes darkened when he curled a damp strand of her hair around his index finger and said, "There are other ways, you know."

She worked to find her voice, but it came out all raspy and aroused. "Other ways for what?"

"To get your panther to show."

His voice was so full of emotion and tenderness it made her abandon any rational thought. "How?"

"Passion."

Chapter Eight

Slyck brushed the pad of his thumb over her plump lips and watched her face suffuse with color. As his panther clawed to get out, he leaned into her, conveying how much he wanted to ravish her. Here and now. Not that he thought she'd balk at the idea, because everything in her beautiful blue eyes told him she needed this as much as he did.

He slid his hand over the smooth bare skin on her arms, and watched the bumps that formed in its wake. She gave a little shiver of excitement and bit down on her lower lip. He could tell her breasts were swollen, achy, and hot beneath her light summer dress, and he had every intention of soothing away that incessant longing with his tongue.

He watched her eyes cloud with need when she murmured, "Slyck . . ."

"I know, Jaclyn," he whispered back, the agony in his voice

matching hers. He pinched his eyes shut, let out a slow breath and added, "Trust me, sweetheart, I know."

The sound of thunder rumbling in the distance propelled him into action. He ushered Jaclyn into the house and closed the patio door behind them just as the clouds sliced open and frigid rainwater blanketed Serene in a cool summer bath.

He quickly moved through the rooms, shut the open windows, and pulled the curtains closed to give Jaclyn and himself their much-needed privacy. Then he made his way into the bathroom and brought back a big cotton towel. He rushed back to the kitchen to find Jaclyn exactly where he'd left her, still standing just inside the patio doors, a puddle forming at her feet, looking like a drowned cat. With her hair plastered to her forehead, she stood there wide-eyed, staring up at him. She'd never looked more beautiful. God, she literally took his breath away. His body shook at the intense emotions he'd never experienced with a woman before.

His heart softened when she began shivering. "Poor kitten. Let me take care of you." Slyck began to peel her soaked dress from her body. He worked slowly, taking his time to savor the magnificent sight of her pert breasts as they spilled from her clothes. He dropped to his knees, carefully lifting one foot at a time as he removed the dress and turned his attention to her gorgeous, passion-drenched pussy as her unique feminine scent called out to him. Once he had her completely naked, he towel-dried her quivering body with the utmost care and noted the way she carefully watched him with those seductive bedroom eyes of hers. His clothes brushed against her flesh as he stood, and her whole body quaked in response.

"Still cold?" he asked quietly.

She lowered her voice to match his. "Yeah."

He gathered her into his arms, rubbed his hands over her body, and offered his warmth. "Hot shower?"

"No."

Surprised at her answer, he inched back to look at her, and arched a questioning brow. "No?"

She shook her head and wrapped her arms around his neck, pulling him back to her, the look in her eyes making no qualms about what she wanted. "Hot tongue."

He grinned at her boldness. Acutely aware of her heat and desire and the way it reached out to him, he backed her up against her kitchen table. Damned if he didn't like a woman who knew what she wanted. Slyck gripped her slim hips, lifted her clear off the floor, and set her on the table.

With easy, gentle movements, he leaned into her and brushed his lips over her eyes, her nose, her mouth, then moved to her neck. Her body trembled and he fought the urge to unleash the beast and ravish her. He slid a hand between her thighs, positioned his mouth near her ear, and murmured in a low voice meant to entice, "You know, since I wasn't invited to your party, I never did get fed tonight."

Her legs began to inch open; the delicious scent of her arousal reached his nostrils. "I think there is still some dessert left. Strawberries and cream, I believe," she purred.

"Mmm, cream. My favorite."

Slyck gently pushed on her shoulders, easing her backward, until she lay flat on the table before him, completely naked, save for the come-hither smile she was wearing. Goddamn, she looked good enough to eat. He stepped back and slowly walked around her, deciding to do just that.

He heard his voice tremble when he said, "You look so fucking hot, Jaclyn." Jesus, no woman had ever made his voice tremble before.

As the rain pounded against the patio door, and thunder rumbled in the near distance, the lights inside the house flickered. He felt her body tense. If there was one thing he knew, kittens feared lightning storms—and Jaclyn really was only a kitten. One who needed to be handled with the utmost care and sensitivity.

"Don't be afraid, Jaclyn." He ran a gentle hand over her breasts, brushing the undersides every so slightly. "I won't let anything hurt you."

"I know," she whispered. She blinked up at him and spread her legs even more, putting herself in his hands, and showing him just how much she trusted him.

As she submitted to him in human form, his panther howled with pleasure and tried to claw its way out, needing most desperately for his mate to submit to him in her natural, primal state. But he didn't want to frighten her with its presence just yet, so he focused on her throbbing clit and caged the pacing animal inside him.

"Now this cream. Where is it?" he asked, his imagination kicking into high gear.

As if she knew how naughty his thoughts had turned, she gulped and nodded toward the kitchen counter.

Slyck grabbed the bowl of homemade cream, dipped in a spoon, and took a taste. "Delicious." He came back to her and pushed a finger inside her tight cunt. Ecstasy flitted across her face. She groaned and arched into him. "But not as delicious as your cream," he added.

He pulled his finger out and licked it, slowly, longingly savoring the sweetness. Her taste fueled his hunger and had him itching to plunge into her hard and fast, but he forced himself to slow down before he lost all control and went at her like a primal beast in heat. Which pretty much summed up how he was feeling.

Jaclyn licked her lips as she watched him and he could practically see her heart thudding against her chest. Slyck caught a glimpse of her flaming birthmark. He touched it with the cool spoon and then dragged his hand higher, until he reached her full breasts. He spent a moment teasing her tight nipples before he made his way to the hollow of her neck. As he approached her mouth, she opened her lips for a taste. He redipped the spoon and offered her a small sampling.

She flicked her tongue across the spoon and then shook her head. A wicked gleam danced in her eyes. "That's not the cream I want to taste, Slyck."

Jaclyn reached out and cupped the bulge in his pants. She angled her head until her mouth lined up perfectly with his crotch. "I want to feel your cock in my mouth. I want to taste your cream."

"Oh, Jesus, Jaclyn," he groaned, his body clenching with need as he pictured that sweet little mouth of hers wrapped around his cock, her hot, hungry tongue laving the length of him. "Believe me, sweetheart, I want that too, but not yet." Disappointment crossed her flushed face. "Later, I promise. First I need to taste you."

When she opened her mouth to protest, he cut her off and distracted her by saying, "I'm going to start here." Slyck scooped up another spoonful of cream and put a dollop onto the peak of each tight nipple. He trailed a milky-white path down her chest and over her stomach, stopping to put a drop in her belly button. "Then I'm going to stop here." When he lightly brushed the spoon over her hot cunt, her hips came off the table in anticipation.

"And?" she asked, eagerly, not even bothering to mask the raw excitement in her voice—a trait that he positively admired.

He grinned, loving that she felt free enough to release her uninhibited nature with him, that she no longer kept her sexual prowess or her blatant femininity hidden beneath staid attire.

"Well, then I plan on pushing my tongue high into your pussy so I can tongue-fuck you." He swept his gaze down the length of her. "Once I have you quivering, I'm going to lick your clit so thoroughly, you're going to come like you've never come before. And just when you think you've had enough, that you can't take any more, I'm going to put two fingers inside you and make you come for me again."

As he offered her a detailed itinerary of how he was going to pleasure her, thunder rumbled close, and Jaclyn began panting with wanting. Satisfaction rolled through him. He loved that he did this to her. Lightning flashed overhead, and the lights inside the house flickered off.

Her soft hand reached out to touch his face, the heat from her palm filling his soul with warmth. He nodded toward the chair beside him as he dropped the spoon and inserted a finger into her throbbing pussy. "Then, once I have you nice and creamy, I'm going to sit in that chair, pull you down onto my cock, and spend the rest of the night fucking you. By the time I'm done with you, kitten, you won't even remember your own name." He gave her a cocky grin and added, "But I'm going to leave you so well fucked, you'll sure as hell never forget mine." She moved against his finger, riding it so hard, he could hardly stand how hot it made him. He put his mouth near hers and spoke in whispered words. "You see, sweetheart, ever since I watched you fuck that rubber cock, it's all I've been able to think about. I want you to resume that position, but I want to be the one beneath you this time."

Lightning flashed again, and he caught a few flecks of green shining in the depths of her blue eyes. Holy fuck! He drew another quick breath as her *We-Sa* reached out to him. Like humans, kittens were born with blue eyes, gaining pigmentation as they aged, or in Jaclyn's case as she became a mature, fully changed panther.

"What is it?" she asked, reading his body language as their hot gazes collided.

He pulled his finger from her cunt and kept his voice light, even though his panther was quivering with excitement, anxious to meet its mate in their primal form. "Nothing," he said. The last thing he wanted to do was alarm her or break the moment by telling her that her panther was trying to emerge. "The storm is close."

She curled her fingers through his hair, and her voice hitched when she said, "I don't normally like storms. But it doesn't seem so bad right now." She gave him a small smile. "Actually, it's kind of cozy being in here with you, listening to the wind and rain pounding against the house."

As her words warmed him deep, his protective instincts flared. Slyck bent and captured her pouty lips with his. He kissed her slowly and gently as emotions welled up inside him. God, he could hardly believe he'd found her. His mate. He almost wept with joy.

He ran his hands over her nakedness and felt her shiver. He inched back and glanced at her body, pleased at the way she was sensuously stretched out across the kitchen table, so open, so willing—his to do with as he pleased.

He'd never seen her look more beautiful or needy. A lump lodged somewhere deep in his throat, and sweat collected on his brow as he perused her. "I love seeing you like this," he whispered and stroked her puckered clit with the pad of his thumb, a light, continuous caress that made her squirm.

Slyck shook his head and groaned. "Look at you, baby. You're all warm and wet and open for me." He continued to stroke her pussy while he glanced into her green-blue-flecked eyes. He spent a long moment just looking at her before he furrowed his brow and questioned, "I know you have a very sexual nature, Jaclyn, but you're not like this with other men, are you? It's different with me, isn't it?" He wasn't sure why but he really needed to hear her say it.

She was so caught up in the moment, he could tell it was hard for her to speak. She pulled in a breath. "You seem to know an awful lot about me, Slyck." Her voice was nothing more than a soft, strangled whisper.

"And you know the reason why, don't you?"

The vulnerable look in her eyes was all the answer he needed, for the time being. He brushed his lips over her damp forehead, and breathed in the sweet scent of her hair. Desperate to taste her entire body, he dragged his wet tongue over her neck and continued on a downward path until he reached her nipples. "Beautiful," he murmured as he wrapped his lips around one hard bud and drank in the cream.

She gasped and writhed beneath him. Her reactions told him just how sensitive her nipples really were. After thoroughly cleansing both breasts, he angled his head to see her. Her eyes flashed with dark desire.

"You like that, sweetheart?"

When she nodded he brushed the soft blade of his tongue over her tight peak again, inserted his index finger into her moist cunt, and felt her small tremors take hold. Heat flared through him. Oh yeah, very sensitive, indeed. She was ready to come just from nipple stimulation. But he wasn't ready to bring her over just yet. The night was still so young, and his panther wanted to play.

With slow, deliberate movements he ran his tongue over her body, lapping up every last drop of cream until he reached her pussy. His eyes moved over her naked sex. *Ah, Jesus.* She had her hot pink cunt spread so wide-open for him it nearly obliterated all his control.

Jaclyn touched her hand to her clit, which forced Slyck to momentarily close his eyes against the southern flood of heat.

"Slyck, I need to come," she whispered, a note of desperation in her voice.

He shackled her wrists and put them above her head. "It's my turn to touch. Now bend your legs."

After she obliged he dropped to his knees and pulled her to the end of the table, and keeping his promise, he pushed his tongue all the way up inside her.

"Ohmigod," she cried out.

He dipped into her juice and then slathered it all over her clit. "You're very swollen, baby," he murmured from between her thighs. He gave a light brush with his tongue and watched her sex muscles flutter.

"Harder. Please. I'm so close."

He could feel the tension rising in her. Hell, he was just about ready to explode himself. "No need to rush things," he said calmly, yet feeling anything but.

"Yes, rush things," she demanded. God, he loved her enthusiasm. The light flickered on long enough for him to see moisture glistening on her hot cunt. The sight made him wild with need.

Burying his face between her legs, he gave her pussy his undivided attention. He pushed into her tight pink core, stretching her with his tongue.

"That's it, Slyck. That's so good."

In no time at all, Slyck took her to the edge of oblivion and kept her hovering there as his mouth indulged in her sweet cream. His cock pushed so hard against his zipper, pleasure turned to pain.

He slipped a finger inside her and stroked her G-spot. He stole a glance at her. Her fingers gripped the side of the table as her dark lashes fluttered shut. Gorgeous breasts bounced as she drove herself against his finger. Lust gathered between his legs. Goddamn it, he needed to fuck her.

She lifted her hips from the table. "Slyck, I'm—"

He let out a long growl as she came in his mouth. Her sweet scent seduced all his senses. When her tremors subsided, he quickly climbed to his feet and looked at her. She looked so damn sexy when she peaked.

"Jaclyn, I need to fuck."

He grabbed her hand and helped her to a sitting position. Her long hair fell forward to cover her breasts. She brushed her bangs back from her flushed face. "Sit on the chair, Slyck. Let me ride you," she said breathlessly.

"You first."

He ignored her quizzical look, scooped her off the table, and sat her in the chair, his eyes never once leaving her breasts. He dipped two fingers back into the bowl of cream and gently covered her cleavage in the syrupy-sweet substance.

She smiled up at him as realization dawned and then cupped her breasts and squeezed, forming a nice little channel for him to fuck.

He shook his head and swallowed. Hard. "Goddamn, girl, that's the hottest fucking thing I've ever seen." He shed his clothes in record time, widened his legs around hers and shimmied closer. Grabbing the back of the chair for support, he bent his knees and pushed his cock between her lubricated breasts.

Sweet mother of God!

As he began fucking her beautiful tits, her tongue flicked out to brush over the tip of his cock with every upward thrust.

"I stand corrected," he said, his entire body shaking with pleasure. "That's the hottest fucking thing I've ever seen."

Jaclyn grinned up at him, and lapped at the come dripping from his slit.

"You keep that up, girl, and I'm going to come."

"Well, you did promise me a taste."

"Don't start that, or I'll never get inside your pussy." He slipped a hand behind himself and stroked her, his finger circling her sopping wet clit. Her cunt rippled in response. "And I think we both want that."

Her edgy laugh turned to a heated moan when he brought his hand to her nipple and brushed it with the pad of his thumb, turning it such a pretty shade of pink. Slyck continued to fuck her cleavage. As her gorgeous tits milked his cock, his entire body throbbed for release. She felt so goddamn good it was all he could do to suppress his release. Okay, he needed to stop now before he shot off a load. He pulled back, lifted her from the chair, and took a seat.

Panting, he said, "Come here, baby." He cupped her hand and pulled her to him. "Come ride me."

Eyes glimmering with dark sensuality, Jaclyn slid her legs around his and tried to plunge downward. Slyck held her hips and carefully guided her, slowly, so she could feel every inch as he filled her. Her cunt closed around him, warm, hot, tight. So fucking good. His teeth clenched and he drew a quick sharp breath as he concentrated on the erotic sensations.

"More," she cried out in a haze of arousal. She swatted his hands away as though desperate to be filled to the hilt. He could feel her body shake with sexual frustration. A rush of tenderness overcame him. He relaxed his grip and let her push downward.

After she lowered herself onto his cock, he completely filled her in ways she'd soon understand. God, it was such a deliciously snug fit. She began rocking against him, driving his cock in and out at a fevered pace, making him so crazed that his mind nearly shut down.

He clenched his teeth. "Baby, you feel so fucking good wrapped around my cock. You have no idea how much I needed this. How much I needed to be inside you."

She brushed her lips over his. "And you have no idea how much I love the way you fill me."

Slyck put his hands around her waist and held her to him, savoring the moment as they joined as one, physically, mentally, and emotionally.

When she grew restless, he grabbed her hips and pounded into her, hot, hard, upward strokes that fucked her deep and made her come again. Her hot liquid poured over his cock and dripped down his balls. "That's it, baby. Keep coming for me."

And come she did.

Slyck lost count of how many times she'd orgasmed for him. With her eyes closed in bliss, Jaclyn gripped the back of the chair and impaled herself on him, taking every inch of his thick cock deep into her body. His cock swelled inside her warm, tight slit, soaking in her heat.

The storm picked up outside, smashing against the windows as they moved together in perfect sync. Slyck brushed his tongue over her nipples, never wanting the night to end. A warm, comfortable, intimate silence encompassed them as they continued to fuck.

Deciding he wanted to see her beautiful body sprawled out beneath him again, he murmured into her ear, "Keep your legs around me." With his cock still buried deep inside her, Slyck stood and carried her to her bedroom. He gently deposited her on the mattress and then resumed his fucking.

As the need for completion pulled at him, he bit down on his lip, wanting to hold off for as long as he could. He continued to fuck her, and when he saw exhaustion pulling at her body, he slowed long enough to let her get her second wind, and then he fucked her some more.

His balls ached for release and his cock throbbed, and still, they fucked. After one last deep push, he said, "Do you want to feel my come inside you, sweetheart?"

"You know I do," she whispered and kissed him long and deep, pulling his tongue into her mouth.

With that, he splashed his seed high up inside her and watched her face light when she came again, her hot cunt muscles gripping his stiff cock so hard, a new hunger began to grow inside him.

"Neat trick," she murmured into his mouth as her pussy continued to spasm.

"It's not a trick. It's because you're my mate. My seed makes you orgasm."

As though not wanting to think about that at this particular moment, she didn't respond. Instead she nuzzled against him and let her body go slack. He circled his arms around her slender waist and held her tight.

Well into the wee hours of the morning, he made a quick trip to the bathroom to clean up and then came back with a cloth for her. After washing her up, he crawled in beside her, pulled her in close and just stared at her. Jesus, he still couldn't quite believe she was here with him.

When she pressed against him, he slipped a hand between their bodies and lightly brushed a finger over her pussy. "Are you sore, sweetheart?"

She gave a soft, contented moan. "A little."

"Let me make you feel better."

Slyck shimmied downward, climbed between her legs, and rested his head against her thigh. Using the soft blade of his tongue, he gently licked her pussy. Small, easy strokes to help soothe away the sting of his frenzied lovemaking. "Why don't you try to get some rest."

"Uh, how am I supposed to rest with you doing that?" she asked, her legs widening involuntarily.

He cuddled in closer and just licked her, softly, slowly, deciding to give her one final sweet delicate orgasm before she succumbed to sleep. After a few gentle laps, her breathing deepened and she came for him again. That brought a smile to his face.

"Good night, babe," he whispered and continued to lave her clean. A few moments later, he heard her give a soft sigh before drifting off to sleep. Slyck remained between her thighs, and brushed a soft finger over her birthmark as it continued to change color. Gone was the itchy red welt, leaving behind a golden yellow pigmentation. A replica of his.

He closed his eyes, and with no intention of venturing too

far away, he let himself drift off. He'd put Jaclyn to sleep with his tongue, and he had every intention of waking her the same way.

Jaclyn woke with a smile on her face and looked to her right to see the gorgeous guy who'd put it there. Sometime during the night, she'd pulled him from between her legs to her mouth so she could taste his sweetness as she hovered somewhere between sleep and consciousness.

With his arms over his head, he now lay on his back beside her, looking sexy, warm, rumpled, and completely delectable, and in that instant she decided to put off her worries for just a little bit longer.

She slid her tongue over her bottom lip and stifled a moan. His head was turned to the side; his dark hair fell over his face. She was about to brush it off and wake him for another round of scrumptious sex when another, more delicious thought struck her. She never did get to taste his cream.

She carefully lifted the blankets until she exposed his naked body. Her gaze leisurely traveled over his bare flesh. Once again her heart softened when she took in the scars marring his sun-kissed skin.

She followed one scar down until it disappeared into the patch of dark hair on his pubis. That was when she glimpsed his magnificent cock. Her body tightened with memories of their night together. Just the mere sight of his morning pudge had her breasts swelling and her well-fucked pussy moistening. Even at half-mast, his size was impressive. Every nerve in her body came alive with longing.

Jaclyn shimmied lower and insinuated herself between his muscular thighs. Deep in sleep he spread his legs for her. She moistened her lips, opened wide to accommodate him, and brought his semierect cock into her mouth.

She licked and sucked and lightly brushed her tongue over his balls. When his cock began to swell in her mouth, she knew she'd awakened him, and her pulse gave a little jump of excitement. With his hard shaft still in her mouth, she glanced up at him and caught his smile. Every fiber of her being felt the new closeness between them. God, how she'd love to wake him up like this every morning just to see that sexy smile of his.

He moaned in appreciation and shifted beneath her. "You sure know how to wake a guy up," he said in a smooth voice that curled her toes. Warm fingers touched her hair, moving it away from her face so he could watch his cock slide in and out of her mouth. She liked that he was watching. It made her feel so sexy and desirable.

"But I wanted to wake you up like that, Jaclyn." She flicked her tongue over his slit, and he drew a sharp breath. "Not that I'm complaining, mind you," he quickly added, prompting her to continue with a smile.

Jaclyn chuckled around a mouthful of cock, loving how crazed she made him.

Slyck pushed another strand of hair from her shoulders, and Jaclyn angled her body so he could better see his cock as he fucked her hot, hungry mouth.

"You are so sexy, Jaclyn." The softness in his voice filled her with warmth.

She moaned and drew him in deeper. Her tongue flicked over his head, drinking in his precome.

She heard his throat work as he swallowed. "Do you like to suck cock, baby?"

Jaclyn closed her palm over his length and began stroking as she circled her velvety tongue over the tip of his cock. After easing his swollen dick from her mouth, she tipped her head, and wanting to be honest with him, she whispered, "Only yours, Slyck." Deep inside her soul, she knew that after Slyck, she'd never enjoy such intimacies with any other man.

She watched his eyes soften as his hand touched her cheek. His loving touch made her heart swell. Her throat clenched with longing. Needing a distraction before she went to mush in his arms, she said, "I want you to come in my mouth. You promised I'd get to taste your cream."

Slyck tossed his head back and grabbed a fistful of her hair as her words filled him with lust. "Baby, you're killing me, here."

Giving him no reprieve, she turned her full attention back to his pulsating dick and sank it to the back of her throat. Her aroused aroma filled the air. She couldn't believe how much she loved the texture, taste, and scent of him. So much so that she could spend the rest of the day right where she was, licking and tasting his cock without a care in the world.

"Your mouth, baby." His head rolled to the side. "Oh God, it's so hot."

He began pulsing in her mouth, and she picked up the tempo, desperate to taste his cream. When a violent shudder overtook him, she stilled her movements, positioned the head of his cock at the opening of her mouth, and stuck out her tongue.

He gripped the back of her head and drew a shaky breath. "So sexy," he whispered as his seed spurted onto her tongue.

Jaclyn moaned in bliss and drank in every last drop. After she swallowed and licked him clean, the strangest thing happened.

Her eyes widened. "Slyck," she whispered with effort.

He smiled at her and pulled her to him. His voice dropped an octave. "Ride it out, kitten."

Her breathing turned labored and her mouth went dry. Heat poured through her body and moistened her skin. Her vision went a little fuzzy around the edges, and her sex muscles clenched and pulsed. She could feel the rippling approach of a powerful orgasm. Good God, what the hell was happening to her? She gripped Slyck's shoulders and concentrated on the glorious sensations.

"Oh. My. God," she cried out as her nipples puckered and her body vibrated in heavenly bliss. She took her time riding out the orgasm, nurturing the release for as long as she could before she relaxed against Slyck.

Enclosed in the circle of his arms, she nestled in closer. "What the hell was that?" she asked after she managed to get her breathing back to normal.

"It doesn't matter how I fill you, babe. You're my mate and my come is meant to pleasure you, no matter how you take it into your body."

She wiped her forehead with the back of her hand. "Well, that certainly makes me want to give you a blow job every day."

He laughed. "That might be nature's point." He cupped her

chin and tipped her head until their eyes met. "A male never takes pleasure without pleasuring his mate in return. It is the way of the panther."

With a strong compulsion to touch him, she ran her hands lightly over his chest. "Your kind is very different from my kind. Most men I know are more than happy to take without giving anything in return." It suddenly occurred to her what she'd said: that she'd admitted to herself that he was different, that he wasn't human.

"You are my kind, Jaclyn," he reminded her. Slyck dropped a soft kiss on her forehead. That small, affectionate gesture tugged at her heartstrings. He climbed from the bed and her stomach churned with his physical retreat.

"Where are you going?" she asked, hating that she sounded so needy.

"Your reputation, remember."

"It's still dark out. What about the bogeyman?"

There wasn't a trace of humor in his voice when he said, "I am the bogeyman, Jaclyn." His eyes turned serious as he sat down next to her, the cushiony mattress dipping under his weight.

Jaclyn glanced down at her birthmark, noting the way it had changed color again. As Slyck's hands stroked her arms, she paused to consider her feelings for him. There was no denying that he'd given her the most satisfying night of her life. And speaking of her life, this was the first time she had felt whole, completely alive. What she was doing before wasn't living—it was searching. Searching for the one and only man meant for her.

Unsure whether she wanted to know the answer, she cleared

her throat and asked, "Everything you said, about me, about this town and the people in it—it's true, isn't it?"

He brushed his thumb over one flame on her birthmark. "Yeah, baby, it's true."

"Which means you were telling the truth about my biological father. You actually—"

Sadness washed over Slyck's eyes and he seemed at a loss for words. "Jaclyn. He . . . I . . . ." He swallowed, and rested his forehead against hers.

God, how could she live with that knowledge or even come to terms with the idea that this man she was falling for was the same man who had taken her parents from her?

Pushing that through to the back of her mind for the time being, Jaclyn clasped her hands together and tried to quiet her heart. "What's going to happen to me?"

She watched his eyes darken, his expression change. Unease crept into his voice when he said, "I won't let anything happen to you."

Her chest tightened. She wanted to believe him, but how could he guarantee that? "Slyck—"

He cut her off, anger flashing in his face. "I've spent my whole life searching for you, and I have no intention of losing you now."

She glanced at her arms, surprised to notice at some point her hair had grown darker, coarser. She got quiet for a moment as she sorted through everything and then asked, "What do we do now? Where do we go from here?"

"For now we pretend nothing has happened. Outside the privacy of our homes, you can't be seen with me."

She put her hand over her stomach to ease the ache. "And yet I can't be without you. Not without it hurting."

Her words stilled him, and once again he rested his forehead against hers. In a voice that was low and soft, he whispered with conviction, "I got us into this, sweetheart, and I'll get us out. I won't let you down. I promise."

As she watched him wage an internal war, she thought it best not to ask how.

Chapter Nine

After another five days of intense training, Slyck was pleased to see that Drake was finally starting to gain control over the undisciplined animal inside him. Still, it would take time, practice, and many dedicated hours before he fully mastered the skill. As he watched the younger panther walk circles around him in the basement of the old town hall, Slyck let his mind wander to Jaclyn.

Jaclyn . . .

His heart pounded harder in his chest just from thinking about her. If only he hadn't filled her with his seed that first night, if only he'd been stronger, less selfish. She could have walked out of Serene and back into her old life, and then they wouldn't be in this mess. Yeah, he thought to himself solemnly, had they not mated, she never would have begun the transformation process and she could have gone on to live and die like any other mortal.

But how could he have stopped himself from doing what was

so natural, what had been pulling at him for centuries, what was meant to be. She was his mate.

His everything.

And now, after mating with him and having been filled with his seed, she couldn't leave their town without him, or her panther would die because they'd only just bonded, and she hadn't gained enough strength from him yet. Nor could she stay. And how could Slyck just up and leave with her, abandoning his pack? He'd spent a lifetime taking care of them, keeping order, and protecting them. How could he just walk away from his brethren? They needed him every bit as much as Jaclyn and he needed each other.

He was so lost in his thoughts, he hadn't properly prepared himself for Drake's calculated lunge, and before he knew it, the younger panther had him on the floor, flat on his back, locked down in a submission hold.

Drake flashed perfect white teeth and growled at his victory. "What's the matter, old man? Can't keep up with a kitten anymore?"

Slyck let out a sigh and shook his head, conceding defeat to his first-in-command. Maybe it really was time for the younger panther to take his place.

"Well-done, Drake. I take it you've been practicing."

Drake purred with Slyck's praise and then nodded.

"Good," Slyck shot out. "Now get the fuck off me before I show you what this *old man* can still do."

Drake laughed good-naturedly and climbed to his feet. He held his hand out and pulled Slyck up with him. Slyck could feel the young panther's eyes on him—a knowing look.

"Maybe you should be practicing what you preach," he shot off casually.

Slyck didn't bite. Instead he growled and offered Drake his back while he went in search of his clothes. Here Slyck had been teaching Drake to bury his emotions during battle, and all the while he'd been completely caught up in his.

And, Jesus, talk about practicing what you preached. Since finding his mate, he'd been doing nothing but breaking policy and acting with his own best interests at heart. As far as Slyck was concerned, that was completely unacceptable conduct that lumped him in with the likes of Vall. Slyck shivered at that last thought.

Morphing back to his human form, he glanced at the clock and began to pull his clothes on. He had just enough time for a quick bite to rejuvenate himself and a shower before he had to make his way back to the hall for the emergency meeting that had been called earlier that day. A meeting that had everything to do with Jaclyn.

Night had fallen as Slyck made his way down Mulberry Lane. Walking restlessly, he ignored the fierce pull as he strolled past Jaclyn's house. He saw her inside the bay window, her hands clasping and unclasping as longing flitted across her eyes. It amazed him how much had changed since the first time he'd spied on her through her lace curtains.

Pulled by the sight of him, Jaclyn stepped up to the glass pane and peered out. God, she suddenly looked so small, scared . . . fragile— like a kitten torn from its mother's loving embrace at birth.

When their gazes collided and locked, his entire world turned upside down. His pulse leapt and his heart crashed against his chest, and despite the cooler air after last week's storm, his entire body broke out in a sweat. His physical need to be with her, to soothe away her worries, proved almost unbearable.

His gut clenched with want as he cut across the street and rushed inside his house. He stripped off his clothes in an effort to cool his heated body down. Struggling to keep his raging panther at bay before it took over and demanded to mate with its life partner, he bolted up the stairs and made his way to the shower as he diligently worked to avoid glancing at Jaclyn through his bedroom window. Christ, he needed a clear head before he met up with the other guides. The last thing he wanted to do at the meeting was to react with emotion.

He stepped into the bathroom, turned on the spray and climbed in, all the while worrying about the emergency meeting. He'd heard the rumblings around town, folks fearful of the outsider and all her prying. Slyck fully expected that tonight's meeting would end with her future decided—with straws drawn to decide who would claim her. And by God, he had to win. It suddenly occurred to him that if he did, that could solve all their problems, but if he didn't . . .

He quickly brushed that thought aside. The consequences were too horrible to consider. He couldn't lose.

He wouldn't lose.

Jaclyn was his—no one would ever take her from him. The thought of her had his cock swelling, and his lust-drunk mind reminiscing about how her sweet body had rocked sensuously against his, how she had felt so right in his arms.

An invisible band tightened around his chest. Even though

he'd spent his whole life waiting for her, he certainly wasn't prepared for the emotions she pulled from him.

Slyck knew the only way he'd be able to keep his thoughts off
Jaclyn and focused during the impending meeting was to release
the pent-up tension inside him. With that last thought in mind,
he pictured Jaclyn's gorgeous plump lips wrapped around his hard
shaft and let his hand drift downward. A low groan crawled out of
his throat as one large palm closed over his throbbing appendage.

"Goddamn it," he bit out and threw his head back.

As the needlelike spray hit his body, he closed his eyes, letting
his imagination take him to the depth of his desires while his fingers worked overtime to take the edge off. Erotic visions of Jaclyn
standing before him, his for the taking, rushed through his mind
as he stroked his length.

As he recalled the taste of her sweet nectar, he stroked faster,
his lips tingling, his mouth aching to press against her beautiful
cunt until she cried out his name in heavenly bliss.

"Jesus," he whispered under his breath, as he remembered her
clit hardening in his mouth, the way it felt against his hungry
tongue, the ease with which he could bring her to climax.

Senses exploding, he dragged in air. With his orgasm merely
a few strokes away, his hands began to work harder over his engorged dick. He began shaking, trembling, and panting. When his
dick began to pulse, crying out for release, he swallowed. Hard.

He squeezed his eyes shut, picturing Jaclyn's tight, creamy sex
muscles gripping his rock-hard cock as he pumped in and out of
her welcoming pussy.

"Fuck . . ." he groaned out loud as pressure mounted inside

him. He cupped his sack and stroked his dick faster. With his cock thickening to the point of no return, he bit down on his bottom lip, his brain no longer functioning.

He grunted something incoherent, stroked once more, and stilled his movements. A second later, he shot hot come into the cool spray and gave a low growl of contentment.

Hands falling to his sides, he worked to regulate his breathing. A long while later, cock flaccid, he washed up and prepared for the night ahead.

Less than an hour later he walked out into the star-studded night and made his way down Main Street. As he climbed the steps back into the hall, a sense of foreboding overcame him, making his skin tighten and crawl. Putting on his best hard-assed face, he entered and made his way to his chair. As soon as all the seats were filled, and everyone was accounted for, Harmony began the meeting.

"I'm sure you all know why I called this meeting."

After a round of nods, she opened the floor for discussion. "What is the consensus?"

"I say we change her," Vall said, placing his big, beefy paws on the table. "My pack is furious after she tried to feed chocolate to one of the pups. Christ, the amount of theobromine in one of those small chocolates could have taken a grown wolf like me out. What's she going to divvy out next, Tylenol?"

"And let's face it, after her party, and the way we treated her, she's still here and ever determined to make friends," Quinn volunteered, his dark eyes flashing in anticipation at the chance of acquiring a new pack member.

"I think you all know my thoughts," Devon offered, giving them a devilish grin, his yellow demon eyes flashing in excitement.

Harmony turned to Slyck. "Slyck?"

Slyck kept his face blank and remained emotionless as he looked around the room, disliking his odds. He had a twenty percent chance of winning, which also meant he had an eighty percent chance of losing. Winning could solve Jaclyn's and his problems, but losing would only multiply the ones they already had. Fuck, he didn't like this. He didn't like this at all.

"Will her family be suspicious if she doesn't return?" Slyck studied the reaction of those before him as he anguished over the odds. He couldn't risk it. Not with Jaclyn. There had to be a better way. Christ, he really needed to buy time until he figured this mess out. "After all, Jaclyn is a rich, pampered city girl who is here simply to raise cosmetics sales," he answered, knowing she was anything but. "And it might look suspicious to her family if she suddenly decides to take up permanent residence here."

As everyone absorbed his statement, the room seemed to grow exceptionally quiet, save for the drone of the fluorescent lights overhead, which suddenly seemed to have grown exceptionally loud in the hall.

"That's a valid point," Harmony finally said, breaking the quiet, her knowledgeable violet eyes studying Slyck as she went on to say, "but she certainly doesn't seem to be in too much of a hurry to go home. And she is asking some very insightful questions, don't you think?"

"It's not like we haven't changed rich, pampered city folk before," Devon pointed out. "And she's single. Always the perfect candidate. Besides, once we turn her, she'll become loyal to her pack—we all know that."

"What's the problem, Slyck? She's just another ordinary girl," Quinn volunteered.

Slyck bit the inside of his mouth. The circumstances surrounding her were far from ordinary, nor were his feelings for her. Slyck remained silent, cautious as he bartered with Jaclyn's future. The last thing he needed was for the council to learn she was the offspring of a rogue; otherwise she was as good as dead. Vall would demand her termination, per mandate rules, and then challenge Slyck's leadership.

Slyck could feel Vall's suspicious eyes on him, his pewter glare cutting though his shield as easily as Quinn's razor-sharp incisors sliced through ripe flesh.

"What's the matter, Slyck? You sweet on her or something?" Vall asked.

Slyck fisted his hands and worked to control his anger. "I'm looking at all the angles, Vall, trying to be smart about this, to think about the *town*'s best interest."

As though taking personal offense at Slyck's words, Vall sprang to his feet so fast his chair went flying backward. Slyck remained seated. Shifting during a meeting or challenging one's dominance was strictly prohibited when all the members sat around the oaken table and closed the circle.

Eyes taunting, Vall baited him. "What's the matter, kitty, afraid of the big, bad wolf?"

Slyck's fingers twitched, but once again he refused to take the bait. He wouldn't stoop to Vall's level.

Suddenly, Vall's face began to elongate and the sound of his bones crackling was like music to Slyck's ears. Vall's sharp fangs extended, and a long golden mane covered his flesh. The fierce, violent energy swirling through the long hall called out to both the demon and the vampire, which had Devon and Quinn on their feet in record time.

Digging deep to keep his panther in check and show his unwavering control, as it itched to claw at Vall, Slyck slowly stood and turned to the lycan. He met his gaze unflinchingly and put his face close, nudging the beast's temper. He watched the lycan let his anger control the animal inside him, and knew it was one of his nemesis's greatest weaknesses. Irreverent fool that he was. During the change, the man became most vulnerable. At that moment, while still in his human form, Slyck could have easily taken out the wolf, but chose not to.

Harmony banged her hand on the table. Reproof in her tone, she snapped, "Enough."

Devon and Quinn resumed their seats, but Slyck wouldn't budge, not until Vall backed down.

"Slyck, Vall," Harmony said, anger in her usually calm voice. "Enough."

With that, Vall snarled and shook off the call of the beast. After giving Slyck one last warning glare, Vall took his seat.

"Let's get back to the matter at hand, shall we?" Harmony said, quickly getting everyone back on track. "So a show of hands, then."

Slyck had no choice but to go with the majority; otherwise he'd raise suspicions, and after that little battle of wills, it was the last thing he needed. He couldn't risk it. Not with Jaclyn. All five council members raised their hands.

"Majority it is, then." Harmony stood, unlocked the cupboard, and brought out a container with five straws. Beginning with Devon, she walked around the table and held the container out in offering, claiming that last straw as her own.

She sat down, then glanced around. "A show." All five members held out their straws, and when Slyck saw the smirk on Vall's face, he knew that his worst nightmare had just come true.

Oh fuck!

Slyck could feel his blood run cold as his mind raced. No fully transformed panther had ever turned into a lycan from a bite before. In the past, when they'd gone head-to-head, a lycan bite did one of two things: temporarily weakened the panther or, on a few rare occasions when the panther was too young to combat the virus, killed them. Like decapitation, a lycan bite could prematurely end all nine lives.

Slyck swallowed the bile rising up from his stomach. Without having gone through her first transformation, Jaclyn wasn't equipped to deal with such a bite. She was still vulnerable, susceptible to turning lycan after a bite until her panther showed. He needed to speed up the process if he wanted her to stand half a chance of battling and surviving a bite from a lycan elder.

The sound of Vall's voice pulled him back. "Looks like I've got some work to do," the lycan said, gloating like the depraved bastard he really was.

"See to it that it's taken care of before the next full moon," Harmony added. "The sooner this is dealt with, the better."

Despite his best efforts not to, Slyck flinched. He quickly tried to cover it up by returning his straw to the container, but he knew that action hadn't gone unnoticed by the lycan. And no mat- ter how hard he tried, he couldn't seem to control his galloping heart rate, either. Fuck. He suspected the mongrel had heard that too. Slyck needed to get out of there, to warn Jaclyn, to put a plan together before Vall tried to leave his mark on her.

Working to keep his voice casual, he said, "So if that's it, then, let's wrap this up. I'm needed at Vibes." Not that he had any intention of heading to the club. He needed to get home and keep a watchful eye over Jaclyn.

Harmony tapped the table and closed the meeting, with all five species going their separate ways. Or at least they should have all gone off on their own. As Slyck moved down Main Street, he felt Vall's hot glare on his back. The bastard was following him.

Annoyed, Slyck had no choice but to enter his nightclub. He somehow needed to escape Vall's watchful eye so he could figure out what the fuck he was going to do to save his mate. It'd be a cold day in hell before he let Vall touch Jaclyn. And since, ac- cording to Devon, hell was thriving quite nicely with no foresee- able freeze in the near future, that cold day would be a long time coming.

Chapter Ten

Jaclyn awoke with a splitting headache. In fact, everything ached, from the tips of her split ends right on down to the tips of her cold toes. She blinked her eyes open carefully, and cringed when the bright morning sun cut through her windowpane and burned her sensitive retinas. Much aggrieved, she rolled back over, groaned out loud, and fought off the sudden feeling of nausea.

Good Lord, she never got sick. Maybe the odd sniffle every now and then, but she'd never been down and out with the flu before. Now she felt like she'd just gone ten rounds with a transport truck. And not only had the truck won—it had backed up over her to go another round.

She swallowed and took note of her thick tongue and scratchy throat. Jesus, what the hell was the matter with her? Could this really be the flu? Who the heck came down with the flu in the middle of summer, anyway?

With her aching body damp from fever, she kicked off her

light cotton covers and forced her rubbery legs to the floor. Immediately chilled, she crawled from her bed and held on to the wall as she padded across the carpet and made her way into the bathroom. After brushing her teeth, her tongue, and even the insides of her cheeks, she turned on the shower, hoping she'd feel a little more human once the warm spray hit her body.

The hot water felt good, but it only temporarily soothed away the ache. Once she climbed from the shower, her skin grew clammy and cool again as pain inched its way through her body. She hugged herself to stave off the shivers.

She quickly dried off and threw on a pair of jeans, along with a heavy knit sweater, despite the glorious, albeit blinding, sunshine outside. Once dressed, and feeling slightly warmer, she slipped into a pair of fuzzy slippers and, with slow, easy steps, padded softly to her kitchen, where she forced herself to choke down some dry toast.

After she'd managed to swallow the flavorless bread, and surprisingly keep it down, she fished her sunglasses out of her purse and made her way to work, stopping at the drug mart to pick up some Tylenol on the way.

Sunray, who looked like her normal gorgeous self, met Jaclyn at the front entrance of the department store. With the way her friend sparkled on this warm summer morning, it was a good thing Jaclyn had worn sunglasses; otherwise she'd have been blinded by the dazzling glare. Maybe that was why she was named Sunray, because she was just as bright as the sun's rays. Jaclyn gave an easy shake of her head and tried to concentrate. Her fever had obviously caused her mind to wander off track. Maybe it was even making her a little delirious.

Silvery eyes narrowed as Sunray pulled open the heavy glass door and gestured for Jaclyn to enter. She angled her head. "Hey, girl, you look like hell."

Jaclyn let out a heavy sigh. "That's probably because I feel like hell."

Sunray paused and let her glance race over Jaclyn. "You sure you want to be here?"

Jaclyn pushed her hands deep into her jeans pockets and curled her fingers around her medicine bottle. "I'm sure after a little while I'll be as right as rain." And a half a dozen Tylenol.

As midmorning neared, Jaclyn certainly didn't feel as right as rain. Even after the chalky medicine, she felt more like a tree ripped from its roots in the midst of a category-five hurricane. Her skin itched terribly, yet it was so sensitive, it hurt to scratch.

Deciding to leave her post at the cosmetics counter, she took a quick trip to the bathroom. After splashing her face with water, she glanced at herself in the mirror. Her hand flew to her chest, and she gasped in surprise.

"Jaclyn, do you need help?" The soft concerned voice came from behind her.

Jaclyn squinted, trying to blink away the green flecks in her eyes before her friend glimpsed them. When Sunray's hand touched her shoulder, she fished her sunglasses out of her purse and spun around.

Sunray's head came up with a start. "You're not okay," she said matter-of-factly. "Not okay at all." Uncertainty flitted across Sunray's eyes as she assessed her.

Spears of fear whipped through Jaclyn's blood, chilling her to the bone. Oh God, did Sunray know what was happening to her? What would that mean for her? For Slyck?

"I have the flu," Jaclyn said quickly, addressing her friend's concerns, even though deep down she knew her sickness had nothing at all to do with a germ bug. By small degrees Sunray's body tightened visibly. "Or maybe it's just allergies," Jaclyn offered. "Other than that, I'm fine, really," she quipped lightly, a task that took a great amount of effort. She leaned against the sink for support and flashed a smile, or at least what she hoped passed for a smile.

Sunray regarded her with wide eyes as though she could read Jaclyn's every little secret. Shock crossed her friend's face when she nudged Jaclyn toward the door. "You need to get out of here, Jaclyn. Fast. Before . . ." She stopped midsentence when the door to the washroom opened and a customer walked in.

Sunray spoke quickly, "Go." She worried her bottom lip and then leaned in and whispered, "I'll cover for you."

Jaclyn nodded as panic gripped her hard. She rushed back to her section, shut down her cash, and made her way outside. Even with the sunglasses on, the bright sunshine still cut through the dark lenses and stung her oversensitive eyes. She pulled up the long sleeves on her sweater and glanced at her arms. The hairs had grown coarser and darker.

Even though Slyck had warned her to keep her distance from

him while in public, until they figured out a plan of action, she needed him now, more than ever.

Since she'd been watching him for days, she knew his routine well enough to know that he'd be at Vibes, preparing for the night shift. She also knew that this early in the morning, Vibes wouldn't be open to the townsfolk.

As she moved down Main Street, a vaguely familiar scent reached her newly sensitized nostrils. She couldn't quite put her finger on it. When she inhaled again, it hit her. Wet dog. She glanced around but saw no one. Even still, she had an intuitive sense that someone was following her.

Instincts sharpened, and acting as if she didn't have a care in the world, Jaclyn weaved in and out of a few different stores, picking up a couple of items to make it look like she was shopping. When the scent subsided, she carefully made her way around the back of the building that housed Vibes. In her weakened state, she dropped her shopping bags and was barely able to lift her arm to knock on the service-entrance door. While she waited, she prayed that Slyck was inside, because no way could she walk up to his house and knock, not without raising suspicion. And certainly not with the gut feeling that someone was stalking her.

She wrapped her arms around her waist and cradled her stomach. A few moments later the door opened, and one very surprised Slyck stood there, looking at her. He glanced past her shoulder and circled his hands around her waist, hauling her inside.

"Jaclyn," he murmured and dragged her into his arms, his mouth on her eyes, her nose, her lips as though he couldn't get enough of her. "This is dangerous, kitten."

"I know," she whispered back, feeling so much better in his presence. Her headache had even subsided, and she suspected it had little to do with the Tylenol.

"I've wanted to come to you for days, sweetheart," Slyck confessed. "But I haven't been able to. I'm being watched."

Before she could explain that she too felt she was being watched, he said, "Come with me. We need to talk." Slyck packaged her in his strong arms and escorted her down a long hallway, past the public washrooms and into the back office. The room was small, with only one tiny window, a sofa, a corner desk, and a cabinet full of files. Behind the office door she spotted a small private washroom.

With a nod Slyck gestured toward the sofa. After she sat, he took a seat beside her and edged close until their bodies touched. His warm hand caressed her cold and clammy cheek. His brow furrowed. "Are you okay?"

"I don't think so."

Slyck carefully removed her sunglasses. Something that looked like a mixture of concern and pride flitted over his face when he studied her eyes.

"You're changing," he said softly and gathered her hand into his. "That's why you feel ill."

Oh God, she could hardly believe this was happening. But it was happening, she reminded herself, and like everything else in her life, she had to face it straight on. Starching her spine, she pushed past her fears and asked, "Will it always feel like this?"

He gave her hand a comforting squeeze. "No. The first time is the worst. It'll get easier each time," he reassured her.

She searched his face when he got quiet. "What is it?"

He crouched down in front of her, his mouth tightened. "Presenting my panther will help bring on the shift," he offered in a low, soothing murmur. "But I don't want it to alarm you, sweetheart."

Jaclyn palmed his face as a bone-deep warmth moved through her. Common sense would have dictated that she run. Run as far away from Serene as possible. But she was past the point of denial and needed for some unfathomable reason to see his panther. She murmured low, "Show me." Jaclyn held her breath, preparing herself the best she could to witness the transformation for the first time.

Without his eyes ever leaving hers, Slyck broke their intimate connection, stepped back, and removed his clothes. His warm, earthy male scent reached her nostrils and curled around her. She inhaled, savoring his rich aroma, noting how his familiar smell helped ease the tension inside her.

As she studied his beautiful scarred body, she watched his skin stretch and darken. Wincing, she clasped her hands in her lap at the sound of his bones shifting and crackling as his body elongated. Even though she'd braced herself, when all was said and done, nothing could have prepared her for the pain that crossed over his eyes as he transformed. Nor could she have prepared herself for the sight of the beautiful black panther that now stood before her, or those magnificent green eyes that could surely see into the depths of her soul.

Too astonished to even breathe, Jaclyn let her jaw drop open, and she took a long minute to just stare at him. Her heart pounded and her entire body broke into a sweat. A low, unfamiliar primal sound rose up from the depths of her throat.

When the panther before her—Slyck—heard the rumble from her animalist growl, it began pacing, purring, and brushing up against her legs.

She sucked in air. Her gaze slid over his panther form, and for a moment she felt like she was drowning, suddenly finding it harder and harder to breathe.

"You're so beautiful," she said with effort, tentatively stroking his shiny black fur. The room began spinning, her body tingling as her fingers slid over his smooth back. She blinked her eyes and tried to shake off the light-headed feeling. Something was happening to her, something she had no control over. Her heart began pounding as full-blown panic gripped her.

Before she knew it, Slyck had morphed back and nestled himself on the floor between her legs. His knuckles brushed her cheek, and the tremendous connection between them helped her nerves settle.

"I need you to concentrate, Jaclyn, to let go of all your fears and inhibitions. Just let the shift take place. It's natural. Don't fight it," he coaxed.

She tried to follow his advice—she really did—but the more she worked at it, the more worked up she became. Completely dismayed, she blew a heavy breath and pounded her hands against the sofa in frustration.

Slyck moved in close and began kissing her, derailing her ability to concentrate. The warmth of his flesh ignited a fire in her.

He hastily began unzipping her jeans, bombarding her with heat and desire.

With her attention diverted, her breath caught on a gasp, and she shot him a smoldering glance. The look in his eyes reflected her desires. "What are you doing?" she asked, arousal replacing frustration as his fingers caressed her flesh.

He pulled her pants to her ankles and tossed them away. In one quick movement he roughly ripped her panties from her hips and discarded them. His eyes grew intense and the urgency in his voice both excited and frightened her. "Saving you from death, or the very least a life as a 'damned' dog."

Jaclyn's libido roared to life. Her head fell to the side, and her skin flushed hot. She was so consumed by need, she didn't understand what he was talking about. "I guess neither one of us is a fan of the canine," she murmured, her passion-drunk mind barely able to hold a coherent thought as he ripped the rest of her clothes from her aching body.

His voice came out in a heated whisper. "You'd be nothing more than a chew toy for Vall." He tapped her thighs, nudging her legs apart. His nostrils flared as he lowered his head and brushed his tongue over her inflamed clit.

Oh good God, his mouth did the most delicious things to her.

As he devoured her, some small coherent part of her rattled brain realized he was talking about Vall. Why the hell was he talking about Vall at a time like this? And what was it he'd said she'd be to him? A chew toy?

She palmed his muscles, and without censor she asked, "And what am I to you?" She gyrated against his burning mouth as it pressed hungrily to her cunt.

His eyes, dark and needy, flashed to hers. "You're everything to me. You know that." The soft cadence of his voice caressed her all over and brought on a shudder. He slid a thick finger into her pussy while his thumb brushed her clit. Blistering heat exploded inside her and spiraled onward and outward until her entire flesh burned with pleasure.

She pushed against him and said, "I know. I guess I just needed to hear you say it. So it could help me make sense of all this."

A second finger joined the mix, and she could no longer think. Oh God, she desperately needed him. Desperately needed to feel his cock inside her. Hungering for him with an intensity that made her shake, she asked, "So you're saying you can save me by having sex with me?"

"Yes, kitten. That's exactly what I'm telling you."

"Then what are you waiting for?" she asked, her hips coming off the sofa. "Save me." Her aroused voice came out sounding shaky and unstable.

Need pumped through her veins, and her mouth watered as she took in his beautiful body and rock-hard cock.

He captured her hands and hauled her off the sofa. "Wrap your legs around me," he rasped.

When Jaclyn pounced onto him, he backed her up until she hit the wall and crushed his chest to her breast. His lips crashed down on hers, his tongue thrashing against the inside of her mouth. A low growl crawled out of his throat as fierce need burned in his eyes. In one quick thrust, he impaled her and began pounding into her hot, wet pussy. Each powerful thrust drove her harder and harder against the wall.

Her breasts pressed into his skin, her nipples rubbing sensuously against his hard muscles. She rocked her hips, taking every inch of him inside her. Her body blazed with lust, and she'd never felt so wild or frenzied before.

He burrowed deep, making her delirious with need. As hunger clawed at her insides, soft quakes began at her core, making her crazed, frantic. Slyck continued to drive deeper and harder as she burned with need. She could feel his cock swell and pulse as he filled her with his seed. Panting, and clawing at him, she gave herself over to her orgasm as he released high inside her.

A long while later, when the tremors had fully subsided, his gaze met hers. A mixture of emotions passed over his eyes when he lowered her to her feet and stepped back. Before she could reach for him, to haul him back, pain overtook her, and her body collapsed to the carpeted floor. It was happening. Slyck dropped down beside her and put his mouth close to her ear.

"Stay strong and ride it out, kitten. I'm here for you." His hand touched her shoulder in a comforting manner.

Jaclyn could hear her bones shift, feel her mouth and limbs elongate. She swallowed down the fear and watched her skin stretch and darken, her nails extend to razorlike claws. She shot Slyck a quick glance and could hear the thunder of his heart as he watched her with concerned, loving eyes.

She let out a low moan and tried not to concentrate on the pain. Her nerves began tingling, her body convulsing. Minutes felt like hours as her final transformation took place. Summoning all her bravado, she dropped her head and called out to him.

"Slyck—"

"I'm here, sweetheart."

When she looked up again, she saw pride and possessiveness burning in Slyck's beautiful green eyes as she took her next breath as panther.

"Look at you. Jesus, just look at you," he whispered. "I've never seen such strength and beauty."

He too morphed, joining her in his animalistic form as he began rubbing up against her. Silence ensued while he offered her time to get used to the change.

"Oh God, this is so—" She stopped midsentence, and with surprise ringing in her voice, she said, "We can communicate."

"Of course," he responded. "But we can only communicate with other panthers in this form."

Her knees wobbled slightly, and she drew a steadying breath. "It feels so—I don't know—weird but amazing at the same time." In fact, it felt a little erotic, stimulating. Jaclyn went down on her haunches and lifted one palm to examine it. She brushed it over her face, grooming herself. "I can't imagine ever getting used to this."

Slyck nudged her head with his own, and she could feel the passion rising in him, reaching out to her. His primal essence completely overwhelmed her. When she caught his glance, she could feel his primitive urges as baser instincts kicked in. His control was weakening, his need to take her strengthening. Everything from the heat in his eyes to the sensuous way he moved instinctively told her he needed to lay claim to her—a final marking that would bind her to him forever.

His scent aroused the animal in her, and her entire body responded with need, spasming with pleasure. Fire and heat curled through her.

Understanding the implications of her actions, she stretched her paws out in front of herself and gifted him with her body in panther form. As she submitted to her alpha, offering herself up to him, he growled low and deep. Her uninhibited responses urged him on.

Slyck mounted her from behind and in one quick thrust pushed into her. Jaclyn moaned, fully comprehending the importance in what they were doing. "You are mine, Jaclyn," he announced, his voice low, firm, savage.

Something deeply intimate and animalistic passed between them as he sank into her heat and left his final mark on her. Warmth moved through her as he branded her as his for eternity, and for the first time in her life, she truly understood what it meant to feel safe, cherished, and loved. Understood what it meant to belong.

He spent a long time inside her, their bodies joining as one while they moved in perfect rhythm. When she felt him throb, she knew he was close.

"Tell me you are mine, Jaclyn."

"I'm yours," she murmured. "And only yours."

She shook and pulsed beneath him as he filled her with his seed and brought on her release. With that final mating, her mind cleared, and it was as if her entire life now had a purpose.

His breath came in a low rush. *"We-Sa . . . ,"* he whispered and held her to him as she rode out the waves.

Minutes later, with their mating ritual complete, Slyck lay down beside her. She nuzzled in close. "How do I shift back?" she asked, perplexed.

"By visualization. Relax, push your panther away, and visualize yourself in your human form."

Jaclyn did what he told her to, and a moment later, they both morphed back to their human forms. She glanced at her hands. "Shifting back didn't hurt near as much."

"It'll get easier, and shifting will come naturally, especially when presented with strong emotions. But over time, and through guidance, you'll learn to control it and use your panther and our bond as strength."

Jaclyn fell silent for a long time and tried to take it all in.

"Hey," Slyck whispered, breaking the quiet. When she met his eyes, he smiled at her and warm familiarity moved between them.

"Hey, yourself," she said back as a shiver raced through her. He pulled her in tighter and her naked body soaked in his warmth.

"Are you okay?"

She nodded, unable to vocalize exactly what she was feeling.

"Let's get you off this floor, sweetheart." He climbed to his feet, helped her up, and gestured toward the sofa. His tender concern made her womb clench.

Slyck gathered up her clothes. When his hands connected with her jeans, her bottle of medicine fell out of the pocket and rolled across the floor. Slyck snatched it off the carpet and turned it over in his hands.

His eyes narrowed. "Did you take one of these?"

"Yes." Jaclyn shifted on the sofa, laying herself out, and patted the empty spot beside her. She felt a need for his intimate contact at all times.

Slyck sat down and brushed her damp bangs from her forehead. His distinctive, familiar aroma teased her senses. "Do you take them often?"

She gave a quick shake of her head. "No, I never get sick. At first I thought I was getting the flu, so I took one for fever, but it actually made me feel worse."

"That's because cats don't tolerate Tylenol very well, kitten. Especially if you've never had it before." His eyes softened when he added, "It could kill you."

She shook her head, flabbergasted. "I had no idea. I guess I still have so much to learn."

She saw possessiveness in his eyes when he said, "I'll teach you everything, Jaclyn. I'll protect you and teach you how to use your panther and our bond as a strength."

Slyck stretched out beside her, and she gently touched his scars. As their bodies melded together, she thought more about the panther species and what it might actually mean to be one. "I thought all fairy-tale creatures had special healing abilities. What about these?"

He ran his lips over her forehead while his strong, comforting arms circled her and pulled her in tighter. "We all have different abilities. Regenerative healing isn't one of ours."

"And the others?"

"Demons, vampires, and lycans can all regenerate. Witches and panthers are the only ones who can't."

She crinkled her nose and gave that more thought, suddenly remembering what he had said before he made love to her. "Speaking of the others, why did you say I'd be a chew toy for Vall?"

He blew out a heavy breath and shifted restlessly, and she sensed he was trying to hide the truth. His hair brushed her cheek when she tilted her head to see him.

"Slyck?" she questioned.

He took a moment as though weighing his words carefully before he delivered the cold, hard truth. "I didn't tell you this before because I'd hoped it wouldn't come to it, but our council has decided to make your stay permanent."

"Permanent?" she echoed.

"Straws were drawn—" His voice broke off, like he was trying to spare her the ugly details.

She put her hand on his chest. Her throat constricted and her mind raced. She was intelligent enough to figure out the outcome. "And Vall got the short end," she volunteered. Which explained why he was following her. He planned on marking her, turning her to a lycan. She paused to consider things further. She glanced at Slyck again and began, "And you needed me to be fully turned because—"

Frowning, Slyck narrowed his eyes. "Because if he tries to bite you, you'll have a defense against him," he elaborated. "Until your panther showed, you were vulnerable. There was a chance Vall could have turned you into lycan. At least now we don't have to worry about that." Despite trying to soften his words, the unease in his cadence hadn't gone unnoticed.

"So now what do we have to worry about?" She drew a fueling

breath and took a moment to compose herself the best she could under the circumstances. "What if he does manage to bite me?" she probed. "What then?"

He inclined his head, his dark hair falling forward. "The best we can hope for is that it weakens you," he confessed.

She arched a brow and could feel his heart race beneath her hand. "The worst?" she countered, even though the angst in his tone and the way he'd tried to avoid eye contact had already answered that question.

He lifted his chin to meet her questioning gaze. His eyes swept over her face slowly, apologetically. Instantly aware of the way his body tightened beneath her fingers, she demanded, "Tell me."

"You're only a kitten, sweetheart. The virus from a lycan bite can only weaken a mature panther, but on rare occasions, it can poison and kill a young body such as yours." His voice came out rough, fragmented. His nostrils flared; the muscles in his jaw flexed. "It's rare, Jaclyn, but we won't let it come to that."

"So even if his bite doesn't kill me, one taste of my blood, and he'll be able to figure out I'm panther, right?"

"Yeah, there's always that."

"So, since I'm the offspring of a rogue panther, either way I'm dead."

Her blood raced and her mouth went dry as she marveled at the turn of events and all that she'd gone through over the last couple of weeks. She scraped her teeth over her bottom lip. "Does this kind of thing happen often? Humans getting marked?"

"No, and only with the people who refuse to leave, or ask too many questions about the town. We need to turn them and bring them into the brethren in order to ensure that our secret society remains a secret."

When he caressed her lightly, feathering his fingers over her arms, her heart tightened. God, he was so full of power and strength, yet capable of such exquisite gentleness when he touched her.

Confusion crept into her voice. "Who's to say once a person is changed that they don't expose this place?"

"It's not like that once you've been changed. You're here on your own free will because you *want* to be with your brethren, *need* to be with them. You can't bear to be away from them. Your pack comes before anyone and everything else, so much so that we even go so far as to sacrifice one life for the greater good."

She rolled her shoulders. "Why couldn't they just accept me as panther when I showed up? Why would they think I'd expose the town?"

"Because your father was a rogue, and because I covered up his treachery, and because deep down, we're all primal beings ruled by instinct. I could plead with the council to let them know you're not a threat, but I can already tell you it wouldn't matter and they'd terminate you. Trust me. Right now we're better off not letting them know. Plus I can't let Vall challenge my authority until I'm certain Drake is ready. Otherwise the entire town could be in jeopardy." Seemingly weary, he pinched the bridge of his nose as though trying to ward off an impending headache. "I thought I was doing what was best for the town," he murmured under his breath.

Jaclyn traced the scar just below his ear, her heart going out to him. "Where do we go from here?"

Frustration passed over his eyes, his brow creased in concern. "I'm working on that." Slyck fell quiet, lost in his own thoughts.

After a moment of silence Jaclyn said, "I felt him following me, Slyck. Just this morning."

He tensed and drew her body in tighter. "He didn't see you come into the club, did he?" he rushed out.

God, she felt so protected in his strong arms. Without conscious thought, she snuggled in closer and shook her head. "I was careful." After she felt him relax, she continued. "When will he try to mark me?"

"He has until the first full moon, which is less than two weeks away, but I think he'll bide his time and see if I react. Marking you and taking me down in the process, especially if he knows what's between us, would give him the utmost pleasure."

Slyck cursed and fisted his hands. Jaclyn could feel his pulse pick up tempo. As though to calm himself, he softly brushed his cheek over her hair and lowered his voice when he explained, "Which is why we have to be extra-careful. We can't let anyone know you're my mate, and we can never ever let our guard down."

She swallowed and put her hand on her stomach. "I think Sunray knows."

"Sunray?"

"Yeah, she saw me this morning at the department store. I think she even saw my eyes, but I can't be sure. She was really worried about me. Told me to get out of there and that she'd cover for me."

He paused to consider that for a moment before saying, "Even though she's a lycan, she's not like the others in her brethren. Many years ago, when she was trying to come to terms with what she was, she used to spend a lot of time at the bar. And in a strange sort of way, with both of us feeling alone in this community, we bonded as friends, and I suspect we can trust her to keep our secret." Then his gaze went to her medicine bottle, and suddenly, as if a lightbulb had gone off in his head, his eyes lit.

"What is it?" Jaclyn asked.

He kissed her full on the mouth, and something that looked like hope entered his eyes. "You're brilliant."

"I am?" She could almost hear his mind race, formulating a plan.

"Yes, Sunray is just the woman to help buy us some time and turn the predator into the prey."

Chapter Eleven

After listening intently to Slyck's extremely risky yet still workable plan, Jaclyn put a call in to Sunray at the department store. Sunray readily agreed to meet Jaclyn for drinks after nightfall. It was clear she understood that they needed to talk.

To make their meeting look as inconspicuous as possible, they met up at the crowded bar, just two women sharing a margarita after work hours. Jaclyn could feel Vall nearby. He sat, watching and waiting. Even though she couldn't see him, his pungent scent impregnated the smoky establishment and stung her sensitive nostrils. Her skin prickled, and she fought back a violent shudder.

Jaclyn kept the conversation light, exchanging pleasantries only, even though Sunray's silver eyes held many questions. Jaclyn was pretty certain Sunray could feel her stress, despite her efforts to bank her tension. When they finished their drinks, they casually walked back to Jaclyn's place for a swim as though neither had a care in the world—an act not uncommon for coworkers and friends.

Jaclyn suspected Vall wouldn't intervene, especially since he'd planned on bringing her into the brethren anyway, and not only would that mean she'd eventually have to bond with Sunray; it also meant she'd have to bond with every other member of his pack as well.

As soon as they stepped across the threshold of her rental, Jaclyn's cat hissed at Sunray and bolted to the basement. The poor thing was obviously frightened by the intruding canine. Jaclyn made a mental note to give Ruby extra attention later on that night, and maybe even a few special treats.

Both women stopped walking through the dimly lit room when they spotted Slyck leaning against the doorjamb. His arms were folded across his chest, and his expression was serious. Jaclyn had never seen him look so intense.

As their eyes penetrated the darkened bungalow, Sunray shook her head. "What the hell is going on?" she demanded, and took one measured step backward. Silence fell among them all as Sunray watched them with uncertainty.

Trying to handle the situation as delicately as possible, Jaclyn cupped Sunray's elbow and guided her into the living room. She gestured toward the sofa and took a seat beside Sunray. Slyck positioned himself on the coffee table in front of them, and with his elbows planted on his knees, he leaned forward.

Sunray's curious gaze went from Slyck, to Jaclyn, to Slyck again. "You marked her," she stated. Slyck nodded in confirmation. Flabbergasted, Sunray threw her hands up in the air and asked, "Are you fucking insane, Slyck? Vall told us he'd be bringing Jaclyn into our brethren, but after I saw her eyes today, I figured out what you'd done." Sunray blew a long, slow breath, her eyes widened with apprehension, and when she turned to Jaclyn, she announced, "When Vall figures it out—"

Slyck intervened. "That's why you're here. We can't let him find out. And we need your help."

Her eyes shot back to Slyck. "Why me?"

He got right to the point. "Because I know how much you hate Vall."

She lifted her chin, her eyes questioning, even though she wasn't denying the accusation. "How do you know that?"

He cocked his head. "Because of the way he treats you, because of the way you act around him, and because you won't submit to him. And, because over a bottle of tequila at the bar many, many years ago, shortly after you'd been turned, you told me about the night he changed you."

She gave a slow shake of her head. "I guess I forgot about that conversation." After a humorless laugh, she held her finger up and wagged it. "Tequila is not my friend."

Slyck pitched his voice low, to show the seriousness of the situation. "I love her, Sunray, and I won't let Vall take her from me."

Jaclyn swallowed. Even though his erotic touch had shown her how much he cared for her, it was the first time she'd heard him voice those words. The first time any man had ever told her he loved her, in fact. Her heart twisted and her insides turned to pudding.

Sunray looked down. The deep sadness in the depths of her friend's eyes took Jaclyn by surprise. Sunray grew quiet, lost in her own thoughts.

Reading her distress, Jaclyn flicked on a corner lamp that bathed the room in a soft glow. The gentle rays gave sufficient light for her to see moisture in Sunray's eyes.

"What is it?" Jaclyn asked and captured the other woman's hands in her own.

Sunray took a moment to gather herself and began, "I understand how you both feel. Vall took someone very important from me a long time ago, and I've never forgiven him for it. But I don't see how I can help you, Jaclyn. Vall has every intention of marking you."

"Which is why we need him to mark you, instead," Slyck suggested.

Sunray frowned, her solemn eyes turned to Slyck. "Mark me, instead?" she echoed, and then gave Slyck a look that suggested he was insane. "Do I need to remind you that I'm already a lycan?"

"Which is why his bite won't hurt you. We need for him to think he's marking Jaclyn, when in reality he's marking you."

She shook her head wildly, her long golden mane tossing about recklessly. "It'll never work," she said. "My scent alone will give me away. And, besides, we look nothing alike."

Slyck shook the bottle of Tylenol and Sunray's eyes went wide. "There's nothing a little makeover can't fix, and with these . . ."

Sunray made a strange sound, a mixture of surprise and incredulity on her face. "I always knew you were a crazy son of a bitch, Slyck." She paused and then added, "A crazy son of a bitch who'd do anything for love, which is probably why I like you so much." Then suddenly, as if her mind had gone in another direction, the sadness returned, and her eyes clouded with emotion.

She cast her gaze downward in thought, and she clasped Jaclyn's hand tighter.

Jaclyn touched Sunray's chin and angled her head until their glances collided. Tormented eyes met and locked with Jaclyn's, and in that instant, Jaclyn could feel her friend's sadness and deep loneliness as though it were her own.

Sunray blinked back the moisture and went on to say, "But I understand the extent you would go to to save a loved one." Her voice came out low and shaky. "Trust me, I'd do the same if given the chance." She sagged against the couch and looked heavenward. "God, it's been close to a hundred years, and I still miss him," she muttered almost to herself, angst lacing her words. "I miss our secret meetings in the old, abandoned building near the tracks, and our late-night swims in the school's aquatic center. He was on the swim team and we'd often sneak in." A pause and then: "I have a hole inside me that will never go away, thanks to Vall. He stole my innocence, my life. I hate him. So much so that I recently bought a gun and loaded it with silver bullets."

Jaclyn gasped. "You want him dead?"

"Hell, yeah, I want him dead. But I wasn't going to use it on him. I was going to use it on me, because some things are worse than death, Jaclyn."

"Like what?" Jaclyn asked gently, coaxing her friend to open up.

"Like submitting to Vall. Truthfully, life would be good here without him."

"Why didn't you leave?"

"And go where? These people are my family now. They're all I have. If it just wasn't for Vall . . ." She blinked and attempted a smile. "I was ready to end it all until I met you, Jaclyn. There is something about you, something that reminds me of the man I loved and lost. I can vaguely feel him on you. Smell him on your skin. Like he's come back to me through you somehow."

"Was he panther?" Jaclyn asked.

Sunray shook her head. "No, and I know this all sounds insane, but it's the only way I can explain it."

Jaclyn smiled. "After everything I'd been through over the last couple of weeks, I'm well past thinking anything is insane."

Slyck touched Sunray's hand, bringing her attention around to him. "What about Ciaran, Vall's first? How would he be as a leader?"

"I think he'd be fair, but I won't submit to him, either," Sunray said. "I made a promise a long time ago. . . ."

Head down, looking emotionally battered, Sunray shivered, and everything inside Jaclyn reached out to her. She ached to soothe her friend's pain, to push back the cold and fill the void, if only for a little while. It shocked Jaclyn to think that underneath that sparkly, passionate exterior, Sunray was nothing more than a chunk of ice, completely frozen.

Jaclyn knew there was only one way to help her. Since mating was part of their culture, a primal way to show both love and acceptance, Jaclyn exchanged a long look with Slyck, and reading her intent, he nodded his consent. If there was anything they could do to help Sunray's internal disposition match her bubbly exterior, Jaclyn wanted to try. She was driven by a need to help build the trust among the three of them and show Sunray that they were her family now. Jaclyn inched closer until their thighs touched.

As though moving of their own volition, Sunray's hands reached out to both Slyck and Jaclyn, searching, needing. . . . Slyck dropped to his knees in front of her. "We're here for you, Sunray." The intimacy in his gesture seemed to catch Sunray off guard.

"What do you mean?" she asked.

"We're your family now," Jaclyn explained and raked her fingers through Sunray's soft blond hair. "We want to mate with you tonight, to create an impenetrable bond among us by bringing you into our small circle—to show you how much we care for you." With that, Jaclyn brushed her cheek over Sunray's, and burrowed close to her neck, a low purr sounding in her throat.

"You don't need to be lonely anymore, Sunray. You have us now," Slyck added.

Jaclyn inhaled and noted that, unlike Sunray's aged alpha leader, her friend had a warm, sweet puppy smell. Slyck was right: Sunray was different from the others.

Aware of the heat building among them, Sunray closed her eyes. Sunray squeezed Jaclyn's hand as though understanding and accepting the gift they were offering her. Jaclyn could see the hardening of her friend's nipples beneath her silk blouse. "I've been lonely without him," Sunray admitted, her sweet-scented breath warm on Jaclyn's face.

Slyck touched her cheek and let his hand trail to the buttons on her blouse. "You don't have to be alone anymore, Sunray. You have us now." Jaclyn's hand slid between Sunray's jeans-clad legs, making their intentions very clear.

With her breath quickening, Sunray turned to Jaclyn and licked her lips. Color bloomed high on her cheeks. The desire in

Sunray's eyes and the new closeness among them all prompted Jaclyn into action. She brought her mouth to her friend's and kissed
her deep. With fevered need, Jaclyn greedily drank the passion
from Sunray's lips.

"Come with us," Jaclyn whispered.

Slyck helped the women to their feet and ushered them to the
bedroom. He cradled Sunray in his arms, and gently kissed her on
the mouth before he began to remove her clothes. "Let us both
take care of you," he whispered.

Sunray reached for Jaclyn and drew her into the circle. Three
tongues met and tangled, their moans of pleasure merged, and
soon Slyck helped them remove their clothes before quickly shedding his own.

Slyck backed Sunray up until her knees hit the bed. Jaclyn
guided her to the center of the mattress and shimmied in beside
her. Slyck stood back and watched Jaclyn palm her friend's sexy
curves.

Jaclyn toyed with Sunray's beautiful red nipples. "You're so soft
and sexy," she murmured and found her mouth again. Attuned to
her friend's needs, Jaclyn slid her hand over Sunray's bare skin, going
lower until she reached the apex of her widened legs. Using light
strokes, she brushed her finger over Sunray's inflamed clit.

Sunray shivered violently and moved against her invading
hand. "So good." She motioned Slyck closer and whispered, "Please,
Slyck. I want to feel you inside me."

Slyck's low primal growl filled the room as he pushed a finger
into Sunray's moist heat. A moment later, Sunray's aroused scent
saturated the room and assailed her senses.

The mattress dipped as Slyck moved in closer and sandwiched Sunray between their bodies. Jaclyn's heart crashed against her chest as she reached for her mate and ran her hands over his sinewy muscles and washboard stomach.

Slyck began kissing Sunray's body, his mouth going to her beautiful breasts, her stomach, her pussy. When Jaclyn began to take her hand from the other woman's sex, Slyck stopped her.

"Don't. It's sexy."

Jaclyn grinned at him, her pussy moistening with need and her breasts filling with heated blood as she watched him indulge in Sunray's cream. As he worked his finger in and out of Sunray's feminine heat, Jaclyn leaned forward and pulled one hard nipple into her mouth. As Jaclyn savored the sweet bud, and made love to her friend with her mouth, breath rushed from Sunray's lungs.

"Goddamn, that feels incredible," Sunray whispered, and writhed restlessly beneath her as she raked her fingers through Jaclyn's hair, holding Jaclyn to her breasts.

Jaclyn moved to Sunray's mouth and slipped her tongue inside. When she felt the other woman's sex muscles tighten, she whispered, "Come for us. Let us taste your sweetness."

Sunray met her eyes and murmured. "Thank you, Jaclyn."

"My pleasure," Jaclyn assured her with a smile. With that, Jaclyn slid down Sunray's body and joined Slyck between her long, silken legs. Working in tandem they pushed their tongues high into Sunray's pussy, while Jaclyn paid special attention to her clit. With the tip of her finger, she drew slow, sinuous circles around her beautiful puckered nub.

"Yesss . . . ," Sunray hissed out, and gave herself over to the sensations, offering them a taste of her sweet cream as she rode out her climax.

After Jaclyn and Slyck finished lapping her pussy clean, they turned to each other. Jaclyn's body immediately reacted to the fiery passion in Slyck's eyes. Her nipples tightened painfully, her pussy dripped with desire.

His nostrils flared. "Lie down," he commanded, and Jaclyn nearly came then and there, from his sexy tone alone. "I need to fuck you," he added.

After Jaclyn sprawled out on the mattress, Slyck climbed between her legs. There was a look of contentment on Sunray's face as she ran her warm hands over Jaclyn's naked body and moved close. The flutter of Sunray's lashes against Jaclyn's skin brought on a shudder, as Slyck pushed his thick cock into her and fucked her hard.

Jaclyn's nails clawed at his back, her body spasming. God, she loved the way he filled her.

As he rode her ferociously, driving into her with wild, primal need, his mouth found hers. Even though he was fucking her hard, stoking the flames inside her, his kiss was so full of emotion and tenderness, it got to her in ways that completely astounded her and tangled her emotions in knots. She scarfed her hands around his neck and kissed him back with all the love inside her. Driven by need she bucked against him and felt him thicken with pleasure. Warmth flooded her pussy, as Sunray slipped a hand between their bodies and brushed her clit. "Slyck . . . ," she cried out and held him tight as a powerful climax stole her next breath.

"Jaclyn, kitten . . ." He breathed the words into her mouth as he joined her in release and poured his seed inside her.

Once he had completely released himself inside her, Slyck crawled in next to her and pulled the blankets up. All three snuggled in tight, one against the other. When Jaclyn began to drift off, she heard Sunray and Slyck whispering, Slyck asking her if she really knew what she was getting into, and if she truly understood the consequences of her actions if she got caught. After Sunray's assurances that she was in all the way, they both climbed from her bed and left the room. A moment later Jaclyn heard her back door open and close as the two carefully made their way home before sunrise.

After their long, thoughtful conversation with Sunray, and an evening of lovemaking, Slyck had cautiously returned home and spent the rest of the night all alone at his kitchen table, strategizing and fine-tuning the details of his timely yet risky plan.

It was fortunate for both Jaclyn and him that Sunray had been harboring a deep hatred for Vall for decades now. The strong female lycan had also bonded with Jaclyn over the last few weeks, which made her a very willing partner in his scheme. And her participation was critical for success. They needed her full cooperation if they had any chance of pulling off such a dangerous mission.

After a sleepless night, Slyck had made his way to his club to put things into motion. As midmorning neared, he hurried around Vibes and emptied every bottle of grenadine. After pouring the liquid down the drain, he dropped the bottles into the

Dumpster in the alleyway next to his club, and then hopped into his SUV.

He rarely left the community, had no reason to really. Until today. Of course, going outside the gate during the day wasn't prohibited, provided the inhabitant had a purpose. And since it was Friday night, his busiest night at the club, Slyck had, after emptying the grenadine, given himself a perfect excuse, especially since it was a crucial ingredient in the guard's favorite drink.

Slyck eased his SUV up to the security gate and tipped his head at the demon cowboy on duty. Yeah, that's right: a demon cowboy. It was one of the strange personae the demon had taken on over his lifetime. Why he continued to stick with it, Slyck would never know.

And speaking of cowboys, it was too bad Slyck and Jaclyn couldn't just ride out of town and disappear into the sunset, like Slyck used to do when he lived in the Old West. Talk about a sure-fire way to send his community, and his people in particular, into a tailspin. Sure Vall would love to see him gone—but he'd prefer to see them dead. That, and the overseers would classify them as rogues and undoubtedly hunt them both down. The only way Jaclyn and he were going to make it out of Serene alive was for the townsfolk to think they were dead.

"Morning, Jake."

Jake angled his head, his amber gaze narrowing in curiosity as his leather Stetson shaded the sun from his eyes. "Where are you off to this morning, Slyck?" he asked in a slow, practiced Southern drawl that would have made Clint Eastwood proud.

Slyck clicked his tongue. "Off to get some grenadine," he offered. "Got stiffed on my last shipment." Slyck gave him a know-ing wink. "And I know you wouldn't want to miss out on your tequila sunrise tonight."

Slyck gauged the guard's reaction as he looked him over. Christ, if the guy wanted to maintain his tough cowboy appearance, then perhaps he should opt for a drink that went along with the image. Tequila sunrises hardly fit the reputation of a rough-and-ready cowboy.

Crooked teeth flashed in a devious smile. "No, we wouldn't want that to happen, now, would we?" Jake commented and quickly lifted the gate.

Slyck grinned. Sometimes bartending really paid off.

"Harmony left here earlier," Jake began. "She was mumbling something about needing herbs, and how her garden had gotten drowned out in the thunderstorm last week." Rubbing his palms together, he gave Slyck a wicked grin as mischief danced in his golden eyes. "I wonder what she's got cooking up."

So did Slyck.

With the strange, flirty way Harmony had been acting around Vall lately, always taking his side in a dispute, he worried whether her sudden need for herbs had something to do with her feelings for him. Love spells were strictly forbidden. She knew that. Hell, everyone knew that. Lessons learned long ago taught them all that such magick caused nothing but trouble. And Vall was trouble enough as it was.

Harmony also knew interspecies mingling was prohibited. Suddenly Slyck had another thought, a darker one. Did Harmony too suspect Vall of trying to grow his pack? Was she forming an alliance with Vall should a shift in authority take place—she always did enjoy her place on the council—to ensure herself a position at the top in the canine pecking order?

Pushing those disturbing thoughts to the recesses of his mind to consider later, Slyck made a quick trip to the neighboring community to stock up on supplies. After he had stopped at the beauty salon, the dress shop, the perfume counter, and the optometrist's office, it was just past lunchtime when he passed back through the gates to Serene. With his packages camouflaged, he quickly rushed to the department store, where he met up with Sunray and inconspicuously handed the supplies to her. He then dropped the bottles of grenadine off at Vibes and made his way to the town hall, where Drake awaited him.

"Slyck," Drake greeted as he practiced his martial arts moves in the basement of the hall.

"Drake." Slyck nodded and began to stretch and warm up his muscles. He watched his first-in-command punch the air, using slow, controlled movements, and was pleased to see his dedication. "Been here long?" Slyck asked, noting the sweat on the other man's forehead.

"Long enough," Drake commented, his green gaze assessing Slyck, curiosity stirring in the depths of his penetrating eyes.

As Slyck lunged forward, elongating and preparing his tight muscles, Drake stepped up beside him. The air around them grew heavy, and in that instant, Slyck knew he could no longer put off the truth. Drake had obviously been sensing his tension for weeks now, and it was time to enlighten him, whether he wanted him involved or not.

Mouth set in a solemn line, Slyck stood to his full height and turned around to face his first. He blew a slow, reserved breath and locked his gaze on a pair of curious green eyes. "We need to talk," he declared.

"I kind of thought so." Drake glanced around the empty room. "Is it safe here?"

Suddenly feeling very stifled, practically claustrophobic, Slyck said, "Let's run." He gestured to the set of steep stairs that led outdoors.

As the two men made their way to the running track encircling the vacant dog park, Drake got right to the point. "What the hell is going on, Slyck? Your tension is palpable. I can even smell it on you. And believe me, others outside of our pack have noticed too."

Slyck's thoughts raced to Harmony, and her sudden need for herbs. Once again the disturbing feeling that she knew more than she was letting on worried the hell out of him.

"It's Jaclyn," he confessed, no longer able to hedge the truth.

Drake nodded. "I got that much."

"She's panther."

That seemed to slow Drake's steps. "What the fuck? You marked her?"

Needing to burn off his nervous energy, Slyck picked up the pace, forcing Drake to quicken his steps. He kept his voice low, barely audible over the sound of their sneakers hitting the pavement. "Yes and no. She had panther in her when she came here. I aided in her first transformation. She's my mate, Drake."

Slyck heard Drake draw in a sharp breath and then let it out slowly. Christ, Slyck could practically hear the other man's mind racing as he sorted through the information.

"How is that possible?" he finally questioned.

Slyck quickly went on to explain the rogue shifter, and how he'd covered up his actions because he thought it was the only way to keep peace in the community. He elaborated, clarifying that even though he was training Drake for his leadership role, and no other panther was as skilled or qualified, Drake still needed more training before he would be ready to take over the alpha role should the council deem Slyck unfit to keep his brethren under control.

"Jesus, Slyck, if anyone finds out, they'll kill her."

"It gets worse," Slyck went on to explain. "Vall drew the short straw."

"Oh fuck."

Slyck's breath was coming in ragged gasps; he stopped running and put his hands on his waist as he sucked in air. He wiped his brow and turned to his friend. "I need to know you're with me, Drake. If anything happens to me, I need to know that you're strong enough to take on the alpha position."

Drake wiped the moisture from his own brow with the back of his hand and asked, "What are you planning?"

Truthfully, if Drake took his place on the council, the less his friend knew about his plans, the better. His plans to use Jaclyn as bait. As much as he fucking hated to put her in harm's way, he had to trust that she could pull it off because they needed to buy time until the full moon. With the rest of the community on lockdown during the full moon—a precautionary measure for their own protection—it was Slyck's one and only opportunity to save her. It would take prudence and a timely plan for the three of them to pull this off.

"Just tell me you're strong enough," Slyck demanded.

In a move that took Slyck by surprise, and all the while controlling the animal inside him and maintaining his human form, the young panther pounced and knocked Slyck to the ground.

Drake grinned down at the other man and said, "You tell me."

Chapter Twelve

Jaclyn stood before the mirror and checked her eyes to make sure the new blue contacts covered all her green flecks. Satisfied with the results, she tried to keep her shaky fingers calm as she applied a light layer of pink lipstick to moisten her dry lips. With the knowledge that she needed to cover any traces of panther scent, she reached into her bag and retrieved the new bottle of jasmine-vanilla perfume that Slyck had given both her and Sunray earlier that day. She dabbed some on her neck, her wrists, and her breasts, putting an extra drop between her thighs before tucking the bottle back into her purse and exiting the washroom.

She glanced around Vibes, canvassing the patrons before sidling up to the bar and easing herself onto one of the padded stools. She ordered a fruity girly drink, all the while keeping her back to the door in a show of innocence, and also as a show of ignorance as to what was taking place in the town around her.

She ran her hands over the smooth oaken bar top and stole

another glace around the room. Padded booths lined the perimeter, while square wooden tables were positioned around the small dance floor. Truthfully it looked like any other nightclub in any other small town. The scent of stale beer, pine-scented floor cleaner, and lemon-scented Pledge reached her nostrils. The combination actually turned her stomach. Jaclyn wasn't sure if she'd ever get used to her new, acute senses.

Since the sun had only recently set, the place was still fairly quiet, but she knew it wouldn't be for long. In no time at all the nightclub would be bustling with fairy-tale creatures come to life. She shook her head, hardly able to believe she was one herself. But she could no longer ignore the truth of what Slyck had awoken in her.

Slyck cast her a sidelong glance, which Jaclyn avoided by toying with her straw while she sipped her fruity drink and tried to make it look like she was uncomfortable, like she didn't belong in the establishment—an easy task for sure, since her insides rattled more than dice in a Yahtzee cup.

As she neared the bottom of her strawberry daiquiri, the door behind her swung open, and the sound of heavy footsteps on the wooden floor heralded Vall's arrival. She'd recognize the thunder of those combat boots anywhere. She worked to relax her tense body and keep her heart rate steady.

As he sailed past her, his long golden mane shimmered under the mosaic of dance floor lights. Jaclyn's nostrils flared as the pungent scent of him washed over her. He smelled like wet fur, alcohol, cigarettes, and sex. Jesus, who would have thought a lycan would smoke? Then again, it wasn't like he had to worry about dying from lung cancer.

She used her feelings of restlessness and anxiety to her advantage. Vall lit a cigarette and stepped up to the counter. She sipped her drink, shifted uncomfortably on her stool, and met his steely gaze.

Through the thick fog of smoke billowing around his head, she regarded him with wide eyes, taking in the hard lines of his profile and his cold calculating eyes as he grabbed a drink from the barkeep and stretched out in the corner booth, his back to the wall like a true predator. He drummed his fingers on the table and took stock of the room. From over the wide rim of his whiskey glass—yes, thanks to her new heightened senses, she could smell it from where she sat—he stared at her and scrutinized her every small move.

She swallowed hard, and despite her efforts not to, her gaze automatically went to Slyck as he came out from the back room, a rack of clean glasses in his hands. Their eyes locked in a silent message and the strength of their bond helped bolster her confidence. It also gave her the courage she needed to confront the big bad wolf, face on. She schooled her nerves and took another sip of her icy drink.

Ever determined to carry out the first part of their plan, and force the lycan to make his move on her tonight, she shot him an innocent smile and blinked her long lashes flirtatiously. Thanks to Sunray, she now knew exactly how much Vall liked corrupting young, innocent females and turning them into his obedient, submissive lycans. Just like he planned to do to her once he turned her. The mere thoughts of submitting to him made her skin crawl.

Jaclyn smoothed down the waist of the floral sundress that Slyck had also picked up for her earlier that day. Her actions were twofold. One she wanted to wipe the moisture from her hands, and two—since lycans were primal beings ruled by lust—she wanted to draw extra attention to her cleavage. As Vall watched her he swallowed half his drink in one gulp and swiped at his mouth with the back of his hand.

With the way she was currently dressed—the way she'd been dressing since her arrival, in fact—she sure as hell fit the descriptive requirements as a sweet, innocent woman, his for the taking.

His half-empty whiskey glass gave her an opening. She pointed to his glass and raised a questioning eyebrow. When he nodded, she put in her order for two fresh drinks. After they arrived, she sashayed across the floor. Fortunately the loud music helped drown out the pounding of her heart.

As she approached Vall's table, the tiny hairs on the back of her neck began to tingle. "Mind if I join you?" She held his drink in her left hand and hers in the right while she gave a dismayed shrug and pouted. "Folks around here don't seem too friendly toward me, and since we briefly met the other night, I just thought—" She purposely stopped speaking and waited for his invitation.

When an offer didn't come, she made a move to turn. "Of course, I understand. Sunray—"

That seemed to trigger a reaction from him. His expression hardened; his hand clenched around his glass so hard she was certain it was going to break. He leaned forward and questioned in a deceptively calm voice, "What about Sunray?"

"I know she has to work late tonight," she rushed out. "And since I saw you sitting here all alone, I thought we could just talk or dance or something. I'm not trying to cut in on her guy, if that's what you're worried about." She put on her best innocent face. "Goodness, I would never do anything like that."

She spent a long moment standing there, trying not to fidget under his interrogating glare, before he gave a predatory smile, opened his large hand, and gestured to the empty seat across from him. "Have a seat."

Jaclyn shimmied in across from him. The ice in his refill glass clinked against the side, and a few drops of the amber liquid sloshed over the rim as she slid the drink across the tabletop.

His features soured after he took a huge swig, nearly draining the glass. "What the hell is in this?"

"It's a whiskey blitz." She blinked up at him with wide-eyed innocence. "I asked the bartender to make it special for me." She offered him a flirty smile and neglected to tell him the lemon juice was to mask the taste and smell of the Tylenol. "I thought you looked like the kind of guy who would appreciate a little blitz in his drink." She waved her hand and the movement stirred the smoke from his cigarette. "They're a favorite back home. Very strong," she added for good measure. When he frowned at her, she reached for his glass. "Sorry. I just thought—"

He crushed his cigarette and reached for another. "It's fine."

She didn't have to fake her smile of relief. He brought the glass to his lips again.

That's it. Lap it all up like a good little doggy.

When he found the bottom of the glass, he wiped his mouth

again and leered at her. Her skin crawled as his lecherous eyes went to her breasts.

The music blaring from a nearby speaker caught her attention. Praying the Tylenol would kick in quickly and dull his sharp senses, she gestured toward the nearly empty dance floor.

"Dance?" she asked, and climbed to her feet.

Vall pinched the bridge of his nose, blinked his eyes back into focus, and shook his head. "No."

Mind racing, Jaclyn bent down and fussed with the buckle on her sandals. Damn. She needed to arouse him, to entice him, to rattle him, to leave no question in his mind that tonight would be the night he *had* to mark her.

As he watched her adjust the leather strap, she offered, "Clasp trouble." She then straightened and caught a glimpse of two demons prowling restlessly through the room—the mischief that danced in their amber eyes gave their species away. She concentrated on her purpose and said, "Maybe I'll ask—"

He snatched her hand and she resisted the urge to pull it back. She could feel his sheer strength through his fingers. She instinctively understood this lycan would never exhibit gentleness or kindness toward others. Unlike Slyck. Her throat tightened painfully.

When he slipped his arm around her waist, pulled her close, and then led her to the dance floor, she forced a smile. As her body pressed against his, she could feel his mounting arousal through his pants. The pleasure resonating through his body sickened her. He turned on his puppy charm, and even though it was lost on her, she pretended otherwise. She longed to let her panther off its leash as the fierce, primal urge to claw at his eyes kicked in. She worked valiantly to suppress a shiver and fight down her primitive fight-or-flight instinct.

Shifting on her feet, she severed the lewd connection, but he simply pulled her in closer. Time seemed to stand still as one song ended and another began. She soon lost track of how long they'd been dancing as Vall continued to press his body against her.

Much to her relief, he began to wobble. His grip on her hips increased as he strove for balance. The Tylenol was kicking in. Thank God. Based on his size and weight they'd given him just enough to disorient him and make him nauseous, but not enough to kill him.

She tried for small talk and inched back. "It sure is warm in here tonight." She toyed with the top button on her sundress and added, "I think I might have to jump in the pool when I get home."

Vall's hands slid around her body and rested on the small of her back as he pulled her to him, joining them hip to hip. He gripped her hard, his eyes darkening. "What the fuck was in that drink?" he asked.

Jaclyn tried to keep her heartbeat steady. "You're supposed to sip it. It's quite strong. I've seen full-grown men go down after only two of those." She played up to him. "But I'm sure they weren't a real man like you, Vall."

"Yeah . . . ," he responded absently, his voice dubious.

Thinking quick she added, "Oh, and it has chocolate in it to help sweeten it." She licked her lips. "That's my own addition, just because I love chocolate so much."

Vall cursed under his breath. His feet seemed to move a little slower, his tongue a bit thicker as he continued to mumble a few more unsavory expletives.

It was time to make her move.

She feigned a yawn and staged her exit. "I guess I'd better get home. It's late and I have an early morning tomorrow." She offered him a bright smile. "Thanks for the dance." Jaclyn made a move to go, wondering if he'd try to stop her. When he didn't object she said, "I'll see you around later?"

He turned and stalked back to his table, but not before she caught the calculating look on his face, a look that told her "around" would definitely be a lot sooner than later.

She kept the triumphant smirk from her face when Slyck caught her eyes. She pushed through the front door and made her way out into the night.

After feeling the lycan's reactions to her body, and sensing that he wanted to stop her before she caused any more havoc around town with her love of chocolate, she suspected he wouldn't be too far behind. She didn't have to worry about him losing her trail, not with the way she'd drenched herself in perfume. He'd easily be able to follow her scent and track her into the alleyway, where Sunray awaited her arrival.

Her shoes tapped a steady rhythm as she hustled between the buildings. Jaclyn slipped deeper into the darkness and nodded in passing to Sunray, who now donned a dark wig, the same dress as Jaclyn, and smelled like she'd just taken a bath in jasmine-vanilla perfume.

Jaclyn hunkered down behind the large Dumpster and waited,

all the while trying to calm her ragged breathing. When the stench of the garbage bursting out of the trash bin beside her reached her nose, she resisted the urge to retch. She glanced around, trying not to concentrate on the foul smell, when another scent reached her. Slyck. She could feel him close by, ready to jump in if anything went wrong.

She wondered if he had Sunray's gun. As a last resort he'd probably kill Vall before he let anything happened to either of them. But by killing Vall they'd also be giving themselves a death sentence. Christ, they were damned if they did and damned if they didn't. Which was exactly why this crazy, harebrained plan had to work.

Jaclyn cleared her head and trained her focus on Sunray. With her back to the street entrance, Sunray bent down, pretending to fiddle with her broken clasp the same way Jaclyn had earlier, all part of their risky plan. Her dark hair covered her features and she mumbled low under her breath for effect.

Suddenly the air in the narrow alleyway charged, and a dark shadow prowled closer to her. The deep growl that emanated from the dark figure sliced through the stillness in the air and made Jaclyn shudder. She covered her ears and watched him quickly close the distance, praying he couldn't taste her fear as it hung heavily in the air.

Looking feral and predatory, he advanced with purpose, quietly coming up from behind, so as not to bring alarm to his victim. His stealthy actions surprised Jaclyn, since she took him for a man who would appreciate a struggle. Another time perhaps. Another day, when his system wasn't flooded with poison.

As he loomed over Sunray, he clasped her waist from behind. A primitive growl rumbled deep in his throat, and his lips peeled back to expose razor-sharp teeth. Wasting no time at all, he clamped down on her shoulder, diving hungrily through her dress to reach her delicate skin. The slurping, flesh-tearing sounds turned Jaclyn's stomach. She put her hand over her mouth to keep herself from making a sound, and all the while trying to ignore the bile rising up from her throat, Jaclyn forced herself to watch, to see exactly where he'd broken through her flesh.

Survival instincts kicking in, Jaclyn reached into her purse and pulled out a sack of deer blood, compliments of the town's blood bank. She worked quickly and poured it over her shoulder before ripping her dress. The pungent coppery scent assaulted her senses and made her eyes water. Thanks to a lycan's regenerative healing abilities, Jaclyn didn't have to worry about Vall searching for teeth marks. Come tomorrow morning, she'd be as good as new.

Sunray covered her shoulder with her hand. A loud thud sounded as she dropped to the ground and let her hair fall forward to cover her face. Blood dripped from Vall's mouth and spread across his shirt. He blinked his eyes and looked around, disoriented. Suddenly, he clutched his stomach and sank to his knees. A loud wrenching noise pierced the dark alley as he violently threw up. The two women took that opportunity to switch places. It was fortunate the opportunity had presented itself; otherwise, they would have had to hope and pray that Vall, in his current condition, did not notice that it was Sunray he'd marked.

After a long time, Vall finally managed to pull himself up. He wiped his mouth with his sleeve and mumbled something about chocolate under his breath. Still confused and unstable, he gathered Jaclyn into his arms, carried her to her house, and deposited her on her bed.

She dropped to her mattress like dead weight and remained motionless until he rounded the corner and disappeared from her line of sight. She heard her back door open and close, and listened to the hard pounding of his boots on her walkway. It was then and only then that she dared to gasp and suck air into her lungs.

As she tried to calm her shaking hands, she concentrated on her breathing, amazed that everything had come together. Now if only everything else went so easily.

She paused to consider the rest of the plan. Here she'd come to Serene to bury her provocative ways and play the part of the good girl. Who would have thought she'd have to draw on her feminine wiles to get her out of suburbia alive? Good thing her parents weren't here to witness what they'd consider an act of rebellion. After all, it wasn't like she could tell them that she had to release her wild sexy side because she was a were-cat trying to trick an entire town.

And one lycan in particular.

Chapter Thirteen

Jaclyn slept in late, which, she'd quickly come to learn, was exactly what was expected of any human after surviving a lycan bite or, rather, a lycan "marking." From what Sunray had explained to her, a human needed rest and nourishment while adjusting to the radical changes that would take place inside the body.

She used the quiet time wisely, reading, researching, and learning everything she could about the lycan species, and about canines in general. She'd also come to learn that silver really was the only thing that could kill a lycan, and during their shift, as they morphed from man to wolf, they were defenseless, which made them especially vulnerable to an attack.

Forty-eight hours later, after having studied all things were-wolf, she left her house and stepped out into the bright morning sunshine. And once again, as she ventured into the town, she found herself having to masquerade as something she wasn't.

The first thing Jaclyn did upon her "awakening" was make

her way to the department store for a new wardrobe. Since lycans were as libidinous as panthers, maybe even more so, she couldn't go around dressed in her staid attire.

With Sunray's help she went on a shopping spree, refilling her closet with an assortment of sexy clothing, similar to the ones she'd left behind when she'd first begun her quest to mend her wicked ways.

Feeling much more comfortable and at home in a short flirty miniskirt and sexy top that exposed her midriff, Jaclyn made her way with Sunray to the hairdresser in search of a hot new look for Jaclyn. She asked the stylist to cut off all her long hair, then give her a short, wild, curly bob and light blond highlights that matched the color of a wheat field. The shade looked pretty next to her new silver contacts, even though she couldn't wait to get rid of them so she could proudly display her new green flecks to her alpha mate.

She couldn't afford to slip from her role for one minute, so she paraded herself around town to make sure everyone witnessed the changes taking place in her. She strived to leave no question in anyone's mind that Vall had indeed marked her.

Later that day, during their lunch break, Jaclyn and Sunray stopped by the body-piercing boutique to get belly rings, completing their sexy, sultry look before they headed back to work.

Back at the department store, now that Jaclyn had been marked, she'd suddenly become accepted by the community. The town's women had begun to step up to the counter—an effort to welcome her into their secret society, she supposed. Even the lady whose daughter she'd nearly killed with chocolate had suddenly turned friendly.

They bought skin-care products that they didn't need, and would probably never use, as well as an abundance of makeup supplies. Much to her surprise and delight, Vasenty Cosmetics began to fly off the shelf. After all, wasn't that one of the main reasons she'd moved to Serene in the first place?

Later that night at Vibes, she learned that since Jaclyn and Sunray had been growing tighter by the day, Vall had tasked Sunray with the responsibility of initiating Jaclyn into the brethren. It was Sunray's job to guide Jaclyn through all the changes taking place inside her body and mind. To teach the new "cub" exactly what she'd become before the first full moon and to school her in the ways of the wolf. Sunray was required to stay with her day and night, to help ease her into her first full shift before she handed Jaclyn over to Vall. He'd then take her for a run in the outskirts, and come morning he'd expect her to submit to her alpha and bond with him sexually, in animal form, before he offered her body to the rest of the pack. Jaclyn shivered just thinking about such a horrendous thing.

It truth, it seemed odd that Vall would trust his rebellious alpha female with such a huge task, seeing as how little control he had over her. Then again, perhaps in some way, it was a small offering, a little tit for tat. Vall knew how close Jaclyn and Sunray had grown over the last few weeks. If Vall offered Sunray a new plaything, maybe in return she'd be grateful enough to submit to him—like she adamantly refused to do, but should have done so many years ago.

The two women began spending all their time together, which seemed to please Vall immensely. From working together at the department store, to meeting up at Vibes for after-hours drinks, to ending the night at Jaclyn's place, where a night of real female bonding ensued. They talked about Sunray's past and the man she'd loved and lost, as well as the reason Jaclyn had come to Serene in the first place.

Even though Jaclyn enjoyed Sunray's company, her body craved Slyck intensely. She felt so desperate for his company, her insides hurt. Just knowing he was across the street and she was unable to go to him filled her with turmoil. That turmoil had her panther pacing, urging her to answer the demands of her body.

She ached to be with him, *needed* to be with him more than she needed her next breath, but it was far too risky to blatantly cross the street and go to him. Everyone around town knew how Slyck felt about lycans, and if she and he were spotted together, even briefly, it would raise Vall's hackles.

After many days into her "change," and with the full moon merely three nights away, Jaclyn continued with her daily routine. She'd left the department store and taken a quick lunch break at the neighborhood café. Apparently, before one's first shift, one had a ravenous appetite until their metabolism stabilized, so Jaclyn made sure the townsfolk watched her gorge. While she was sitting near the window, enjoying a sandwich, salad, coffee and blueberry pie, her cell phone rang. She dug into her purse and hauled it out. Her heart lodged somewhere in her throat when she saw the number.

She swallowed her last bite of flaky crust and flipped her phone open. "Hello," she said, feigning enthusiasm. She loved her parents—she truly did—but this was so not what she needed right now.

"Jaclyn, darling, how are you?" her mother asked, in her usual cheerful voice.

"Fine, Mom. Just been busy. I meant to call earlier—"

Her father's voice boomed in on the other extension. "No worries, Jaclyn. I know you've been working hard. I have the sales figures in my hands to prove it."

Jaclyn smiled. She missed them both, and even though they were only a few states over, it felt as if they were a million miles away. "I guess that will make the board happy."

"More like thrilled," he corrected and Jaclyn could just picture the boisterous smile on his robust face. "This will finally prove to them that Jaclyn Vasenty, brilliant, hardworking daughter of Benjamin Vasenty, is just the woman to take over the reins when I retire," he boomed out.

Oh God, her father was counting on her to run his empire, and she owed him that. He'd put all his faith in her, and she didn't want to disappoint him or let him down, not again.

"Which might be sooner rather than later," her mother piped in. "Isn't that right, Benji?"

Benji? She'd never heard her mother call her father Benji before. What the hell was that all about?

Jaclyn crinkled her nose and nodded her thanks to Lily when she stepped up to the table and refilled her coffee mug. Was it just her imagination, or did her mother suddenly sound giddy and a bit flirty with her father? Her parents had always loved each other—that much she knew—but her father was a workaholic who never really made a lot of time for his wife, nor had her mother ever acted like a love-struck teenager before.

Jaclyn took a small sip of coffee and wiped her mouth with her napkin. "What's going on?"

"Oh your father and I just purchased a retirement home in Florida, honey."

"I've spent a lot of years working and building this company, Jaclyn. And now that everyone knows my business is in good hands, I plan on making up for all the lost time I've been away from your mother."

Her mother giggled again and Jaclyn's smile widened. She loved that the two of them were finding each other again after all these years.

"After a few more weeks with these sales numbers, there will be no doubt in anyone's mind just how dedicated and serious you are about running the business. Then you'll be able to come home."

Oh, if it were only so easy . . .

Suddenly her mind raced to Slyck, and how she'd only just found him. Oh God, what would happen to the both of them when the full moon peaked in a mere three days? Would they ever be able to walk out of suburbia alive?

Her stomach knotted and she worked to keep her voice steady. "I am serious about the business. I always have been."

"And I've always believed in you, honey," her father said, and for the first time in her life, Jaclyn actually heard genuine pride in his voice.

Jaclyn pressed the phone to her ear harder and fought the prick of tears. Her emotions were in such turmoil lately that she felt like she was on a roller-coaster ride and the only way off was to jump.

"Oh, Jaclyn, before I forget, I wanted to mention that Caroline's daughter, Katherine, is marrying a nice young doctor. The wedding is in September. I'm sure you'll be getting an invitation any day now."

"Super. Can't wait." Sometimes it took real effort keeping the sarcasm from her voice.

After giving her time to absorb and digest that bit of information, her mother went on. "We're going to take a drive down to see our new home, so we thought we'd stop in to see you before we headed south."

Oh God, no.

Jaclyn increased her grip on her phone. "That's probably not such a great idea," she rushed out, her alarm obvious in her tone. She tried to soften her outburst and began backpedaling. "It's . . . a . . . It's just that I'm so busy and still trying to get settled in, and I'm just getting over the flu, and I have all these allergies." She coughed for effect but in her jittery state ended up hitting her coffee cup. As the hot liquid poured over her table, the commotion drew the attention of those around her. She spotted Harmony's violet eyes trained on her, gauging her carefully. Jaclyn jumped to her feet and tossed napkins on her spill. Lily came back with a cloth and Jaclyn smiled at her in appreciation.

"Are you okay, dear?" her mom queried, which brought her attention back to the crisis at hand.

Her body tensed while she scooped up her purse and made her way out into the sunshine. She sagged against the brick building and ran her hand along the back of her neck to loosen the knot. She tried to keep her voice level as she addressed the worry in her mother's voice. "Yes, yes, I'm fine. Just busy. You guys go on ahead to Florida and we'll catch up when you get back. Have fun. Don't worry about me. I have everything under control here," she lied.

After a moment of silence, her mother spoke. "Is it because of a man, Jaclyn?" she asked. Jaclyn didn't miss the underlying hope in her voice. "Have you found yourself a nice boy in Serene?"

Jaclyn shaded the sun from her eyes and glanced down the street in time to see Slyck making his way back to Vibes. Her pulse kicked up a notch at the mere sight of him, and need gathered in her belly. Even from her distance she could smell his warm, earthy, masculine scent as it perfumed the air. She worked to regulate her breathing and fisted her fingers as the compulsion to scurry across the street and pounce on him whipped through her blood. When their eyes briefly met and held in a lingering look, she locked her knees to keep upright. Slyck turned away and she took in his profile. It was then that she noticed the deep, fine lines fringing his eyes, and the worry shadows darkening his skin. He looked exhausted, like he hadn't slept in a week. Her heart tightened in her chest when he pulled open the door to Vibes and disappeared inside.

"Jaclyn," her mother said again, bringing her thoughts back around. "Is he a nice boy?"

Oh, yeah, Slyck was a nice boy.

A bad boy.

A panther boy.

All of the above. Oy!

She glanced at her sexy attire and her cute new belly ring.

Now was certainly not the time for her parents to visit, not when she was trying to convince the locals she was a libidinous lycan-in-the-making. She took a moment to consider her best approach, one that would keep her mother away.

She drew a deep breath and, focused on keeping the emotion out of her voice, calmly said, "Yes, Mom, I do have a new man. And if my parents showed up wanting to meet him, it just might scare him off. So it's best to just let me take things slowly, and you'll meet him when the time is right." Jaclyn's blood suddenly thickened, fearing that such a time would never come, because they just might not make it out of Serene alive.

Her answer seemed to appease her parents for the time being. "All right, dear, we won't come. You take care of yourself now, and take extra care of that new boy. Make sure you make him a nice pot roast." Jaclyn bit back a laugh. Her mother really was old school, she mused.

"And keep up the good work," her father added, before they both hung up.

Jaclyn let out a slow breath and shoved her phone back into her handbag. With that major crisis averted, she headed back to the department store, and prayed her mother would keep her word.

In his small private office at the back of Vibes, Slyck unlocked his safe, and pulled out Jaclyn's father's file, heavyhearted and saddened that Jaclyn hadn't had the opportunity to get to know him. But, unfortunately, and as much as it pained him sometimes, such was the way of their society. He carefully placed the file onto his desk and moved across the room. As he stretched out on his sofa, his thoughts raced to Jaclyn and the night she'd first presented him with her panther in this very room. The animal in him roared to life, aching to mate with her again and again until the two were left sated, drained. Christ knows, a week out of her bed was a week too long.

He glanced up at the near-full moon before he surged from his cushiony seat. He stepped out into the hall, walked past the washrooms, and made his way out to the front counter. As he went to work preparing for the late-night rush, Drake sidled up to the bar and ordered a beer.

"Hey, Slyck. Look what the cat dragged in." He jerked his head toward Jaclyn and Sunray as they moved sensuously on the dance floor, grinding against each other as if they were very famil-iar with each other sexually. "If I didn't know better, I'd say she's turning lycan."

Slyck lowered his voice and took in Jaclyn's new look. "Then maybe we should leave it at that."

"Too late," Drake countered and took a long pull from the bottle. "Because I already know better."

Slyck glanced around, ensuring their privacy before leaning forward on the counter. He planted his elbows on the hard oaken tabletop and murmured in a low voice meant for Drake's ears only, "Vall only *thinks* he's marked her."

After taking note of the patrons, Drake lowered his voice to match Slyck's. "And it looks like she's got him fooled." He made a slight, inconspicuous gesture with his head. They both took in Vall's lecherous glare as he watched the two women gyrate against each other. "For now, anyway. One false move and he'll kill her, you know."

Slyck fisted his hands and clenched down on his teeth. "I know."

"And just exactly how is it she's going to fool him when the moon is full in three nights from now?"

"She won't have to."

"No?" Drake shot him a dubious look. "Want to enlighten me?"

The less knowledge Drake had about the situation, the better, but at this point Slyck suspected that he had no choice but to fill Drake in, because in the end, he just might need his help. "I'm going to get her out of here."

"And you don't think that will raise suspicion?"

"Not if it's done right."

Drake shook his head and looked down at his beer, as if the amber liquid held all the answers in the universe. "Slyck, I sure as hell hope you know what you're doing."

"And I sure as hell hope you can handle my position when I'm gone."

Drake's head came up with a start. "I can," he assured Slyck, then in a lower voice asked, "So you're leaving then?"

"I've come to the conclusion that I have no alternative." Over the last week he'd spent many restless nights sorting through his options and coming up with only one. It was a difficult choice, yes, but he'd come to terms with it.

"You don't look as confident and secure in your decision as you make it sound."

Truthfully, turning his back on his brethren wasn't an easy choice to make by any means, but it was a necessary one, and now that Drake had learned to control his beast and fight using logic, he felt he was leaving his family in good hands. Drake would now be able to help guide the youngsters and hand down knowledge and skill.

Slyck spoke quietly. "I need to be with my mate. She can't stay here, and she won't survive unless I leave with her. Plus I've been making mistakes, slipping up. The fact that Jaclyn is here proves that fact. Stepping down is best for the community."

"So how do you plan on doing it, Slyck?" Drake's bottle hit the bar with a thud. "How the hell are you going to get through the gates with her?"

Slyck let out a long, slow breath. "As you know, sometimes humans don't survive the first change. It's rare, but it happens. Jaclyn isn't going to survive a wolf transformation, or at least that's what the good people of Serene are going to believe."

"He's not going to let her out of his sight, and he'll want to run with her that first night."

"That's why we solicited Sunray's help. She's in charge of Jaclyn until she shifts. Then and only then is she required to bring her to the den and hand her over to Vall for their first run. Vall plans to initiate her into the pack and make her submit to him come morning, after her first change, but we'll get her out before that happens."

"He'll want to see the body. When he doesn't find one, and you go missing, he'll know."

"The man is all about pride and power, Drake. You know

that." Slyck's voice hardened. "And he'll also never admit to any-one that his lycan ran off with a 'kitten,' now, will he?"

"He'll want to hunt you."

"And you're strong enough to stop him." Slyck shot him a challenging look, his eyes questioning. "Strong enough to take over where I left off, and keep the brethren running smoothly."

Drake nodded his understanding and then took another swig. "And how are we going to account for your disappearance?"

Slyck turned to see two female lycans sidle up to their alpha. A moment later, Vall slipped his hands around their bodies, guided them to the door, and disappeared into the night with them. The closer they got to the shift, the more libidinous they became.

"I'm an old man. No one can dispute that," Slyck answered. "Tired of fighting the good fight, my friend." He glanced around his nightclub with longing, taking it all in one last time. "Imagine if I accidentally forgot to lock up shop and got attacked by a lycan who just happened to wander in, drawn by the scent of fresh blood. There goes my last life."

Expression troubled, Drake said, "But you have two lives left."

"And only you and I know that."

"No one will believe you were so careless."

"You'll make them believe it."

Drake curled his fingers around his bottle. His muscles bunched. "It's fucking risky, Slyck. What if something goes wrong?"

Slyck let out a slow breath. "Then I'm fucked, Drake. Totally and utterly fucked. But if I don't try, I'm still fucked. Hell, we're all fucked."

There was a resigned sigh and Drake's gaze drifted to the dance floor. "Speaking of getting fucked . . ."

Slyck followed Drake's gaze and watched Jaclyn brush against Sunray beneath the colorful strobe lights, their barely dressed bodies moving in sync, sensuously and erotically, the way two lovers would move between the sheets. His glance strayed lower. His slow perusal paused briefly on her belly button. He took in her sexy new belly ring and with heated interest watched the way it glistened under the dance floor lights, calling out to him like a beacon in the night. God, what he'd do to taste that sweet crevice. He brushed the tip of his tongue over his bottom lip with longing.

When his glance moved back to her face, he saw the sparkle in her gaze and the raw desire in the depths of her eyes. In that instant he knew her sexy little performance was meant for him and him alone. As his gaze skated over her a second time, his cock thickened inside his jeans, his fingers itched, and the beast inside him roared to life. It was all he could do to stop himself from crossing that room, gathering her into his arms, and fucking her in primal form.

If Jaclyn couldn't physically be with Slyck, the least she could do was give him something to think about tonight—something to help warm his blood and fuel his memories while he slept alone. As her body swayed against Sunray's, she visualized Slyck sprawled out on his mattress, his thick hands wrapped around his beautiful cock, masturbating as he thought about her. Her entire body shook. God, if she kept that up, she'd melt to the floor in a puddle of want.

With Vall gone from the club, she could now intimately connect with Slyck, even if it had to be from across the dance floor.

She brushed up against Sunray again and ran her hands over her own body, coming perilously close to her nipples and her passion-drenched pussy. As the dance floor got crowded, she moved to the side, to give him an unobstructed view of her actions. Slyck's dark, hungry gaze brushed over her, and she could see pure torment on his face. Jaclyn could relate, because she needed him as badly as he needed her. His eyes tracked her every movement before he turned to talk with Drake. After the two exchanged a few words, Drake replaced Slyck behind the bar, while Slyck disappeared down the hall and into his private office.

Fire burned deep in her thighs, and her body broke into a sweat as she watched him go. As she ached with need, her lascivious mind raced with wicked ideas. With Vall gone, and everyone in the club seemingly preoccupied, Jaclyn turned to Sunray and put her mouth close to her ear. "I'm thirsty. Let's go get a drink."

Sunray eyed her, reading her intent. Blond hair flew to the side as she cocked her head in warning. With her fists planted on her hips, she said, "It's too risky."

Jaclyn gathered her hands in a ball and placed them on her stomach. "I need . . . ," was all she said.

After a long moment, Sunray conceded. "Okay, make it quick. I can only cover for you for so long."

Jaclyn gathered Sunray's hand in hers, and warmth moved through her when she saw tender concern and genuine affection in her friend's eyes. "What would I do without you?"

Sunray squeezed her hand, a silent gesture to indicate that she felt the same. "Go, and hurry."

The two women made their way to the bar. While Sunray engaged Drake in conversation, Jaclyn pretended to make her way to the washroom. Fueled by need, she cautiously crept farther down the hall and despite the "Private, No Admittance" sign, she slipped into Slyck's office. Inside, she found him in his small washroom, one palm braced on the wall, the other wrapped around his hard cock.

Jaclyn gripped the wall for support, because it was all she could do not to impale herself on that magnificent cock. Her body quivered, her pussy moistened with longing, and it became most difficult to speak. "Need a hand?" she whispered, her panther mewling as passion rose in her.

Slyck spun around and, in one swift move, anchored her body to his. Even though his eyes darkened with lust when they connected with hers, he announced, "Jaclyn, you shouldn't be in here."

She tossed him a wicked grin. "I didn't think it was fair to get you all aroused and not do anything about it."

"You can't—"

Partly to stop him and partly to feel his comfort, Jaclyn laid her hand flat on his stomach, her palm connecting with his rigid muscles. The smile fell from her face. "It hurts, Slyck," she began, cutting him off. She swallowed, and when she spoke again, all humor left her voice. "It hurts when I'm not with you."

Slyck sucked in air. His thick muscles shifted as he backed her up until he reached the sofa.

"Lift your skirt," he demanded.

Jaclyn almost sobbed with relief. She bent herself over the sofa, and inched her miniskirt up until she exposed the curve of her cheeks. She widened her legs, granting him access and when her aroused scent reached his nostrils, he gave a low primal growl.

"Jaclyn . . . ," he whispered. His voice seeped into her skin and filled her with warmth.

"Please fuck me," she begged shamelessly.

Slyck splayed his hands over her hips and positioned the tip of his cock at her opening. With one quick thrust he slammed into her. Her mouth opened in a silent gasp. He pushed so deep and so hard, it drove her against the couch. Her nipples scraped against the fabric until pleasure bled into pain. Yet she still couldn't get enough.

"More," she cried out. "Harder."

He slammed into her, pushing and pulling, giving and taking, making up for all of the last week.

When her orgasm finally took hold, she nearly blacked out from pleasure. As Slyck released high inside her, filling her body with his seed, he took her to the moon and back. Life surged through her in ways that baffled her and brought on another climax.

As Jaclyn's body came back down to earth, Slyck spun her around and pulled her in close until her body melded with his. Everything inside her reached out to him. Good Lord, here she thought she'd shrivel up and die in the small isolated town of Serene, only to find out she'd just barely begun to live. That thought was like a punch in the gut, and in that instant she vowed that no one was going to take away what she'd spent her whole life searching for.

"I've missed you," he murmured into her hair, his lips rushing over her flesh.

"I've missed you too." She collapsed against his hard chest. As she breathed in his scent, she pulled it into her lungs so she could call on it later, when loneliness disturbed her soul. Jaclyn pressed a small kiss to his chest and then turned her head to the side to make out an open file on Slyck's desk.

She listened to the rustle of clothes as Slyck got dressed. "I want to give you something," he said and inched away. He stepped to his desk, gathered the file and handed it to her.

Heart aching, Jaclyn brushed her finger over the photo, instinctively understanding that the man in the picture was her natural father.

"I want you to have this, Jaclyn."

She looked into his eyes and saw sorrow and sensed this was his way of trying to give back something that he'd taken from her. Her heart softened and tears pricked her eyes. She couldn't hold her father's death against him. Slyck was a good man who didn't have a malicious bone in his body. She already knew he only ever acted with the town's best interest. "What was he like?"

Slyck came up behind her and pressed his chest to her back, his touch and his body contact comforting her. He put his mouth close to her ear and spoke in whispered words. "He was a good man, Jaclyn."

"Tell me about him. What did he do?"

"He monitored the perimeter." After a moment of silence, he said, "You actually remind me a lot of him." That brought a smile to her face.

She spun around. "How?"

The corners of his lips twitched. "He was a little rebellious, a little hardheaded."

She smacked him. "Hey . . ."

His eyes softened and turned serious. "But he was also intelligent and kind."

Jaclyn felt a lump lodge in her throat. "And my mother?"

Slyck touched her hair and tucked a piece behind her ear. "She was beautiful."

"You met her?" she asked, her eyes going wide.

"No."

Jaclyn looked down. "Oh. Then how do you know?"

"Since you don't look like your father, I can only assume you look like her."

Slyck touched her chin and tipped her head until their eyes met. His warm, loving lips came down on hers. As her lids fell shut, his tender kiss, full of love and empathy, alleviated the pain over her father's termination. It also helped her come to terms with the fact that the man she loved was the man who took her father away from her—the one thing that she held against him. But Slyck was a humanitarian, a man of great character and integrity, and she now understood and accepted it was the way of their people and he'd never do anything to purposely hurt her, or anyone else for that matter. In fact, she knew he'd give his life and go against his own best interests to protect her.

She inched back and looked deep into his eyes. Something in their stormy depths combined with the gentleness and compassion she met there gave her great comfort and soothed the lifelong ache of never having known her biological parents.

Chapter Fourteen

Jaclyn awoke to dark skies and angry winds. The perfect match for her mood, she decided. She hadn't seen Slyck since she'd slipped into the back room with him two nights ago, and her body now ached terribly.

After she had stretched out her limbs and fought off the pangs of longing, her gaze strayed to her window and her heart leapt. As she focused on the brand-new day, reality came rushing back in a sobering whoosh.

One more night until the full moon.

She leaned over and tapped Sunray on the shoulder. "Time to get up." Sunray mumbled something about puppies needing a lot of sleep, and rolled back over.

Chilled after shedding her covers, Jaclyn hugged herself and climbed from the bed. When she stood she noticed her sore thigh muscles—a beautiful reminder of her frenzied lovemaking with Slyck. She padded to the bathroom and hopped into the shower.

The water helped warm her body but did little to lighten her foul mood. After drying off, and slipping into a pretty formfitting shirt that was high enough to show off her belly ring, and a flirty white skirt, she applied her makeup, put in her silver contact lenses, and made her way to the kitchen.

Her gaze strayed to Slyck's house and her glance caught his silhouette in the window. Tall. Broad. Muscular.

Hers.

His eyes glistened in the darkened room, and she could only guess that he was longing for her just as badly as she longed for him.

The sound of Sunray moving around in the bedroom pulled her focus. When she heard the shower turn on, she sauntered to the kitchen to whip up breakfast for the two of them. Would the day ever come when she and Slyck could share a relaxed meal together?

After filling their stomachs with waffles, cream, and fruit, the women made their way to the department store. Just before lunch hour approached, Jaclyn spotted a couple near the front entrance. Despite the damp weather, both were dressed in bright Hawaiian shirts and knee-length shorts—which reminded Jaclyn of retired Floridians. They were asking for directions but were receiving only cold, snide remarks from the locals. Obviously, they were outsiders who'd stumbled upon Serene because they weren't expecting any temporary residents.

But that voice . . . it was familiar.

Jaclyn's heart lodged in her throat. Surely to God it wasn't.

A strange sound crawled out of her throat and gained Sunray's attention. She came rushing over.

"What is it?" Sunray asked, her silver eyes flashing from Jaclyn to the front entrance with unease.

Jaclyn gulped and pointed toward the couple coming her way. "My parents."

"Oh shit," Sunray bit out. She pushed Jaclyn behind her. "Quick, go. They can't see you like this. Run over to women's apparel and find something appropriate."

Moving quickly, Jaclyn grabbed a pair of cream-colored dress pants and a matching blouse. She tore the price tags off and rushed to the dressing room.

Once she was satisfied that it was a look her parents would expect and appreciate, she sauntered back to her counter and opened her eyes wide in delight when she spotted them browsing the shelves.

"What a surprise," Jaclyn said, her voice a little too high as she threw her hands up in the air.

Her mother gave her a peck on the cheek, her short blond hair brushing over Jaclyn's face. Jaclyn turned to her father and glanced up, taking note of his dark tan and how the sun had lightened his thinning brown hair.

He gave her a wink and went on to explain, "Been on the golf course." He in turn appraised her. Dark brown eyes opened wide, and a smile broke out on his jovial face when he took in her appearance. "You changed your hair."

Her hand automatically went to her short curls. She nodded and flashed a smile. "I cut it off. I thought the shorter length looked more professional." His grin widened, seemingly pleased.

"What kind of contacts are those?" her mother asked, squinting as she peered into Jaclyn's eyes. "What an odd color," she commented.

Oh damn, she'd forgotten about those. "I find it gives me a sophisticated look," Jaclyn said and folded her hands behind her back. She took that moment to redirect the conversation. "So you decided to come along anyway, even after I told you it wasn't necessary."

Her mother gave a sheepish, half-guilty grin, and wiggled her fingers with excitement. "I just couldn't wait to meet this man of yours."

Jaclyn worked to keep the annoyance out of her voice. "He's working late, so you won't be able to meet him." She quickly changed the subject again. "Have you had lunch yet? Let's go back to my place, and I'll make something."

"We wouldn't want to put you out," her father said. "Let's just go to that nice café we parked by."

Oh hell.

Ten minutes later Jaclyn sat across from her mother and father at the café. Outside, heavy rain beat against the plate-glass window in a quick, steady rhythm that matched her heartbeat. She was antsy and wanted to get her parents out of town before they started noticing the strange goings-on. She practically scarfed her food down in record time.

After glancing around at the other patrons, her mother leaned in and whispered, "Have you made any friends? The people here don't seem too friendly."

"It's a small town, Mom." Jaclyn shrugged and brushed off the comment. "They're just cautious of outsiders."

Her mother's head wiggled from side to side like one of those bobblehead dolls. "Well, I certainly wouldn't want to spend any more time here than I had to."

Precisely.

"And what about that gate?" her mother probed. "Don't you think that's odd?"

"Coyotes," Jaclyn explained. "Plenty of coyotes." Good Lord, weren't the lies just effortlessly flying from her mouth? "It's for our own protection." Jaclyn bit back a sardonic laugh. It sure hadn't taken her long to start justifying things and protecting the town. She took a big bite of her pie and finished it off.

Marie placed her hand over Jaclyn's and frowned. "Jaclyn, darling, you need to slow down before you get digestion problems."

"I'm fine, Mom."

Keeping her hand there, Marie went on to say, "Oh, did I mention that Caroline's daughter, Katherine, is getting married next month to a nice young doctor?"

How they went from digestion to Katherine getting married was beyond Jaclyn. "Yes, Mom, you did." Jaclyn eased her hand away and reached for her coffee.

"So what does this boyfriend of yours do?"

Smooth, Mother. Real smooth.

Jaclyn resisted the urge to roll her eyes. "He owns a nightclub."

Her mother starched her spine, disapproval apparent in her body language. "Oh."

"He's also on the town council," Jaclyn added in his defense, then realized she didn't need to defend Slyck to her mother. He was a wonderful man—a man with integrity and honor. Not only that, he was intelligent, capable, and thoughtful, and she was damn proud of him.

Just then Vall walked into the restaurant, looking and smelling like a wet dog. Jaclyn resisted the urge to crinkle her nose in distaste, then blinked quickly, trying to dispel the vision of his attack on Sunray. But the memory sparked vividly, and she feared the image had been permanently etched into her brain. She noted that there wasn't a trace of softness to be found in Vall's arctic eyes as they catalogued the café. They were as cold and bleak as a Chicago winter. His curious glance went from Jaclyn to her parents, to Jaclyn's formal business attire.

Jaclyn crossed her arms across her chest and leaned into the table, but her efforts to camouflage her staid clothing were too little, too late.

Harmony and a few of her coven sauntered in behind Vall. They slid into the booth behind Jaclyn, but not before she caught the inquisitive look in Harmony's violet eyes.

"I need to get back to work," Jaclyn said lightly. "Can't help get those numbers up if I'm not there," she added.

"That's my girl," her father piped in, and threw his napkin down onto the table.

"Can we have a tour of your house first?" her mother asked, and Jaclyn knew she was stalling. It was her not so subtle way to hang around longer in hopes of getting a glimpse of Slyck.

The rain had slightly lightened as Jaclyn hustled them back to her place and gave them a two-minute tour. After guiding them back to her front room, she glanced at her watch. "I guess you'd better get going if you want to make good time before nightfall."

In no hurry to move, Jaclyn's mom picked up the pretty blue vase and carried it from the coffee table to the windowsill. Jaclyn followed the movement and smiled. Like mother, like daughter. It must have been the socialite instilled in them both. Always adjusting the little things and striving to make their home perfect.

Her mother turned intense blue eyes on her and Jaclyn knew she was getting right to the point. "So do we get to meet this man of yours before we leave?"

Without thought Jaclyn moved her gaze from the vase to the damp sidewalk. The sight of Slyck passing by drew all her focus, and she found herself walking to the rain-splashed window, drawn to him like metal to a magnet.

"Is that him?" Marie asked, stepping up beside her. Jaclyn didn't miss her disapproving glower as she took in Slyck's wet, mussed hair, worn jeans that hugged his body to perfection, and his tight T-shirt, which displayed washboard abs and a body designed for sin. Not only was he gorgeous—he was the sweetest, gentlest, kindest man Jaclyn had ever met, and she wouldn't allow anyone to say otherwise.

Not even her mother.

When her mother made a *tsking* sound, and gave a quick shake of her head, Jaclyn felt her entire world shift. Suddenly weary and tired of her mom's disappointing glares, and the way she was always so quick to pass judgment based on appearances, Jaclyn lifted her chin high. She had no desire to upset or disappoint her parents, but she was an intelligent woman who made smart choices, and maybe it was time her mother knew it.

Over the last few weeks, Slyck had given her confidence in

herself, helped heal her old wounds, and taught her to appreciate, embrace, and love herself for who and what she was.

"Yes, that's him."

"But darling, he's so, so—"

Jaclyn spun around to face her mother. The quick movement seem to take Marie by surprise. "You really shouldn't judge him until you've met him," Jaclyn stated.

Her mother waved a dismissive hand. "But, Jaclyn—"

Undeterred, Jaclyn continued. "And I won't let you meet him until you can start accepting people for who they are." Her voice began to rise. "He's a wonderful man, and I love him," she announced loudly. Just hearing herself vocalize those words made her legs go weak.

She loved him.

The way Slyck had suddenly stopped midstride and the way his tender, heated glance locked on hers told her that he'd heard those three powerful words.

"I love him," she repeated, and laid her palm on the cool window in search of his heat.

Displeased, and looking for an ally, Marie turned to Benjamin. "Benji—"

As emotions poured through Jaclyn's body, she noticed her nails extend to claws as her panther fought to protect its mate. She quickly shoved her hands behind her back and said, "I'm a grown woman, Mother, and you raised me to make good choices, which I do. Now it's time for you to step back and see how good a job you've done."

Her mother opened her mouth to speak, but her father cut

her off. "That's enough, Marie," Benjamin piped in. "I think it's time for us to go. It looks like Jaclyn has everything under control here. When she's ready for us to meet him, she'll introduce us."

She gave her father a grateful smile and leaned in for a hug, her panther fading. Just then Ruby jumped into her mother's arms, breaking the tension surrounding them.

"Ruby," Marie said, delighted.

Jaclyn suddenly had a lightbulb moment. "You need to take her with you." Jaclyn had no intention of leaving her cat behind, and this gave her one less thing to worry about when making her escape.

"Really? Is it because of the coyotes?"

"Yes. Now you really need to go." She touched her mother's back and ushered her toward the door. "I've been away from work far too long."

With that, Jaclyn herded them all back to Main Street, where her parents had parked their car. After seeing them off, she hustled back to the store and changed out of her damp clothes and back into her sexy outfit.

Jaclyn made her way back to the cosmetics counter, relieved that she had ushered her parents out of town so quickly. The minute she looked into Sunray's eyes, her vision went fuzzy around the edges, and she knew something very bad was going down. "Oh God, what is it?"

"It's Vall."

Jaclyn gripped the counter. "What about him?"

"He changed his plans."

Oh Jesus, this was not good. Not good at all. Jaclyn sank to her stool and glanced at Sunray with apprehension. She could feel the blood drain from her face.

"He's bringing you into the brethren tomorrow, before the full moon, to keep an eye on you."

As if the bottom had just fallen out of her world, her body went ice-cold. "Oh God, I need to talk to Slyck."

As Slyck wiped and restocked the drink glasses, placing them in the overhead rack above the bar, the sound of his service-entrance door banging open pulled his focus. He quickly tore his thoughts from Jaclyn and glanced across the room. He took one look at Drake's distraught face, and the tension in his body as he stormed toward Slyck, and Slyck knew something was wrong.

"What?" Slyck asked, squaring his shoulders.

"Sunray came to see me," Drake rushed out, breathless like he'd just finished running laps at the track.

Slyck's body stiffened. "Why?"

"She thought you'd need me."

Slyck stopped drying the glass and stood stock-still. "Out with it, Drake," he bit out in annoyance. He was in no mood for cryptic words.

After Drake wiped his damp hands on his training pants, he ran anxious fingers through his dark hair and stepped up to the bar. With his eyes intense and his brow furrowed, he said, "It's Vall. He plans on bringing Jaclyn into his pack tomorrow, before sunset."

The glass Slyck had been holding slipped from his hands and shattered on the hard floor. His pulse pounded, his blood roared through his veins, and the air rushed from his lungs in a whoosh. Ignoring the shards of glass at his feet—acting on pure instinct— Slyck moved like a lightning bolt and jumped over the counter. He let out a roar of fury and turned his body to push past Drake.

He felt his blood drain to his feet as he digested Drake's words. "I need to get her out of here now," he announced with alarm in his voice.

Drake stepped in front of him and put his hand on Slyck's chest to still his movements. He spoke in a low voice meant to calm, but it did little to ease Slyck's ragged nerves. "Sunray thought you might react this way, which is why she came to me first."

With full-blown panic urging him on so he could barely comprehend what Drake was saying, he gripped Drake's hand. He made a swift move and twisted Drake's wrist until he released his willful hold. "Get the fuck off me, Drake. I have no intention of standing back and letting Vall touch her."

Drake's eyes narrowed in frustration but he held his own. He receded until his back was pressed to the exit door, blocking Slyck's path. "Listen to me, Slyck. You need to stop, separate yourself from your emotions, and think about this. Logically."

Leaning over his friend, Slyck said, "Fuck logic. I'm not going to sit around and let Vall engage in every debauched activity known to mankind with my mate. Now move."

"Just—"

Slyck cut him off with a glare and, with his voice deceptively mild, said, "I'm going to get her. Now get out of my way, before I make you get out of my way."

"And you'll get her killed." Drake widened his stance and

continued to hinder Slyck's escape. "You'll get us all killed, even Sunray, and you'll throw this town into chaos, breaking down everything that has taken years to build." In a tone that was dark, dangerous, and serious, he asked, "Is that what you want?" Drake put a placating hand on Slyck's shoulder and held firm. "You know that's not what you want, Slyck."

Oh, Christ, everything was falling apart and the situation was escalating beyond his control. "Unless you have a better idea, you need to get the fuck out of my way," Slyck retaliated, even though in the back of his mind some small, still logical part of his brain was telling him that Drake was right, and that he needed to listen.

Drake watched him for a moment and then said, "Sunray told me she can still get Jaclyn out before the full moon."

Arms folded across his chest, Slyck paused and waited for him to elaborate.

"She said she'll watch over her and figure out a way to distract Vall before the run."

"How?" Slyck snapped.

"I don't know, but she said you'd have to be close by, because when it goes down, it's going to go down fast."

Slyck's stomach dipped, and his shoulders dropped. He cast his eyes down in thought as his throat closed over. "Sunray's not yet physically strong enough to take on Vall."

"Maybe there are other ways for her to take him on." With his voice low and unsure, Drake asked, "Do you trust her, Slyck?"

Slyck's head came up with a start, and he didn't even hesitate to say, "Yes."

"Even though she's a lycan?"

Everyone knew how much Slyck distrusted lycans, but Sunray wasn't like the rest. What was Drake getting at? "Yeah. I trust her. Why?"

Drake's face tightened warily. "You in no way think she's working with Vall. Playing you for a fool?" he asked, his words planting a seed of doubt in the back of Slyck's mind.

Slyck paused to consider that option, then met Drake's gaze unflinchingly. "No. She's with us all the way."

He watched Drake physically relax. His firm answer seemed to appease him, even though Slyck now had a sick, apprehensive knot in his stomach. He truly believed Sunray had integrity. Truly felt that she had Jaclyn's best interests at heart, but he also knew Vall could be manipulating her somehow, holding something over her.

Drake's voice broke his concentration. "Then you'll have to trust her enough to believe she'll get Jaclyn out. It's our only option."

Feeling restless and edgy, Slyck sagged against the wall and worked to regulate his ragged breathing. "They mate before their run, Drake." His fingers fisted at his sides, and his pulse beat at the base of his throat so hard he thought it would burst. "So help me, if Vall touches one hair on her head, I'll rip him to shreds with my bare hands."

"Sunray won't let that happen."

Slyck grimaced and worked to curb his anger and emotions, desperately trying to draw on his logic instead. "Sunray can't guarantee it."

"And there is no guarantee that you'll both escape from here either, Slyck. The guard might not be on duty during their one and only compulsory shift night, but the pack will be running, and you're both at risk." Drake dug into his back pocket and hauled out a key. "But this might help speed things up."

The overhead fluorescent light reflected off the metal in Drake's hand. Slyck stepped back, momentarily surprised. "You stole the key?"

"Hell, yeah," Drake said, trying to lighten the mood. "It's not like you can climb the fence on shift night. I'm not interested in cleaning up fried kitty come morning." He shoved the key back into his pocket. "I'll replace it right after you escape."

Slyck pounded his fist on the wall in frustration. "I don't want you there, Drake. It's too dangerous."

"Which is why I need to be there. What kind of alpha leader would I be if I wasn't there to protect one of my pack?"

Slyck's mouth lifted in a grateful smile, any fears or worries he had of Vall manipulating Drake now gone. Drake would make one hell of a leader.

Slyck faced his friend and met his glance straight on. "You know the consequences if you get captured." It was a statement, not a question. Slyck pressed his lips together, thinking how the community would be affected if they were both caught in the action. "Maybe it's best if you don't—"

"We won't get caught. Besides, you took care of me for years. Now it's my turn to take care of you. I'll open the gate just before the full moon, you get Jaclyn and get out, and then I'll shut it so none of the mongrels follow. I'll also have a car waiting for you on the other side. Then I'll explain both yours and Jaclyn's absence to the council in the morning."

Slyck patted him on the back, respect apparent on his face. "You're going to be one hell of a leader, Drake."

"Trained by the best," he said. "Now you need to lie low until tomorrow. Get out of here and go home. I'll take your shift tonight. You sit tight, and then make your way to Vall's den an hour before the full moon." With that, he turned around, pulled open the service entrance door, and disappeared behind a wall of heavy rain.

Slyck returned to the bar, cleaned up the broken glass and then shut the lights off. Clouds hung as heavy as his heart as he made his way home. Inside his house he paced and ran over the turn of events until darkness fell over Serene.

He stepped in front of his window and spotted movement inside Jaclyn's house. Everything inside him reached out to her, and in that instant he knew he had to go to her, to see her, to make love to her. They might not have tomorrow but they sure as hell had tonight.

He could no longer suppress his primal need for his mate. He threw on his raincoat, covered his head to disguise himself, and made his way to the back entrance. He pulled the door open and jumped back, both startled and surprised to see Jaclyn standing there, dark slicker cloaking her identity, hand raised to knock.

"Oh God, Jaclyn," he rushed out, and hauled her inside with him.

She tilted her head back to look at him. "Slyck—"

He put a silencing finger against her lips and then held her face between his palms. "I know, sweetheart. I know everything. Drake filled me in." He trailed his fingers over her body and pulled her hood down. "Let's get you out of this." Once he rid her of the slicker, he said, "I thought I saw you at home a minute ago."

A wave of passion overcame him and warmth spread over his skin as she wiped her damp bangs back and blinked the water from her eyes. "It's Sunray. She's covering for us." Her voice was rough with emotions and stirred him in crazy ways.

As he stood there looking at Jaclyn, the air around them charged with electricity. His hands brushed hers, and he dipped his head and covered her mouth with his. Her chest heaved, and when he felt her deepen the kiss with wild abandon, he inched back and said, "Come with me." Slyck gathered her hand in his, led her to the bedroom, and peeled her clothes away, his depth of desire for her stronger than ever.

Glistening green-and-blue-flecked eyes stared up at him as her fingers spiraled over his body, pulling at his clothes. His heart pounded erratically while his panther ached to mate with her.

Profound silence ensued as Slyck quickly shed his clothes and then stood back to stare at the beautiful woman before him. His eyes left her face and slowly tracked down her body as he sorted through matters.

The moon would rise and the moon would fall—that they had no control over—but tonight they had each other, and as long as they were both alive, he wasn't going to waste one minute with her.

He breathed a kiss over her parted lips and backed her up until her knees hit the mattress. She gripped him hard, careful not to sever the connection as he laid her out and crawled in beside her. Long, dark lashes fluttered as she stared up at him in longing, and he saw love shining in her eyes. The way she looked at him flooded him with emotions and brought on a convulsive shudder.

With her mouth poised open, her voice dropped to a whisper and she murmured, "I love you."

His heart skipped a beat, and a maelstrom of sensations whipped through his veins. "I love you too, *We-Sa.*"

His lips found hers again for a slow, simmering, soul-stirring kiss. The way she kissed him back, with such passion, desire, and love, made him feel a little raw and a whole lot vulnerable. When he finally eased away, they were both left shaken.

He breathed in her sweet panther scent and gave a low growl of longing. He gripped the side of her hips and buried his face in her neck. "I love you so fucking much, Jaclyn," he murmured, his voice raspy with emotion. Hands shaky with need, he brushed her hair from her face before he ran his mouth over her body, kissing and touching every speck of her warm naked flesh like he couldn't get enough. A whimper escaped her lips. She quivered beneath him, her body beckoning his touch, his mouth, and his cock, her throaty purr resonating through his body.

Her breasts crushed into his chest, and she pulled him down on top of her. He took note of her quickening pulse, the urgency in her eyes, and the desperate edge in her voice. "Make love to me," she cooed, everything in her voice and her body language letting him know she feared this would be their last and final mating.

He slipped a finger between their bodies and found her wet and wanting. When she let out a little gasp of pleasure, he thought his heart would explode with all the love he felt for her.

The near-full moon outside shone though his window and danced over their bodies, a taunting reminder of things to come. Fuck, were they fighting the inevitable? Slyck pushed that thought aside for the time being and gave all his attention to the woman beneath him.

"I need you inside me," she said, her voice nothing more than a rough whisper. She put her mouth near his; her warm breath brushed his face like a lover's kiss. He heard the tremor in her words when she added, "Slyck, please . . ."

Slyck began trembling from head to toe as he positioned his cock at her opening, and lightly brushed his fingers over her clit in preparation. Needy and desperate, she bucked forward, forcing the head of his cock inside.

A muscle in his jaw flexed and he smiled down at her. "Slow down, baby," he whispered, despite the fire raging between his thighs. He blew out a shaky breath and murmured softly into her ear, "We have all night. And I plan on making love to you until the sun rises."

She began panting heavily as he slowly pushed into her, offering her only an inch at a time. Her warmth wrapped around him and branded his nerve endings. The sweet friction made him throb and he shuddered involuntarily.

He drew a fortifying breath and watched, transfixed, as her eyes took on a darker shade of green. He felt his chest puff up, in pride of his mate. Her pretty pink tongue slid over her sensuous bottom lip, and she spread her legs a little more to offer him better access.

"Oh baby." He let out a low moan as he slid into her—as he slid home. The onslaught of pleasure nearly shut down his brain.

Her arms and legs locked around his, holding him in place as though fearing he'd escape. A shudder rippled through her, and he watched her throat work. The sweet scent of their lovemaking curled around them, and he inhaled, pulling it into his lungs.

With slow, controlled movements, he pumped into her, drawing out and savoring every sensation, every moment in her arms. As his orgasm mounted, he watched the play of emotions over her face and could feel her muscles tighten and clench. Her flesh suffused with color and her eyes darkened with desire. She opened her mouth but no words formed.

Slyck smiled down at her. "I love the look on your face when you come for me." His words pushed her over the edge. In no time at all, her damp heat seared his cock and dripped down his balls.

He continued to ride her, picking up the tempo as he chased an orgasm. As he reveled in the sensations, pressure built inside him, and his throat tightened with emotions. He gulped for air and slammed into her, pushing high and joining them as one.

Unable to hold off any longer, his muscles strained and he let himself go, jettisoning his come high inside her pussy. His orgasm was so intense, his entire body shook violently. As his seed filled her, she quaked beneath him, tumbling into another climax.

"Oh my," she cried out, and clamped her legs around him harder. "I don't think I'll ever get used to that. But I'm willing to try."

As tension drained from his body, Slyck laughed out loud and collapsed beside her. Jaclyn curled in next to him and pulled the blankets up.

"That was beautiful," she purred.

"You're beautiful."

Their lovemaking was soft, intimate, tender, and so damn powerful, it left him in a weakened state. He gathered her into his arms and held tight, never wanting the night to end.

She snuggled close, and when her breathing returned to normal, he said, "Jaclyn."

"Yeah."

"Do you trust Sunray?"

She blinked up at him. "Yes. Why?"

"It was just something Drake said earlier, that maybe she was working with Vall and playing us for fools."

"She's not like that," she responded firmly. "Drake doesn't know her like we know her."

"Do you think she can get you out?"

He didn't miss the uncertainty in her voice when she said, "Yeah."

Not wanting to put a damper on their evening together, despite the dire circumstances, he changed the subject. "So I take it from your mother's scowl that I'm not her first choice for a son-in-law."

Jaclyn laughed, and it filled him with such warmth. He'd yet to hear her laugh, really laugh, and he vowed when this was all over, he'd do whatever was required to make her laugh more often. She jabbed his chest. "What matters is you're *my* first choice." She rolled into him and lightly touched his face. "And, besides, what's not to love? I give her five minutes and she'll be charmed."

"Yes, I suppose I do have that going for me," he teased, then arrogantly blew on his knuckles and brushed them over his chest.

Her hand slipped between their bodies, and when her warm palm connected with his cock, he immediately hardened. The smile fell from her face and was replaced by inviting, come-hither eyes. "Hey, big boy, why don't you show me what else you have going for you?"

He climbed on top of her and spent the rest of the night taking her, again and again.

Chapter Fifteen

"Jaclyn, wake up."

Jaclyn slowly opened her eyes and came face-to-face with Sunray. Her body warmed as memories of her wonderful night with Slyck and the protective way he'd seen to it she'd gotten home before sunrise came rushing back to her mind.

"It's time." Sunray pulled the blankets from Jaclyn's fatigued body and reached for her hand.

Jaclyn's heart missed a beat and she swallowed down her rising panic. "Already?"

"Yeah, Vall wants you to hang out in the den until the shift. If we show disobedience, he'll know."

Jaclyn considered the events leading up to the transformation and the mating that went along with it. "Will he want—"

Sunray shook her head. "Not yet. He just wants you there for safekeeping."

Feeling numb and cold inside, Jaclyn reached for Sunray's

hand and climbed from the bed. She went through the motions—showered, dressed, and followed Sunray to Vall's den, which was situated on the outskirts of the woods, and used only on shift night. It was in the perfect location for the pack to gather, shift, and then run into the woods to feed, or fornicate, or whatever the hell they did.

Sunray unlocked the dead bolt and motioned for Jaclyn to enter. Jaclyn stood by the door and glanced around the cabin. It was much larger than she had expected. It contained three sofas, a fireplace, blankets strewn across the floor, and even a kitchen with a stocked pantry.

With only one small window, the room felt dark and dank, and it smelled stale. Heart racing, she took one measured step inside and inhaled. When she choked on the stench of wet dog, her eyes watered in response. Grimacing with disgust, Jaclyn turned to Sunray and met her glance. "How can they—"

The look in Sunray's eyes stopped her. Shit. Sunray was one of them and she'd just offended her.

"I can't help what I've become," Sunray said softly. "But I do what I have to do to survive. And to survive, I change with my pack, run in the woods, and feed on animal blood."

"Sunray, I didn't mean—"

Sunray held her hand up, palm out. "It's okay. We all do whatever we have to in order to survive, and tonight I'll do whatever it takes to help you survive."

Jaclyn felt her heart pound harder. "Why, Sunray? Why are you doing this for me?"

"Because I care about you, and because I can feel Ray on you.

And somehow I just know you're very important to me and my future."

"Ray?" she asked. "That was his name?"

A small smile touched Sunray's mouth, and she went quiet for a moment. "Yeah."

"You're Sun*ray* and he was *Ray*? Why do I think that's not a coincidence?"

"My name is Sunni. I combined our names after Vall killed him and turned me so I could carry him close at all times and never forget the love we shared."

When she saw the sadness in her friend's eyes, Jaclyn pulled her into an embrace and held her body close. She understood why Drake would question Sunray's values and her loyalty to Vall, but he didn't know Sunray the way Jaclyn did. No one could fake the pain and heartache in the depths of Sunray's silver eyes. Silence ensued as they both became lost in their own thoughts.

Sunray broke the quiet. "Vall is a sneaky bastard, and never to be trusted. Let's just hope Drake is as capable of handling him as Slyck was."

Sunray's words hit Jaclyn like a slap in the face. Jaclyn drew back, flabbergasted. Ohmigod, how could she have been so selfish, so caught up in her own dilemma that she'd never once considered Slyck's position? Not once had she even considered that Slyck would be leaving his pack, everything he'd ever known. Wasn't he the one who said that the pack came first, and that they'd go so far as to sacrifice one for the greater good? She swallowed hard. Oh God, everything he'd done was for her, and if Drake wasn't up to handling Vall, she could be the downfall of his entire community.

How could she allow him to walk away from his people? How could she allow herself to be the destruction of everything he'd spent years building and protecting?

Sunray dropped onto the sofa and gestured for Jaclyn to have a seat.

"What do we do now?" Jaclyn whispered, her heart lodged somewhere in her throat.

"We wait. And I plan."

"How—"

"Don't ask."

The day passed slowly. Jaclyn spent most of the daylight hours pacing, worrying, and praying that they were going to get out of this.

Soon the sun disappeared behind the mountains, and nighttime fell like a guillotine. As the full moon crept higher in the sky, an eerie energy blanketed the small town and made Jaclyn's skin crawl. She sat nestled in the corner, trying to make herself invisible as the cabin filled with creatures. Because she felt like a gazelle caught in the lion's den, her survival instincts kicked in and she pulled her knees to her chest. Except she was a kitten, not a gazelle, and this was a dog pen, not a lion's den, and if they found out what she was, they'd eat her alive and use her bones to clean their teeth.

Heavy boots outside the den heralded Vall's arrival.

Sunray must have sensed her sudden increase in heart rate and burst of anxiety. "Stay calm," Sunray whispered, and Jaclyn nodded, hoping like hell she could follow the advice.

The hinges creaked and Vall strolled in, his presence darkening the doorway. Jaclyn glanced behind him and watched the clouds peel back to reveal a full moon, nearly reaching its peak in the summer sky. Looking virile, powerful, and animalistic, Vall stepped farther inside his den and perused the room, taking stock.

When his eyes met Jaclyn's, a small smirk curled up his lip, and it was all she could do to suppress a shiver. Without his gaze ever leaving Jaclyn, he crooked his finger and motioned for Sunray to join him. She stood and walked over to where he stood. From Jaclyn's distance she couldn't hear the exchange between the two; she knew only that they were talking about her.

A moment later Vall dismissed Sunray and took a seat near the fireplace. A few women sidled up to him, showing submission to their alpha. Making soft growling sounds, they began rubbing their bodies against him seductively, like feral dogs in heat. Seductive music turned on in the background, and the room took on a new energy—heavy, sexual, carnal.

Jaclyn casually glanced around and realized the prerun mating had already begun. Dear God, she was smack-dab in the middle of a lycan orgy. Men and women were shedding their clothes in preparation for the shift. In one corner, a woman began servicing a man's cock while a second man lubricated himself and took her from behind, driving his hard shaft in and out of her wet pussy. Everywhere she looked there were naked bodies engaging in every sexual act known to mankind—or dogkind.

Jaclyn licked her lips and feined interest, especially with the way Vall studied her and was gauging her reactions to the hedonistic acts. She prayed Sunray had something up her sleeve; otherwise the kitty was about to become the first snack of the night.

"Jaclyn." The sound of Vall's rough voice made her pulse leap with fear. She shifted her body and turned to him. Her glance raced over the two women as they tore his clothes from his body and ran their hungry mouths and hands all over his naked torso, paying extra attention to his stiff cock.

He motioned for her to join them. "Come, little one, it's time for your initiation," he murmured, his implication clear in his tone.

Oh fuck.

There was no way in hell she was going to join them, but if she didn't, it was game over. Actually, either way it was game over, because if he got a whiff of her panther, it would drive the canine into a feeding frenzy, and soon the others would join in. She stood there immobilized, trapped like a snared rabbit.

Taking her by surprise, she felt Sunray's hands on her legs, widening them and inching upward to dip beneath her short skirt. Her position exposed her sex to Vall, who had suddenly dropped his hand and stopped beckoning her.

Vall's eyes widened in delight when Sunray pressed her lips over Jaclyn's and giggled playfully. She then positioned her mouth close to Jacklyn's ear and whispered, "Follow my lead. We need to stall."

Jaclyn climbed to her feet and shot a fake seductive smile Vall's way. Sunray gripped her hips firmly and joined Jaclyn and herself pussy to pussy. The two began moving to the sensuous music while Vall watched in fascinated excitement.

Sunray made short work of her clothes, then began to peel Jaclyn's shirt and skirt from her shivering body—she shivered from fear, not excitement. Warm hands closed over her breasts as the two women performed a sexy act for Vall. Jaclyn ran her fingers through Sunray's golden hair and guided her mouth to her tightening breasts. The low growl coming from Vall told her how much he liked that.

Sunray flicked her tongue over Jaclyn's nipples, turning them a bright red, and slipped a finger between her thighs to toy with her clit.

Jaclyn widened her legs and bucked against her. She stole a glance at Vall and watched as he guided one of his women to his cock. The woman cupped his balls, wrapped her mouth around his length, and bobbed up and down as Vall continued to indulge in their erotic sideshow.

Jaclyn glanced at the door. A few lycans had already shifted and taken to the woods, their howls cutting through the ominous stillness of the night. The panther inside her quivered.

Sunray dropped to her knees and pressed her mouth over Jaclyn's sex. Vall growled out loud and began bucking against the woman who was devouring his cock.

Jaclyn cast her eyes down and noted the dark hairs on Sunray's back, a good indication that Sunray was desperately trying to fight off the call of the moon. But for how long would she be able to resist? And if she changed, would she turn on Jaclyn?

Panting hard, Jaclyn moaned in delight and gyrated against Sunray's tongue. A minute later, Sunray slowly made her way back up her friend's body, her tongue trailing a lazy path over Jaclyn's naked flesh.

"We can't make a move until he's seconds from shifting," Sunray whispered into Jaclyn's ear. "Then he'll be lured by the woods and you can escape." Their mouths found each other and their moans of pleasure merged.

"Enough," Vall bit out, his silver eyes darkening with desire. "Bring her to me."

Sunray turned and gave him a seductive, playful grin. "First I want to thank you properly for gifting me with a new plaything," she murmured. At first Vall seemed confused by her words, but as understanding dawned, he quickly dismissed his two submissive playthings. They both shifted and bolted out the door, leaving the den empty except for Vall, Sunray, and Jaclyn.

Sunray dropped to her knees before Vall and he let out a snarling bark of victory.

Oh God, Sunray was submitting to Vall.

Suddenly, Drake's words of warning came back to haunt her. Was Sunray turning on her? Had she been working with Vall all along? Hadn't she vowed she'd never submit to Vall or any other man?

Jaclyn had to be wrong. She just had to be.

Jaclyn shook her head to clear it. No, Sunray would never turn on her. Jaclyn diligently fought off the seed of doubt, hating that Drake had planted it there, but understanding nonetheless that he had only his pack's best interests at heart.

When she heard Sunray mumble, "Forgive me, Ray," under her breath, Jaclyn's heart turned over in her chest, knowing that she submitted to Vall only as a distraction to buy Jaclyn and Slyck more time.

Fierce instinct to protect the ones she loved kicked in. She couldn't, wouldn't let Sunray give herself to Vall like this. Not like this. Not for her. Which was probably why Sunray had never filled her in on her plan. She had to stop this. She'd rather die before she'd see her friend do the one thing she swore she'd never do.

With Vall's attention diverted, Jaclyn crept around the back of the sofa and looked for a weapon, strategizing her next move. Sunray's warning glare stopped her cold; then her pretty face morphed to wolf and she growled Jaclyn away.

In that instant, Vall started to shift. His bones and skin stretched and slid into place, his hair thickened and darkened to a mixture of black and silver. He surged upward, then dropped down on all fours, growling, pacing, and radiating strength.

He was bigger and more powerful than any dog Jaclyn had ever seen. In fact, he was the scariest fucking animal she'd ever encountered. The panther in Jaclyn trembled in reaction to the treat before her.

Sunray's voice pulled Jaclyn's attention as she lowered her head in submission and said to the wolf, "I want to run with you tonight, Vall."

With that, Vall let out a long, overjoyed howl as he brushed against Sunray, as though his new "cub" and her initiation were temporarily forgotten. Legs pumping, his powerful, streamlined body took to the woods. He moved with a speed no mere canine possessed. Before he disappeared into the thick foliage, he glanced back at Sunray, waiting for her to follow.

Long, unsteady strides carried Sunray to the door. When the light of the moon spilled over her, she began shifting. She cast

Jaclyn a quick glance. "As soon as I get into the woods with him, you need to go."

"I can't leave here without you." Jaclyn reached for her, but when Sunray nipped at her fingers, she quickly pulled them back. She tried to reason with her friend, plead with her even, but was unsure if Sunray could comprehend the words in her current state. "When I go missing, Vall will figure it out and kill you."

Jaclyn glanced back out the door in time to see Vall's large, dark-haired body duck into the woods. His howl carried in on a breeze, beckoning for Sunray to join him.

Sunray's glance went from Jaclyn to Vall, back to Jaclyn again. She clutched her stomach and growled. "Jaclyn, please, if you don't go now, I can't be responsible for what happens to you."

Then, suddenly, the pull of the moon became too strong to fight off, and Sunray completed her transformation. Standing before Jaclyn was a golden-haired werewolf, nails extended, eyes glistening, and teeth bared, hungry for nourishment. Growling, Sunray made a threatening step toward Jaclyn. With fear ruling Jaclyn's actions, her survival instincts kicked in. In one fluid movement, she shifted to panther.

Chapter Sixteen

Slyck paced restlessly outside the den. Something was wrong. Seriously wrong. He could feel it in every fiber of his being. He'd watched Vall and his pack take to the woods minutes earlier, but Jaclyn and Sunray hadn't surfaced yet. Had Vall discovered she was panther? Was Sunray unable to distract him or *take him on*? Whatever that was supposed to mean.

No longer willing to wait, Slyck stalked forward, hell-bent on rescuing Jaclyn and getting the fuck out of Dodge. So help anyone who tried to stop him. As he rounded the corner, his thighs connected with something muscular, something hairy.

Something that walked on all fours.

"Jaclyn . . ." He dropped to the ground and wrapped his hands around the black panther mewling before him. "Thank God, you're okay." Jaclyn purred and brushed against him. "Shake it off, sweetheart. We need to get you out of here, and if you stay like this, the wolves will smell you."

He held her tight while her bones slid back into place and she returned to her human form. "Where's Sunray?" he asked as he pulled her to her feet. Slyck tore off his T-shirt and pulled it over her head, covering her naked body.

"Running with Vall."

"Fuck." It suddenly occurred to him just how Sunray had taken Vall on. "Come on, we need to get to the gate while they're all distracted."

Their heavy footfalls echoed in the still night as Slyck and Jaclyn ran through the deserted streets and made their way to the front security gate. He spotted Drake inside the booth, his hand on the controls. They were close, so fucking close to making it, Slyck's body began to shake in anticipation.

"Going somewhere, kittens?"

Slyck spun around and surveyed the street. Vall moved, advertising his presence some twenty feet away. Once again fully dressed, he stood beneath an awning, just outside the grocery store. Instinctively, Slyck grabbed Jaclyn and positioned her behind him, protecting her from the beast.

"Back off, Vall. We're going to walk out of here, and you're not going to do a damn thing about it. If you try, I'll stop you, and trust me, you're not going to like it."

Amusement passed over Vall's face. "Did the kitty just threaten the big bad wolf?"

"So you want to do this the hard way then?" Slyck snarled.

Vall cocked his head, his expression smug. "Is there any other way, kitten?"

Just as Slyck detected movement around them, he identified

a few other members of Vall's pack, his easily led minions. Goddamn it, he really hadn't anticipated an ambush.

"Here, kitty, kitty," Vall taunted, hackles raised. Still maintaining his human form, he kept his distance, using the awning to
protect him from the pull of the full moon.

The pack cantered forward and closed around them. Vall *tsk*ed
and shook his head. "You should never underestimate your op-
ponents, Slyck. You really are past your prime, aren't you?" He let
out a bark of laughter and announced, "I knew what you two were
up to all along. I thought I'd go along, just for the hell of it, and
then take you all down at once."

When Slyck fisted his hands and took a threatening step
forward, Vall laughed out loud and said, "Look around, Slyck.
You're outnumbered." He rocked on his heels, his glance men-
acing. "What were you thinking, venturing outside on a night
like tonight?" He waved his hand toward the moon. "When the
town wakes up tomorrow to find you gone, they'll never blame
me, since I can't be held accountable for my actions in wolf
form."

"But you're not in wolf form," Slyck countered.

Vall gave a humorless laugh and cut his hand through the air,
motioning toward his loyal followers. "Oh, but they are."

"What is it? You need your mongrels to fight your battles,
Vall? Is it because you're afraid to get your hands dirty? Or is it
because you're afraid of me? If you want me, come and get me
yourself."

Vall let out a growl of fury and dropped to his haunches.

Strike one.

That's a good little doggy. Let your anger take over until you can't fight the shift, Slyck mused silently.

Jaclyn wrapped her hands around his waist and whispered in his ear, "Where's Sunray?"

Slyck trained his focus on the pack and did a quick count. They were outnumbered by at least twenty, and Sunray was nowhere to be found.

His eyes shot to Vall. "Where's Sunray?" When Vall didn't answer, Slyck pushed. "I guess she opted not to run with you after all." Jesus, he hoped she'd managed to get out of the gate already.

Eyes enraged, Vall snarled, stepped out from the awning, and advanced with purpose.

Strike two.

"Don't worry about her. I fucked that ridiculous kitty fetish right out of her," he crooned.

Slyck peeled Jaclyn's hands from his waist in preparation. "Bummer to learn she only submitted to your wolf to save her kitty friends."

"Bullshit. She's mine, always has been, and she wanted to submit to me." Vall ripped his clothes from his body as anger whipped through him and the pull of the moon became stronger. His bones began to shift, but he continued to fight the inevitable transformation.

Strike three.

Slyck angled his head and instructed Jaclyn to get in the control booth with Drake, but to walk slowly. Any quick movements would attract the wolves.

"Guess she had to turn to her panther friends for *companionship* since her alpha wolfie couldn't do it for her." Slyck licked his lips and offered Vall a coy grin. "And here I never thought I'd ever acquire a taste for puppy."

Vall twitched, and then unable to fight the pull any longer, his bones began to slide and his skin to stretch.

You're out.

Running at breakneck speed, Slyck covered the distance between them in mere seconds and pounced on Vall. Summoning every ounce of strength and power he possessed, he drove his fist into the other man's throat. Vall let out a deep guttural sound right from his belly, then lunged upward. Slyck pounced, gained purchase, and began mauling the hound. The sounds of cartilage popping and bones crunching echoed in the night. Vall yelped and dropped to the ground.

Vall's snarl fueled the other lycans into action, and they rushed forward, frothy saliva and fresh blood dripping from their muzzles. Slyck could feel a set of fangs slice through his flesh, ripping his skin from his body. Claws dug and teeth clamped, and he feared there was no way in hell he was getting out of this alive, because the wolves would tear his head clear off his shoulders, and rob him of any lives he had left.

As that last image filled his mind, he thought about Jaclyn and how they hadn't been bonded long enough for her to live on without him. She too would be robbed of her life, and he couldn't, wouldn't let that happen. A new energy pumped through his veins, giving him a strength he had no idea he possessed.

It was the strength from their bond.

Drawing on that strength, he tore the rest of his clothes from his body and shifted.

Scowling, Vall barked at his wolves, and then surprisingly, one of his loyal followers turned on him, sinking his teeth into Vall's backside and spurring the others on. Vall's low whine rent the air as, one by one, they all turned on him. How was that for love and devotion? Treating his pack like shit and bullying them had finally come back to bite him in the ass.

Literally.

Jaclyn's stomach knotted and her body broke out in a sweat as she regarded the tumbling weed of fur and claws. The sickening sound of skin ripping and animals howling and the pungent coppery scent of blood saturated the air had her panther itching to surface. But her little panther wasn't strong enough to take on one dog, let alone a whole pack.

Oh God, she needed to help Slyck. She needed to do something, anything. And she needed to do it fast. But what? How? Her gaze scanned the street until she came to the department store. Guns. The department store had a gun section.

Working to keep herself invisible, she crab-walked to the security gate, where Drake stood guard, fighting off a few stray lycans himself. With his back to the gate, metal bar in his hands, he dodged a set of canines and cracked the beast over the head. The animal fell with a yelp, blood splattering across the pavement. It remained motionless, but Jaclyn knew that after a few moments, it would regenerate and be as good as new.

Jaclyn pressed her back to the booth as one of the lycans turned on her. She maintained eye contact, not wanting to show fear or give the wolf any reason to attack. Lips peeled back to expose pointy fangs, it prowled closer. Its wolf nostrils flared, and she suspected it got a whiff of her panther scent.

Blood pounded in her ears and her nerves tingled. "How do I get into the department store?" she shot out to Drake, feeling her way along the booth in hopes of finding the door, getting inside, and securing a weapon of her own. "I need to get guns." The sounds of animal cries reached her ears and her heart raced. She worked diligently to fight down the panic. Fuck, she needed to move fast, before it was too late, but she couldn't do a thing with this damn dog at her heels.

Drake came around to her side and swung his weapon like a baseball bat. The lycan squealed and rolled backward. A second later it climbed to all fours and shook its head, dazed. "The bullets won't kill them," he exclaimed, then turned his attention back to the lycan as it prepared for another attack.

"But these ones will."

The feminine voice came from behind, and Jaclyn spun around to see Sunray standing there in her human form, completely naked, gripping a gun, white knuckled. She squeezed the trigger, and the sound of gunfire cut through the air and startled the dogs. They tucked tail and ran, instincts driving them to seek safety in the woods. Only Slyck and Vall remained in the middle of the street. Both were injured and bleeding, yet they continued to fight.

Jaclyn reached for her friend but pulled her hand back when Sunray snarled and began morphing, her skin sliding away. "I don't know how long I can fight it," she cried out, her voice cracking like broken bones.

"Give me the gun," Jaclyn spoke softly, and with slow, unhurried movements, she stepped forward.

The gun fell to the ground as Sunray dropped to her knees in pain. Jaclyn kept a close eye on the wolf as she stooped to pick it up. "Easy, Sunray," she whispered. "I'm not going to hurt you."

Gun in hand Jaclyn stood up and walked backward. When Slyck roared behind her, she twisted around and pointed the gun. Jesus, she couldn't pull the trigger, couldn't tell who was who as they struggled on the ground. When she thought she had caught a flash of wolf fur, she squeezed her index finger, discharging the gun. The hot silver rocketed from the chamber. The sound cracked the air and the smell of sulfur curled around her. She glanced at the two still animals, and suddenly the world around her went hazy. The gun fell from her hand and clattered against the pavement as she waited for movement.

"Slyck . . . ," she whispered. "Get up."

Breathing heavily, Drake came up beside her. Three injured lycans crawled away from him to safety. Drake's hand closed over her shoulder and squeezed, a gesture meant to calm. She turned to face him and watched a smile pull at his mouth.

Confused, she fixed him with a stare. He gestured with his head and said, "Look."

Jaclyn spotted Slyck morphing back to human form. He climbed to his feet, his naked body broken and bloodied.

"I'll go open the gate again," Drake said. "There are clean clothes in the car for you both."

Her heart soared like a leaf caught in an updraft, and she bolted forward. She threw her arms around Slyck and kissed him with all the love inside her.

"Easy, baby," he murmured and kissed her back.

Jaclyn cringed and inched away. "Oh, sorry," she whispered almost giddy with relief.

Slyck's grip suddenly tightened and she heard him curse under his breath. In wolf form, Sunray moved toward them.

"Where's the gun?" he bit out.

Jaclyn stepped in front of him and positioned her body between man and wolf. "No, Slyck, don't."

His muscles tightened and he bit out between clenched teeth, "Jaclyn, she doesn't know what she's doing."

"Yes, she does. She won't hurt me. She's proven that to me already." Jaclyn pointed to the open gate, and in a low but firm tone, she said, "Go. Run. Stay safe, and at sunrise meet us in the next town. We'll be waiting for you."

Sunray bared her teeth and took one small step forward. Slyck widened his stance and prepared for an attack. Sunray turned her eyes on him and growled, then swished her long golden tail and spun around. With strong, rapid strides, she raced through the open gate.

Drake came back and touched Slyck's shoulder. "You need to get out of here now too. Vall's first-in-command, Ciaran, is a good man who has the town's best interests at heart. Tomorrow I'll meet with him, and together we'll cover for tonight's carnage. I'll tell the council you two fought, and both ended up dead, and Sunray got caught in the cross fire. I'm not sure anyone in this town will be sad to see Vall go anyway, not even his own pack. In fact, I think they'll be grateful."

Jaclyn spotted the uncertainty in Slyck's eyes when he nodded and mumbled something under his breath that sounded like *Harmony, Herbs, and Incantation.*

He put his hand on the other man's shoulder and began, "Drake—"

Drake must have seen the unease in his friend's eyes as well because he cut Slyck off and said, "It's time for you to go, Slyck. You've lived your life for everyone else. Now it's time for you to have a life. You deserve this."

Bile rose in her throat now that the moment to leave was upon them, and she began wringing her hands together. Oh God, she couldn't ask him to leave everything he'd ever known because of her, she couldn't be that selfish. Nor would she be responsible for the downfall of his community. They needed his strength, his power, and his command.

She took a moment to run over the events of the last month, her mind searching for an answer and coming up with only one.

Jaclyn took a step back as she came to a decision—she knew what she had to do. With her fate sealed, she began to walk away, slowly. Sure she'd die, but life without Slyck wasn't a life she was interested in living, anyway.

"Jaclyn, what are you doing?" Slyck turned toward her as Drake made his way back to the security booth.

His questioning tone stopped her cold. She swallowed and met his gaze unflinchingly. "You have to stay," she answered, deadpan.

He furrowed his brow and in two strides closed the distance between them. He cupped her face and she bit back big hiccupping tears. The tenderness in his tone nearly dropped her to the bloodied ground when he said, "What are you talking about, sweetheart?"

She lifted her chin and met with deeply tortured, beautiful green eyes. "I saw your uncertainty, Slyck. You can't leave your pack. Sometimes you have to sacrifice one for the greater good. You told me so yourself."

She felt his body tremble and saw the worry in his eyes. "Jaclyn—"

She tried to keep her own voice steady but failed miserably. "Your family needs you, Slyck."

"You're my family now, Jaclyn, and we need each other. I've prepared Drake for my position." He spoke softly and pressed sweet kisses to her forehead, her nose, her mouth. "And now with Vall gone . . ."

"But your hesitation . . ."

"I can't deny that leaving my pack is hard, Jaclyn, but I also know it's right, and I've come to terms with the decision. Everything I've ever done was for my community, and maybe it is time I did something for myself. I think I deserve that. We deserve that."

She gulped.

"Baby, don't think for one minute I'm letting you walk out of here without me. I've spent a lifetime searching for you, and whether you like it or not, you're stuck with me."

Relieved, Jaclyn let out a big, inappropriate, unladylike snort. She swung her arms around him, and when he spun her, she spotted Vall crawling across the pavement on his belly, leaving a big streak of red in his wake.

"Oh shit."

Slyck pivoted, and the second he spotted Vall, he pushed Jaclyn to safety, but before he could counterattack, Vall got a shot off and Slyck fell to the ground at her feet.

She dropped to the ground beside him. "No," she cried out, and wrapped her arms around him, offering him her strength, her life.

The sound of Vall scraping across the pavement propelled her into action. Acting on instinct, and barely aware of what she was doing, Jaclyn bolted across the pavement and flung herself on top of Vall. She grabbed the gun and shot him again, ensuring this time he was dead once and for all.

As she crawled back to Slyck, her eyes stung and she finally broke down. "Slyck—" she cried out, and cradled his head in her hands. "Oh God, no." She scanned his body, searching through the numerous gouges on his skin for the bullet wound. When she saw a hole through his heart, she buried her face in her hands and cried. She stayed there for a long moment, choking on her sobs.

Slyck had been right when he said that someday she'd understand the power of the bond between them, because not only could she *not* live without him—she didn't *want* to live without him. She lay down beside him, accepting that they would die together—the way it was meant to be, the way she wanted it.

"Jaclyn."

She scurried backward, startled. Her eyes sprang open.

"Slyck!" she screeched, her gaze racing over his body. "How? The bullet. Your heart. It's not possible. We don't have regenerative abilities. You told me so yourself." Her words came out hurried and broken.

"Um, we have nine lives. Did I forget to mention that to you?"

Oh. My. God. Of all the frigging things to forget to mention.

She looked heavenward, briefly squeezed her eyes and prayed for strength. "Yeah, you did," she murmured, then turned her glance to him and asked, "How many do you have left?"

He gave her an apologetic, lopsided grin that turned her insides to mush. "Why?"

Her heart filled with love as she smiled down at him. "Because you scared me half to death, and I'm about to kill you again for forgetting to tell me that vital piece of information."

He laughed out loud and pulled her to him. "I have one left, sweetheart, and I plan on spending every minute of it with you. Every day I plan on teaching you how to tame your panther and use it as a strength." He gave her a wink. "And every night I plan on unleashing your wild side and showing you the power of our bond. Like I told you, you're stuck with me, whether you like it or not."

Epilogue

Jaclyn put the last of her files into her briefcase and looked around her beautiful new corner office. Every time she glanced at the "President" sign on her desk, or on the outside of her door, it brought a smile to her face. Everything in her life had fallen into place, and sometimes she had to pinch herself to prove it wasn't just a dream.

Her stint in Serene might not have been all it was cracked up to be, but her ability to restructure and move product certainly proved to the board that she was serious about the business and that Benjamin was leaving his empire in capable hands. Of course, she hadn't expected to walk away as a were-cat, with the most amazing man in the world at her side, either. In fact, there were moments when she'd thought they'd never walk away from Serene at all.

Her thoughts wandered to her parents and she smiled, pleased that her mother had fallen for Slyck's charm, and had readily accepted him into the family, even if he preferred jeans and T-shirts over dress pants and white collared shirts. Perhaps she and Slyck would join them in Florida over the Christmas holidays later this month after all.

Since coming home, Jaclyn had taken on another new image and used her middle name, Marie. Even though they never expected anyone to come looking for them—the entire community of Serene thought they were dead—they felt it best to cover all traces. And, of course, now that she was a good girl, the *Chicago Social*, in their quest to capture misbehaving debutantes, no longer had any interest in her, which allowed her to remain quiet, behind the scenes, and out of the spotlight.

Her mother was happy with the new name because it matched the new, good-girl identity, and it just happened to be her name, as well. Slyck took on the name of Sam, one of his old identities, and Sunray . . . well, Sunray kept her name in memory of Ray.

Jaclyn smoothed down her long skirt as she stood and reached for her winter coat and scarf. After slipping out of her sensible pumps, she pulled on her knee-high winter boots and glanced at the freshly falling snow. Once she was sufficiently dressed for the cold Chicago winter, she stepped out onto the white sidewalk. Jaclyn no longer minded dressing the part of the good girl in the day. Not when she could go home every night and be so very bad with Slyck.

Speaking of Slyck. Both he and Sunray had left the office earlier that day and headed back to Sunray's place to cook Jaclyn a special birthday dinner. She was certainly looking forward to the meal, but truthfully, she was more interested in the dessert afterward.

With Slyck's knowledge of policing, Benjamin had given him a position as head of security before he had retired. And, with Sunray's persuasive techniques, she was now on the marketing team. Jaclyn liked having her new family close by at all times.

As Jaclyn made her way down the street, she stopped to talk to a few of the shopkeepers, picked up a couple of Christmas presents, and exchange happy holiday greetings as well as hugs and kisses. Continuing on her way home, she walked past Risqué. She paused for a moment and smiled as she glanced at the entrance door.

"Shall we?"

The deep, familiar voice came from behind. She spun around and came face-to-face with Kane. Her eyes lit up as she leaned in to hug him. He held her to him long and hard. His warm masculine scent, a sharp blend of spice and a sensual aquatic aroma, impregnated the air and filled her senses with joyous and wonderful memories. She wasn't sure if his scent came from cologne or if he spent a lot of time in a pool.

After she inched back, he narrowed his questioning eyes and examined her, like a hunter studying its prey, and for a quick moment she wondered exactly what it was he did for a living. "You seem . . . different," he said.

"I am different," was all she offered.

He touched her arm, and held the door open. "Coming?"

She shook her head no. Now that she'd found the one man who completed her in every way, she had no need or desire to frequent the nightclubs. "I have everything I need at home," she said.

Kane frowned and she sensed a deep sense of loneliness stirring in the depths of his soul. Strange how she'd never noticed that before. Then again, before she was a were-cat, she didn't have these cool heightened senses.

In a thoughtful gesture Kane lifted her collar and pulled it around her neck to keep the gusting wind from nipping at her exposed flesh. "I'm happy for you, Jaclyn. Really, I am." With that, Kane turned to leave and Jaclyn picked up her pace and made her way to Sunray's. She slipped inside her friend's warm, cozy condo, and Sunray helped her remove her scarf and jacket. Jaclyn caught a glimpse of her husband in the kitchen, and her heart leapt with joy. Slyck stopped what he was doing and came her way, a loving smile on his face.

Before Sunray hung Jaclyn's coat up, she pulled the winter gear to her nose and inhaled. Suddenly her eyes widened, and her jaw dropped open. "Ohmigod . . ."

Jaclyn tore her attention from Slyck and glanced at her best friend. "What?"

Sunray buried her face in the coat again and drew a deep breath. "It's . . ."

"It's what?" Jaclyn waved her hands and prompted her. "Jeez, girl, don't keep me hanging."

Their eyes met and locked as Sunray told her, "It's Ray!"

"Ray?" both Jaclyn and Slyck said in unison. "You've got to be kidding me," Jaclyn added, incredulous.

Sunray's chest rose and fell rapidly as a prick of tears formed in her eyes. "I always knew you were important to me, Jaclyn. Important to my future."

Jaclyn grabbed the coat and inhaled the medley of scents. Her mind raced. Good God, she'd hugged so many people recently, it was hard to pinpoint the exact scent that Sunray had recognized. She drew the collar to her nose and concentrated, sifting through all the aromas until one—one that smelled like spice and pool water—triggered something in the back of her brain, something Sunray had told her about Ray.

Kane!

Jaclyn lifted her eyes slowly and smiled. "I think I know where to find him."

About the Author

A former government financial officer, **Cathryn Fox** graduated from university with a bachelor of business degree. Shortly into her career, Cathryn figured out that corporate life wasn't for her. Needing an outlet for her creative energy, she turned in her briefcase and calculator and began writing erotic romance full-time. Cathryn enjoys writing dark paranormals and humorous contemporaries. She lives in eastern Canada with her husband, two kids, and chocolate Labrador retriever.

Turn the page for a sneak peek of the next novel in the
sizzling Eternal Pleasure series

Impulsive

BY CATHRYN FOX

Available from NAL in June 2010

Chicago: A Century Ago

Hurried steps carried Ray Bartlett across town; his dark clothes as well as the black sky masked his foolhardy presence. As he approached the train tracks, the silhouette of the old abandoned building on the other side of the railroad came into view, prompting him to reach into his pocket and pull out the heavy tin can he always brought with him—a familiar beacon in an eerily unfamiliar night.

"Here, kitty, kitty," he called out as he gently shook the scratched and dented container of sardines, letting the thick oil inside slosh about in an effort to herald his approach. He pitched his voice low, knowing the sound would carry in the breeze and alert the lone occupant of the building to his presence, and signal her to free the latch. He darted a glance around and hoped like hell he'd gone undetected by any resident gangs, should they be lurking about. After all, he was a far cry from his elite Gold Coast neighborhood, and he was now setting foot into Chicago's seedy south side—a testament to his foolhardiness, for sure.

As he took note of his shaking fingers, he slid the can back into his breeches and stuffed his hands into his coat pockets to still his rather unusual jitters. His discomposure was partly because he'd snuck out of his dorm—and should he get caught, the consequences doled out by his headmaster would be most severe—and partly due to his excitement in seeing the girl waiting for him on the side of town where he had no business frequenting—the side of town the folks in his social circle avoided like a diseased wharf rat. But, unlike him, they didn't have Sunni Matthews waiting for them.

Sunni...

God, his heart raced and his body grew needy just thinking about her. She had a certain energy about her: a spark, a light in the darkness that filled him with a deep warmth and unearthed things inside him he'd never felt before.

Everything from the way her golden hair framed her porcelain skin and the way her beautiful blue eyes sparkled with love and laughter, to the way she trusted him completely and thoroughly with her body, heart, and soul rattled his emotions and practically rendered him senseless. Ribbons of want—no *need*—worked their way through his veins because he knew he was only minutes from gathering her into his arms, pressing his mouth to hers and paying homage to her lush body until the early hours of the morning.

As he took in the shape of the slumbering structure tucked just inside the woods, a mixture of joy and sadness invaded his thoughts. He was thrilled to spend a few stolen moments with Sunni—he ached to embrace her, to feel her naked body against his skin—but it pained him to know that he'd wake up tomorrow between a set of starched white sheets, and she on a dusty cot. His heart twisted and his stomach clenched. He halted his forward momentum and took a moment to fight down the feeling of helplessness, as well as the pang of loneliness that ate at his guts like a thousand hungry cockroaches.

Soon, he reminded himself. Soon they'd be together forever, and he'd make things better for her. It was a promise he'd made to her a long time ago, and a promise he intended to keep.

Off in the distance the whistle of an approaching train pulled him back to reality. The high-pitched whine broke through the unnatural silence as he carefully counted the wooden sleepers and made his way over the tracks—tracks he knew better than to cross. Yes, it was dangerous, maybe even downright suicidal to venture into this part of town, but it was a damn strange thing how love affected one's ability to make rational decisions.

He ducked into the woods and glanced around, camouflaging himself amongst the towering maple trees and densely packed foliage. As he stepped onto the overgrown walking path, he once again took note of the strange quiet surrounding him. Not even the cacophony of the bullfrogs living in the swamp just beyond the tracks could be heard. It was as if someone or something had scared them silent. That thought aroused the fine hairs along his nape as the long, unkempt weeds and gangly blades of grass climbed up his breeches and pawed at his ankles.

He blinked his eyes to adjust to the dim light and took two measured steps forward. Because there had just been a week of heavy rain, the heels of his patent leather shoes sank in the wet, moss-laden ground. Ray turned the collar of his wool sack coat up against the cool autumn breeze and carefully picked his way forward, his heart pounding harder and harder with each approaching footstep.

Overhead the tightly knitted clouds peeled back to reveal a full moon. The bright beams broke through the canopy of high leaves to provide sufficient light for him to see the dark metal latch on the door, still just a few feet out of reach. His lips turned up in a smile, and he shook the can again to let Sunni and the menagerie of tomcats seeking warmth and shelter inside know that it was he who approached, not some gang member sneaking up on them unsuspectingly.

Taking him by surprise, a low noise came from behind. A noise not at all unlike the growl of a wild wounded animal. Survival instincts kicked in, and he glanced over his shoulder in time to spot a shadow moving in the distance, weaving in and out of the trees in a drunken, nonsequential pattern and keeping a wide berth as it circled.

Ray narrowed his eyes and peered into the darkness. The shadow sat low, crouched on all fours. He took it to be some sort of dog, but bigger than any canine he'd ever encountered. Ray was not a small man by any means, but to take on a rabid dog without weaponry would certainly make him a dense one.

As his pulse kicked up a notch, his skin prickled in warning and propelled him forward. Moving swiftly, his long legs ate up the short distance to the building in record time. Before he could reach the latch, a low noise serrated the air and stopped him dead in his tracks. His blood ran cold and he swallowed hard, the strangled sound carrying in the wind as he slowly turned in the direction of the growl. He took great care not to make any sudden movements while he tracked the shadow as it continued to come closer—closing in on him. A moment later a large canine stepped into the clearing and two pewter orbs flashed beneath the full moon.

What the hell kind of animal has pewter eyes?

A burst of adrenaline propelled Ray on, and he yanked the door open with much more force than was necessary and charged inside. With his breath coming in quick, unsteady gasps, he slammed the door behind him and collapsed against it, using his body weight to seal it shut.

The light from the candle flickered as Sunni approached. Her palm closed over his cheek and the warmth of her hand drove back the cold of the night. "Ray, what is it?" she asked.

With concern dancing in her eyes, she looked past his shoulder at the secured door. "Were you followed?"

He shook his head, and let the tension drain from his body as he took pleasure in the alluring sight of Sunni and the seductive way the soft candlelight fell over her petite frame like a halo. As he drew in her distinctive floral scent, his heart swelled and his cock thickened, forcing him to struggle to find his words.

He widened his hands to show the animal's excessive size. "Wild dog," was all he managed to get out as his blood raced south.

She frowned. "I thought I heard the same dog earlier when I snuck in here." Just then one of the many tomcats hissed at the door and then turned its attention to more pressing matters, like the food in Ray's breeches. He brushed up against Ray's leg and pawed at his pocket, and the can of sardines he knew would be inside. As a few other cats moved closer and joined in the chorus, Ray pulled out their food.

Sunni carefully positioned the candle on the ledge next to them, away from the boarded windows, and went to work on feeding the hungry felines. After opening the can and placing it on the floor, she turned back to Ray and furrowed her brow. "What should we do?"

"Let's wait it out." Every instinct he possessed warned him of danger, causing a foreboding shiver to prowl through him. It took effort to keep his voice even when he added, "With any luck it will just lose interest and wander off."

Her fingers intertwined in his hair, and in an obvious attempt to lighten the mood, she went up on her tiptoes and whispered, "I'm not afraid of any wild dog attacking me when I've got a protector like you, Ray."

Ray slid his hands around her back to anchor her to him. His edgy laugh churned with passion. "Maybe it's *me* you have to worry about attacking, Sunni." His erection pressed insistently against her stomach, and he diligently fought down the overwhelming urge to tear her clothes from her body and ravish her like an animal in heat. A torrent of emotions washed over him, but he knew he'd never act purely on primal impulses, not with her, not with his Sunni, because it was never just about sex with her and she deserved so much more from him.

Her blue eyes gleamed with mischief and she caught her bottom lip between her teeth. "Speaking of attacking, what on earth shall we do to occupy ourselves while we wait for the mongrel to lose interest?"

She looked at him with pure desire and his body responded with a quiver. God, he loved her openness, her sense of adventure. He'd never had the inclination to divulge—let alone indulge—his secret fetishes to the girls in his social circuit. Sunni had never looked at him like he was a circus sideshow for wanting to tie her up and have her at his mercy. He wasn't sure where that deep-seated need to dominate her had come from, only that it was strong, and was not to be denied. Ray could just imagine how the women in his neighborhood would react to his unusual desires. Nevertheless, Ray only ever wanted to share those intimacies with Sunni.

His mind raced back to her playful question and considered the invitation in her voice. "Do you have something in mind?" he asked.

She palmed his muscles then slipped a hand between his legs to cup his aching cock. She gave a breathy, intimate laugh and playfully responded, "Maybe not something in mind, but definitely something in . . . *hand*."

As desire jolted through him, they exchanged a long, lingering look, and any fears he had about the rabid dog abated. His fingers tightened around her waist, and he pulled her impossibly closer, crushing her small body to his.

"Sunni," he murmured as he captured her mouth in a slow simmering kiss, "you do have a way with words."

Eager hands slipped under his coat to massage his muscles, and her throaty purr resonated through his body. "And here I'd rather you had your way with me."